THE
LITTLE
BOAT
ON
TRUSTING
LANE

THE LITTLE BOAT ON TRUSTING LANE

MEL HALL

 FREMANTLE PRESS

Mel Hall is a writer and musician based in Walyalup (Fremantle), Western Australia. Her fiction has been longlisted for major writing awards, such as the Peter Carey Short Story Prize (2019), the Fogarty Literary Award (2019) and the Carmel Bird Digital Literary Award (2018). Her novella *The Choirs of Gravediggers* was published by Ginninderra Press in 2016, and her short fiction has appeared in *Westerly*, *The Sleepers Almanac* and other Australian journals.

This book is dedicated to Laurie Steed,
who believed from the beginning.

THE BOAT

'Close your eyes. Observe the breath. Do not try to control it. Let it not rush. Let it not be slow. Let your breath fall into its natural rhythm. Okay. We have found the sites of pain. Richard has discovered the energy centres presently affected. Acupuncture needles have been placed at the appropriate sites, whether actual pain-sites, or those connected to the relevant meridians. All that is left now, is to breathe, and release this deposit. Richard has asked that you reflect, to meditate on this extra-earthly substance. What does it mean to you? How is it speaking to you, in your life, in this moment?'

Finn drew a deep breath, catching sight of her pants. Were they too loud for work? She shook her head, and kicked her heels together – a trick Richard once showed her to shift unwanted thoughts.

'Now it is my task to assist in this final stage of your session.'

Finn closed the file. Eloise – a first-time Receiver – lay on the therapy table. A blanket covered her lower legs. She had been suffering from abdominal pains. It seemed this deposit was here to teach her about letting go. Needles encircled her bellybutton. Finn leaned over and patted Eloise's shoulder. No matter what Finn felt outside of the therapy room, when she was here with a client, she was dedicated to making them as comfortable as possible.

'Are you warm enough there, can I get you another blanket?'

'I'm good,' Eloise nodded, her eyes still shut.

And there were the pants again. 'Happy pants' everyone called them: large, billowy trousers with a print of pink elephants. At least they clashed with her blue T-shirt, covered in sunflowers. No-one at work could accuse her of curating the outfit. Finn clicked her heels again.

'Okay, now I am here to help with the expulsion of your shapes.'

'My what?'

'Sorry,' Finn chuckled, shaking her head, 'I am here to help with the release of your deposits. Eloise, are you ready to let go?'

The woman nodded again, a tear streaking her left cheek.

'Now, I want you to really visualise this deposit. What shape is it? Do you know its colour? If you were at the grocery store, what fruit would it be? A spiky rambutan? An overripe custard apple? A bright Granny Smith? Or something wild and hairy, like a stalk of fennel? Or perhaps it resembles a heart, like an artichoke?'

Eloise didn't respond, but Finn knew not to panic.

'Okay, let's picture a long, winding river ...'

'I can see something! But, I don't know if it's right.'

'Eloise, it's impossible to be wrong.'

'How can you be sure?'

'I can't. But if an image is coming up for you, even if you can't make it out clearly, then this is the image we must move towards. What is it that you see?'

Finn pulled up a stool and perched behind Eloise's head. She watched the upside-down mouth as it opened and closed, pointed chin moving up and down. The words seemed to come out long after the mouth's movement, as though the speeds of sound and light had grown further apart. The pink elephants were dancing in the corner of Finn's vision. She realised she had never seen Richard clicking his heels together. Maybe his unwanted thoughts were wanted.

'It's red!' Eloise announced, causing Finn to jump. 'Waves and lines of red! But they're moving so quickly! They're burning up, like sparklers!'

'Good, that's really great,' Finn said with a smoothness she knew didn't belong to her. It was a smoothness that belonged to someone who didn't have doubts about their pants, or any part of their existence. Did this make her a fake? Heels clicked. 'Now let's scan over your body. Where do you feel this red is burning at its hottest point? It won't necessarily be the site of pain. Let your inner gaze move, starting at your temple, between the eyes, moving down the cavity behind the nose, now slowly traversing the depths of the throat ...'

'It's my lower back!'

Finn dashed to Eloise's right side. She hovered her open palms above the exposed abdomen. She closed her eyes, focusing on the message of light. She imagined her hands were a vacuum cleaner, sucking this thing up, out, and away.

Eloise moaned, her breath short and shallow. She reached a small scream, which ended abruptly. The silence was always a surprise. People say it's like childbirth, but with emptiness at the end.

'Oh my ...'

Eloise's shoulders tensed again. Her eyes flicked open, gaze fixed above her.

Finn glanced up at the white.

'I felt this huge surge through my navel,' Eloise gushed, 'and then ... look, can you see?'

Finn smiled in a way she hoped was knowing rather than condescending. She shook her head. No, this was real. She was no fake.

'It's this mass of unspooled, winding scribbles. They're neon pink and red strands, all rushing and intertwining. It's like they are pulsating, like they are alive.'

Eloise turned on her side. Her eyes followed an invisible arc, across the ceiling, towards the porthole. Finn felt her own shapes, the feather-like tickle in her chest.

'Eloise, this is so beautiful. Richard will be very impressed.'

'Oh, they are starting to fade!' Despite her worried tone,

Eloise's shoulders were now relaxed. The blanket had fallen to the floor. 'Now they're just really small.'

'The expulsion of a deposit is the birth of new meaning. It's the possibility for change.'

'But I didn't know it would be beautiful like that.' Her disappointment was audible.

Finn laughed, 'Yeah, I know. They're not exactly demons, flying outta hell. Welcome to your new life.' She rested a hand firmly on Eloise's shoulder. 'I will call in Richard now. He'll remove the needles. And make sure you're hydrated.'

Eloise stared through the porthole. The glowing strands of red wound over the trees, towards the sea.

❁

Richard usually had a cup of coffee while Finn conducted the extraction. Today he considered taking his break on the roof, where driftwood wind-chimes clacked their music. That would be a place to welcome the day, with open arms, open chest, shoulders rolled back.

Richard sipped his coffee, and pushed at his sacrum. It always hurt now, the whole geography of his sit-bones. Too much sitting was to blame. But who can blame you for getting old when you didn't know you would.

Richard had found yoga helpful in the past. It was a way of relieving loneliness as well as physical discomfort. But eventually, classes became confusing.

Turn the muscles of the inner thigh outwards, rotating the right hip towards the wall, right hand extending to the ceiling, gaze reaching past fingertips to an invisible point beyond, maintaining even breath, but don't try to control the breath, moving in time with the teacher, in time with the women surrounding on their mats, all moving in unison to the chanting devotional music, and don't forget the heel of your left foot needs to line up perfectly with the arch of your right, but forget all that now because we're moving to another pose, and Richard, it's okay that you're wobbly, it's okay that you're laughing, because if you were wobbly and serious, if you were wobbly and proud, that would be wrong, that would not be yoga.

He welcomed contradictions in life, but how could one possibly move so fast, and stay correctly aligned? Even in slow-flow vinyasa classes, apparently simple rounds of sun salutations were like a set of sophisticated dance moves. Doing it in your own time. Your own time?

'Every pose is just a way to the next pose,' the teacher would say.

This meant that yoga was a code, and every pose was a smaller code, and it was essential to master each pose to crack the next one. Like that ever happens. If there was a sequence of eight poses, Richard – on a good day – remembered the first, the last, and nothing in between.

'Whatever you do is perfect,' the teacher lied.

But Richard was well aware that his sun salutations did not resemble anything people refer to as yoga. He did seem to win points for being a yoga-class-clown though. The class broke into laughter whenever he attempted a tree pose and failed to even press his foot into his lower calf without the assistance of a wall.

'You bring so much lightness,' a lady next to him said, before flipping up to a headstand.

His humour was appreciated, and he appreciated that. But his humour became a barrier too. It was a 'glass ceiling', his teacher said, keeping him from 'further growth'.

Flocks of women in tights covered in prints of birds and the galaxy liked to laugh too, but was their laughter a mask for annoyance? Was it easier for the class to stay on track now that he was gone?

Since parting with yoga, Richard was left with an aversion to the belief that how you sit or where you sit has much bearing on the rest of existence and how the universe may choose to treat you. And so, instead of climbing the ladder, to drink in the sunshine while he soaked up caffeine, he slumped back on the couch.

As he sipped, listening to the patter of Finn's counsel, Richard stared at the photograph. He knew there were more important things that deserved his attention. The leaky tap in the bathroom. The crack in the kitchen window. That widening hole in the floor next to the toilet. And then there were all those letters from the council that he'd 'reposted' in the gap between the fridge and the pantry.

But even thinking about these things brought a flood of dark energy to his fingertips. It wouldn't be right. He needed good energy in his fingers to finish the session.

And so, Richard sat, leaned back into the couch, and stared at Serena.

❁

The Pleiadian Goddess hung outside the door to the therapy room. Her lips were large and pink. Wisps of golden hair fell about her blue eyes. The Pleiadian constellation surrounded her bodice, which erupted from green clouds. The words 'FIND YOUR HOME PLANET' shouted from the sky, which was festooned with lotus flowers.

'Pleiadians arrived in Scandinavia in ancient times and bred with the locals,' August had gushed when she arrived that first time, with the painting on her bicycle. 'That's why Nordic people look the way they do. Tall, thin, blue-eyed and angelic.' August's eyes were wide and sincere.

Finn and Richard had been sitting down, sipping coffee after a few extractions. August had arrived noisily, her bike jangling with tiny bells and rainbow spokes. Silver tinsel was wrapped around the basket, where a plush alien sat; her 'extraterrestrial navigator'.

Back then Finn was the only helper. Back then Richard was still performing extractions.

Finn wondered how August had managed to transport the painting on her bike. The canvas was almost as tall as her. Richard was loud with his gratitude, exclaiming at her sensitive rendering of the elf-like subject. He wandered off to boil the kettle. Back then, Richard boiled the kettle when guests arrived. He offered tea, coffee and shoulder rubs. Things change when you have two helpers.

Finn was puzzled by the picture. 'So, Pleiadians are superior extraterrestrials who happen to resemble what was once called the "master Aryan race".'

Finn shook her head, though August's eyes beamed wide. Her eyes were like satellites: open to goodness, refracting it out to the ether, irony lost as space-junk.

Finn sidled past the painting and into the main cabin. There she found him, asleep on the couch.

'Richard!'

She tapped his shoulder. Richard's face had become red with spots, an imprint from the couch fabric. Finn noticed his glasses had fallen to the floor. She picked them up and placed them on the coffee table.

'Come on, Richard, you need to wake up. It's time to take out the needles.'

He let out a gasp, but remained oddly still. Then his back stiffened. Finn knew what was coming. She spun away as the sound erupted.

'Richard!'

She crossed over to the galley, escaping the smell. The sink was full of mugs, plates and glasses. Finn switched on the kettle, then began to search for a mug that looked relatively safe.

'What's wrong, my Finn?'

'You have to ask, don't you. What's wrong is, you reserve the best version of yourself for people who aren't me.'

'Consider it a compliment.' Richard heaved a yawn. 'To you I show my truest colours.'

Finn rolled her eyes. She was crouched on the floor, opening cupboards, in search of coffee. 'Nothing ever has a proper home in this kitchen.'

'That's because we're on a boat!' Richard exclaimed, somehow leaping from the couch. 'We're travelling together, across the universe! We, and our coffee mugs, are of no fixed address!'

'Ha.'

Richard thumped across the floor, and Finn felt the whole boat shake. Sometimes it seemed like the boat moved as part of his body. But then, it was probably just that no-one walked as heavily on their feet as he did. Richard leaned on the bench, looking down at Finn. His glasses sat crookedly on his face. There was something of an edge, a glint of nervousness in his eyes.

'You look terrible, Richard.'

'Thanks!'

'Are you okay?'

'Never been better!' He was almost shouting.

Finn pulled out the coffee jar. It was stowed behind a seventies food processor she had never seen before. She slammed the cupboard shut, noticing a new crack in the wall, next to the fridge. She didn't have time, though, to think about things like that. And besides, Richard was the one who should care. This boat was his house. He should be the one worried about keeping it shipshape.

'I've gotta go soon.'

'Oh?' Richard's eyebrows pointed upwards. 'I was hoping you might stay here a bit.'

'What, and wash all your dishes?' Finn chuckled, though she knew she'd sounded serious.

Richard gave a high-pitched giggle. 'Well, that's not what I was thinking necessarily. But if you ever offer, I'll always be grateful.'

'I'm sorry and not sorry, but I have work, then I have a doctor's appointment. I won't be back until the circle starts.'

'What kind of doctor?'

'You know, a real-world doctor.'

'What? Why are you doing that?'

'Mum's making me do annual check-ups. I'm just ticking the box, keeping her happy. I'll be here afterwards. You need to get in there, Richard. Eloise can probably hear us.'

'Yes sir.'

Richard gave a salute, then began to prise himself from the bench. Sometimes it seemed as though every vertical object was just a prop to help him stay upright.

'Have you got any more appointments today?' Finn asked.

'Or you might ask, do I have any more disappointments? Why is it that disappointment is not the opposite of appointment? Or perhaps it's not the opposite. Perhaps we are disappointed when we have missed our appointment with joy.'

Finn continued her search for a clean spoon.

'Oh, just Joan,' he yawned, not seeming to expect an answer. He scuffed over to the fridge. 'Shit,' he said, looking in.

'You don't have any yoghurt?' asked Finn.

'I could give Joan a cup of milk instead. I did that last time and it was okay.'

'Surely milk is more comforting. Perhaps you could warm it.'

Richard smiled, placing a hand on her shoulder. 'Warmed milk? You really go the extra mile, Finn.'

She blushed an unwelcome blush. Richard didn't notice, thankfully. His gaze had moved on to a box of cornflakes.

'Have you ever noticed that the breakdown of contents will say corn: fifty-seven percent, sugar: eleven percent, but the figures never add up to one hundred? Why is that? Do they think we're stupid?'

'Do you think she'll ever come back to the circle?'

'Who? What are you talking about, Finn?'

'Joan!'

'Oh. I'll remind her about tonight. Let her know she is missed.'

'Sorely so. Don't we love her.' Finn felt a pang, aware of her lie. Her feelings for Joan were far from love.

'Last I heard, her arthritis was too severe for the stairs at night,' Richard mused, stroking his beard vigorously. 'I got the feeling she was asking for some kind of assistance, but I'm not sure anyone would be quite up to carrying her.'

'That's fair enough, Richard. 'This place has accessibility issues.'

'I know, I know. I'm thinking in the summer to hold some kind of outdoor sessions, on the carpets in the sculpture garden. We could do ecstatic dance, a juggling workshop, maybe a busy bee and some fire twirling... That's as long as no-one from the council drives past and sees the open flame.' Richard frowned into space.

'The council won't just come spying like that.'

'I wouldn't put it past them!'

'Anyway, Richard, you should really get back to Eloise.'

'Done. Easy. Piece of cake-walk in the park.' He grinned expectantly.

'Once again, it might have been funny the first time, whoever that first person was who was lucky enough to hear it.' Finn stirred a salad server through her coffee, letting it clang in the sink. 'Will you give me a leg-up?'

'Won't it spill?' He nodded at her mug.

'It's only half full.'

'At least it's not half empty!' Richard gave Finn a jovial nudge.

Richard took a deep inhale, then squatted, creating a step with his hands. Finn wasn't convinced of the step's structural integrity, but there was no other way.

'We like to live dangerously, don't we,' she said, pushing her foot into his palms. She grabbed the ladder with her free hand. 'And don't forget to read my story.'

Richard groaned. 'What story?'

'For the circle tonight, remember? You picked the theme "solitude". It's my turn, Richard. I hope you enjoyed your daily workout.'

'Yes, yes,' he nodded. 'Very good. You enjoy the day.'

Finn climbed up towards the utility hole, squeezing herself onto the deck. She imagined Richard watching below as her elephants disappeared into the sky.

THE CARAVAN

August scratched her left thigh. Her legs became so itchy when she sat on the grass. She was cross-legged, inside the annex, listening to her Tibetan singing bowl CD. The sound was a slow and peaceful circling. It made her think of the planets.

The morning was thick with heat and patchouli. August drew a deep breath, then raised her left palm to her forehead. She gently guided her skull towards the earth. With this gesture, she was inviting the sound deeper within. She was inviting the peaceful circling to orbit her third eye.

August let her gaze rest on a single blade of grass. This one was slightly yellow at the tip, and creased at the middle. Like every blade of grass, it held a message. The grass said, 'Steady yourself this morning. Confirm who you woke up as. Repeat your name, six times. Say to yourself: I stand tall. I will move and be moved. It will take much for me to fall.'

August closed her eyes. And then it started.

She felt the hum at the back of her throat. It tickled. She felt thirsty. This was the moment when something emerged from her, something that wasn't of her, but was welcome all the same.

Now her throat was a whispering wall, full of strange sounds. Tones of pink and amber flowed, from her throat, down to her chest. The sounds were deep and rumbling. They soon turned upward, becoming shrill.

A flock of golden specks flew up into her chest. They rose into her mouth, and gave the aftertaste of fresh milk.

They sparkled behind her nose, then danced in the cavities that held her eyes. Finally the specks rose to the base of her forehead.

August bowed her head like she used to in church. The golden specks began to throb, growing brighter. The sounds grew louder. August moved her inner gaze through her body. She looked through the pink, red and the white, the hard, soft and squishy places, until she found the black holes. And then, reaching a final squeal, the specks melted into one beam of golden light.

❁

Each day after her morning meditation, August stepped back into the caravan and breathed in words. The caravan walls were covered in them. Words cut out from magazines. Words pasted on vision boards. Words on cushions. Words on coasters, fridge magnets. Words on candles and plant pots. August looked around the room for inspiration. Some of the sayings were her own creations. Some she had read, in toilet stalls or on café decor, and furiously scrawled down.

BE KIND TO YOUR FUTURE SELF

I CAME TO THIS WORLD TO LIVE OUT LOUD!

LEAVE YOURSELF A WIDE BERTH FOR ALL THE OTHER MISTAKES YOU'LL PROBABLY MAKE

I'M ALWAYS PATCHING WELLNESS LEAKS!

LIFE BEGINS AT THE END OF YOUR COMFORT ZONE

Recently, August had to get rid of a vegan candle Eve had given her. The candle sat at her bedside, bearing the message:

TRANSCEND. On her bed was a large cushion, stitched with the words THERE IS SO MUCH TO LOVE. After August had entered the caravan and read the words THERE IS SO MUCH TO TRANSCEND three mornings in a row, she decided this was a sign in itself. The candle, along with its mischief, was placed in a box, ready for the op shop.

This morning, August only found kind words. She read of loving herself, of the future being bright, and wellness being something to keep grasping for.

All these words brought on a kind of nervous excitement. August began to worry that she might become breathless, anxious even. She closed her eyes and took a deep breath.

'Today, there is so much potential for good in the world,' she said aloud.

Tom was not there. She wished he was. He'd left to help his dad and brother with the harvest. He would be away for an eternity. August sighed. She imagined stepping over to the bed, and brushing a strand of hair from his eyes. She would continue stroking his hair. It was like she was practising a kind of gentleness she wished she could give herself.

His hair had grown so long since they'd moved away from home. But he rarely let it down. This only happened before he left for work, if he had a day's work. Tom picked up the odd shift at a labour-hire firm. And for some reason, before he left, he insisted on brushing his hair in private. He would open the wardrobe doors, creating a small cubicle. At the back of the wardrobe was a square mirror and fluorescent light. Tom would pull his lackey out, flicking long blond curls from side to side. Then, he would pick up the brush.

The sound was like ripping paper as he tore through hair. The hair was being stripped of its curl. The curl became frizz, the frizz was flattened, finally contained by elastic. He would watch his tiny face at the back of the wardrobe, framed by August's fluffy jackets.

August squealed if she caught him in the act. It was like spotting a rare bird in its grooming ritual. She would shuffle up behind him, bumping against the doors, upsetting the makeshift cubicle.

Two is a crowd in a caravan, she imagined him saying. But he would never say that.

Once she managed to fall on top of him. He slumped forward, the wardrobe doors scraping against her back. Later there was a stripe of purple bruise across her shoulder. But she rarely registered physical pain. Scrapes and bruises were as mysterious as life itself. But to Tom, the injuries weren't a mystery. The injuries were a predictable result of being clumsy.

August's clumsiness brought on tides of guilt. The guilt happened when she hurt herself. The guilt happened when she knocked over a small child while she was admiring the flowers carved into a building facade.

August knew that the way she physically related to the world called her safety, and the safety of others, into question. But this wasn't what made her feel bad. She felt guilty because she knew that she was capable of an excitement that could be terrifying, an excitement that could be boundless, an excitement that other people didn't understand, an excitement that always brought anxiety along for the ride. It was the excitement that brought troubles of its own. It was the excitement that was wrong.

Sometimes it felt like any small thing might cause excitement. August could never predict or explain it. She didn't know why the sight of a cat in the street might cause her to run after it. She didn't know why she might be eager to show people how she could move her right and left eyes independently of each other. She didn't know why she needed to wear floral tea-cosies as beanies. Why she *needed* to collect sand at the beach every time she had a special realisation there. Why she needed to then store that sand in a bottle, with a folded plastic letter about the realisation stuffed in on top. Why she needed to line these sand-realisation-bottles along the outside of her annex. Why she needed to buy *everything* she liked in an op shop, telling herself this was democracy, to buy each and every thing you approve of. And now stuffed dinosaurs, cats, gorillas and teddy bears took up half her bed.

August had figured that much out: the guilt was there because the anxious-excitement was there. The excitement made people step away from her when she began to talk, as though her tone of voice was abrasive. And the excitement made her so tired. It was so hard to get anything done when she was excited, because even though she was riled up about all the things she might do, the excitement also made her wish she could just sleep.

Tom let her break things. He let her fall over him. He was her eyes and ears when they crossed the road. He picked up her wallet when she left it on a park bench. He picked lint from her T-shirt, wiped stray food from the sides of her mouth.

Tom never made jokes about her. He never belittled her, but just laughed.

August had made plenty of jokes that Tom was like Samson. But he was even worse than Samson, because even having his long hair seen, let alone brushed by another, let alone cut by another, would mean a loss of his special powers.

August trudged past the vegetable patch, carrying her towel and toothpaste. A month back, the garden was green with parsley, Thai basil, silverbeet and zucchini. Now it was full of crackling yellow grass. The thought of summer gave her a prickle of worry in her throat.

Today August had work at The Heart of Art, an art supplies store in town. She always looked forward to going in. At the store, her excitement was able to settle as she undertook her daily tasks. She unpacked boxes of pencils, stacked piles of coloured card and canvases. She ran the soft bristles of paintbrushes across the backs of her hands.

But then, her excitement also came in handy. When customers asked what her favourite paint was, which canvas or paper had the most appealing texture, August was able to channel her enthusiasm into something that felt productive, sane even.

Her shifts were only a few mornings a week. She always rode away from the store still bubbling with that anxious-excitement. She had recently taken up baking as a way of relaxing afterwards.

August slowly creaked open the door to the house, listening to make sure they were gone. In the house lived Kaye, her husband Dave, and their two children Beatrice and Sebastian. Kaye was the much younger cousin of August's mum, and in the family was always referred to as 'different', 'interesting' and 'a bit of a hippie'. Before having children, the caravan was used as Kaye's photography studio, but after she'd given birth to Sebastian, the chemicals involved in developing pictures began to worry her. She and Dave decided to pack up the studio, scrub the caravan walls, burn sage and Nag Champa, and 'pray that the right soul might be drawn to the place'. The prayer was answered when one day Shirley rang Kaye, mentioning her daughter August was finishing school, that she might need a place to stay. Kaye knew that August was the right person, because she was 'a bit different' too. Shirley wasn't quite sure, when August beamed and announced that Tom could live in the caravan too! But Kaye convinced Shirley it should be fine; the caravan had an annex, there was the possibility of two beds, if that's what might be needed.

And so, Tom and August moved to the caravan four years back, and it probably wasn't meant to go on for that long. But the space just worked. There was the long time, too, when everything went wrong, when August had to go to hospital and move back home for a while. That was when her mind split open, all the brain-stuff came out, and August could never be sure if she'd gathered it all back in again. The brain-stuff was like grain dust, bursting through the air during harvest; golden flecks, floating around August, all the time.

The only thing that was missing in the caravan was a bathroom, but Kaye and Dave were happy for their toilet and shower to be used at any time of day. August liked to go for a shower after their morning ritual had passed. This began at daybreak, when children zombied into their parents' bedroom. There, Dave's large arm would attempt to squash them back into sleep. By six thirty, the house would be abuzz, cartoons on, millet puffs and almond milk over the counter, kettle boiling, stainless steel bento boxes being packed with grapes, cheese and other snacks for Earth Aware Day Care. By twenty past seven the children would be gadding about in gumboots, superhero capes, singlets covered in hazelnut spread, singing, brandishing bubble-blowing wands, a cosmos of sparkling and popping all around them. August loved the kids, and became a kid herself when she played with them, but it was nice to have some space from them too. Being around other people's kids too much could be a reminder of all the things you've been unable to create in your own life.

In ten minutes, Kaye and Dave would round them up, replace gumboots with sandals, pull on clean shirts, give hair a tear-inducing comb, teeth a quick scrub, then pack them into the car. It was as if the personal cosmos that popped and sparkled around each child was reprimanded: packed up, pushed back into their bodies.

After seven thirty-five, August had her chance. She stepped slowly into the kitchen, as though entering a holy place. Dried wildflowers sat in a washtub on the speckled Metters stove. The familiar drone sounded, bees nesting in the chimney. Opening the pantry, August took in the smell of charcoal and sawdust. Shelves were lined with dried spices, arame, herbs and tea leaves. She opened one of the kitchen drawers to find safety scissors, twine, mineral lipstick, bills, a packet of non-toxic oil pastels.

In the fridge there were jars of condiments: homemade sauerkraut and kimchi, jars with kombucha SCOBYs that resembled UFOs, kefir water, homemade nut-milks, soaking almonds, cashew cream, a drawer of organic, wilted vegetables, beetroot leaves reaching out to a large pot of last night's vegetable stew which the kids didn't eat and which would be Kaye and Dave's dinners for the rest of the week.

The whole kitchen smelt old and earthy, like the family had lived here a long time, and would continue living here forever. There was something reassuring in the room's energy. The kitchen reminded her that people lay down roots. They find somewhere to belong. And just for a moment, this could all belong to August too.

THE SHOP

Pure Source Organics was the go-to store for organic papaya, green smoothies for the beach, and the perfect supplements for building up cartilage in the knees.

Occasionally, scent-sitive customers coughed, complaining that someone had been testing the sage deodorant. They would need to be given a glass of filtered water to help counter the reaction.

At least there was only one customer who was allergic to Tuscan kale. This customer always made sure before buying a green smoothie that only the curly variety would be involved.

Vegans came in declaring 'meat is murder' before snatching up their lentil curry pies.

Some would not sit at the tables outside to drink their long blacks with coconut oil. They said: 'No way I'm sitting out there! Too many heavy metals blowing in the breeze.'

Last week, one shopper asked if the bottled water was reptilian, whilst another brought in a Geiger counter, checking the seaweed for radiation. Lately, everyone was talking about the speaker Vashti Tanasi. Her upcoming workshops, 'How to Quantify Vitality', were almost booked out. In the workshops, she would be teaching a range of intuitive tests to perform on fruit and vegetables in order to determine their nutrient density.

Every day, bird-like women stocked up on frozen bone-broth. Every other day, a Polish grandmother purchased unhulled sunflower kernels for her canary, 'but only for special occasions, only for a treat'. And every Saturday, there were those people who hugged for twenty minutes in aisle three.

Finn had always wanted to find a place like this. When she was young, Finn was the kid with the allergies, the one with a dollop of cold-sore cream on her lip, pulling cashew-paste sandwiches from her lunchbox, closing her eyes to imagine that the cool water sipped from a bubbler was real milk. In the beginning, Pure Source was a safe haven, where her special dietary requirements might be taken seriously. But the longer Finn worked there, the more the place frustrated her. It took a while to realise why.

After about a year, she finally worked it out. It wasn't the customers. It wasn't the produce. It was that everyone she worked with was insanely beautiful. Sometimes she even wondered if hiring beautiful women was part of a business strategy.

Look: all our staff buy beeswax candles, wash with goat milk soap, snack on probiotic bars, ingest slippery elm in powdered form, use flaxseed to make eye pillows, smoke damiana leaf, and maybe they secretly drink unpasteurised 'bath milk', although the label clearly states it isn't for human consumption. And they're all gorgeous!

Some days, Finn felt those words ringing through her ears, as clear as memories, though she knew no-one had ever said them. Besides, if workers were hired on the basis of their looks, Finn was not supposed to be there.

Sometimes she wondered if there had been a mix-up in the office. Some beautiful Pure Source employees bumped into each other while wielding paperwork, a huge waft of job applications got flown into the air, collected up, rearranged, Finn's being placed in a 'YES. BEAUTIFUL' pile, right where she didn't belong. But once they had called Finn back, offered her the job, and she'd walked in, ready for her first day, it would have been too awkward to turn her away.

The Pure Source logo was rainbow-coloured, and slightly psychedelic. The whole shop maintained a smell of sandalwood and freshly turned soil. At any one time, if a feminine armpit survey were conducted, you'd find hairiness in the majority.

Hairy armpits shouldn't be of concern, Finn reminded herself. Hairy armpits, hairy legs, hairy everything was very normal to her. But hairy armpits were part of that particular problem of beauty.

Customers and colleagues didn't wear makeup, yet they boasted clear complexions. They all had well-shaped eyebrows, and the perfect number of freckles. In a way, it seemed mean they didn't wear makeup. It was like, 'Yeah, that's right, I am this sexy, without any help.' At least, if they wore makeup, you'd think, 'Hmmm ... I wonder what ugly blemish they're hiding. Oh well, we all have a blemish or two.'

But when they didn't shave, wax, or epilate their underarms, it was like they turned their sweaty pits into cute accessories. The hairy armpits were elevated, because the rest of the bodies they appeared on were just so attractive. The hairy armpit declared: 'I accept my natural state which just happens to be ludicrously hot. This armpit shows that I am a flawed human.'

The armpit was an exception that proved the rule of beauty. And if, for a person like Finn, the hairy armpit was not an exception, but just a part of a body that was consistently hairy and unappealing, then the rule was still that unbeautiful people don't win: unbeautiful people don't rule the world.

If these women were serious about subversion, about overturning stereotypical notions of grooming and beauty, they would let their legs become as hairy as possible. They would wear large clog-like shoes. They would tease their hair into terrible styles, knock out front teeth and wear chunky gold earrings. But maybe on them, all this would look feverishly attractive too.

So, at work Finn felt surrounded by superhuman-beings. They wore shirts with slogans like 'Spiritual is the New Sexy'. They posted hand-drawn flyers for women's circles. They wore tights that gripped their perfectly shaped bums, bums that drew more attention than any bosom ever did. Their hips thrust and bum-cheeks punched side to side as they strode through the store. When the music was loud enough, and featured the right beat, it really seemed like they were on a catwalk.

Unfortunately, there were certain bass-thuds that were impossible not to walk in time with. When Finn was busy, she had that creeping feeling that she too was a model, powering down the runway.

She knew she had that look in her eyes: I'm onto it. I'm busy. I mean business.

And this could all be confused with some kind of sass, some misplaced sexual confidence. Because, Finn knew, she wasn't the kind of girl who was supposed to be strutting her stuff.

Some superhuman colleagues wore lumpy knitted cardigans they'd purchased at the op shop next door, BohoHobo. Others had their hair done at Émigré, where the stylists specialised in cuts that looked like you did it yourself, without all the issues. A few girls wore John Lennon spectacles, fastening henna-dyed hair in topknots. They frowned, complained about sexology assignments, and this all made them look bookish, clever, tired, mature, angry, like they didn't care, while they were still more beautiful than anyone.

Around these girls, Finn was 'the funny one', who kept her hair permanently tied to one side, 'because if your hairstyle is asymmetrical, you don't have to worry about lopsidedness'. She wore loose-fitting happy pants and large T-shirts, because this optimised free movement. She chose shirts that colleagues regarded as 'hilarious', because they featured a cat in sunglasses, lobsters, or a dog in a baseball cap. Despite the loudness of her outfits, she was 'the quiet type' who 'didn't mean to attract attention', choosing the novelty T-shirts from the op shop because they were cheap, comfortable and still had tags on.

'I think it was a present someone didn't want,' Finn said

when Gillian asked her about the shirt featuring beetles crossing a road.

Gillian gave her superhuman laugh. 'I can see why!'

And it was 'so funny' when Finn mentioned the mental alarm that sounded every time she caught sight of her legs. How much she despised her own legs, their white flabbiness, the ever-present rashes, despite attempts to stay away from lactose. And those strange scabs that never heal. Only a fraction of leg needed to be revealed for the alarm to sound inside her head. BEEP! BEEP! BEEP! TOO MUCH LEG!

With every joke she made, every outfit of clashing patterns she walked through the store, Finn felt herself growing further from the superhumans. She laughed at herself, and that enabled others to laugh, though she wasn't always sure that was okay. Sometimes, even, she felt they might be making fun of her.

But whatever their feelings were towards her, Finn couldn't help how she felt towards her superhuman colleagues. Maybe one day she liked them, and one day she didn't. But every day, they did this thing to her body. These beautiful women who Finn worked with made her feel something, like flowers blooming, down there.

Finn tormented herself over these feelings.

Did she want to *be* a girl like this, or be *with* a girl like this? Was her groin throbbing for some lost femininity, some soft part of herself she'd never accessed?

Finn's groin went on pulsating for these women, whom she sometimes despised. It throbbed like a heart – but then, her heart began to thump for a different person altogether.

Finn first met Ethann at the 'Ferments and Pickles' section of the bookshelf. The shapes were clustered tightly in her pelvis, causing intermittent spasms. Finn was stretching, she thought discreetly. She breathed in, and out, trying to see outside the pain. The neatness of spines and block-lettered titles helped.

Some things have edges, she thought, trailing her fingers across books.

She was up to P in her alphabetising. He was carrying an organic bamboo yoga mat. His long hair was tied in a tight ponytail.

He noticed Finn's side-lunge. 'Are you okay there?'

'Sorry? Can I help you?'

'Are you okay?' He spoke in what seemed like a Scottish accent, but Finn wasn't sure.

'Me? Yeah. Just stretching. And working.'

'It's good to do both.'

'Yeah, I try.'

'You're quite red ...'

'Oh, that's normal,' Finn attempted a smile.

He caught her looking sideways at his mat. 'This is much nicer to get a whiff of when you're doing downward dog.'

'Nicer than what?'

'Oh, the smelly plastic mats they have down at the yoga studio. The only plastic I'm interested in is neuroplasticity!'

He chuckled and Finn laughed along, though she wasn't certain he'd made a joke.

'Are you okay, I should be asking,' she faltered. 'I mean, can I help you with anything?'

He thrust out his arm. 'Yes! You can say hello. My name is Ethann. That's with two ns. And, when you're ready, I'd like to talk about broccoli sprouts.'

They shook hands, which felt reasonable as it began to happen. But then as the handshaking went on, Finn realised it was weird. Who shakes hands with customers? Finn became aware of the eyes of colleagues, floating through shelves, drifting about the shop. But a warmth flooded into her palm, up her arm, and for a moment, she didn't care what anyone thought.

'Unusual spelling,' she smiled shyly. Finn dropped his hand, picked up *The Probiotic Promise* and began to fan her face with the book.

'Well, my name was originally Nathan, but then my whole life changed. I did a weekend course in Conscious Manifestation, and afterwards, I just knew I needed to rename myself. I wanted an anagram for Nathan. So, I just pretended the original spelling was Nathen, so I could make Ethann. I always liked that name, no matter how many n's.'

Ethann became a regular, a few weeks back now. He tended to pull his pants above his waistline. Some of the girls nicknamed him 'HHP Sauce', which stood for Harry High Pants. Finn wasn't sure if the 'Sauce' part meant anything. Perhaps it was ironic, or perhaps – and she hoped not – he was something of a flirt?

Ethann's usual purchase was broccoli sprouts. Several times he told Finn how powerfully alkalising they are in your body.

Last Friday, at the counter while he paid for the sprouts, Finn overheard him saying to Gillian – who was the head of the superhumans – that he never ate regular food, only superfood, and that he never used plastics.

'The only plastic I believe in is neuroplasticity!' he said.

Finn felt quietly sad at the recycled line. An urge to protect him. Then she felt concerned. Maybe this was some kind of pick-up line, and he was the kind of person who'd choose a superfood-powered superhuman-being over a strange-looking one.

When he left the store, Gillian roared with laughter.

There were flashes of shiny hair and bouncing bums as girls gathered around her, asking, 'What just happened?'

This afternoon, he came in again just as Finn was rearranging the frozen organic chicken carcasses. He seemed quieter, more contemplative than usual.

'Are you okay?'

'Hmmm ... Yes, I think so.' His weight shifted from one foot to another. 'Well, I work as a cleaner at a couple of pretty fancy houses, and today, well, I think I broke their floor while I was cleaning it.'

'You broke a floor? How can you break a floor?' Finn hoped she didn't sound like an alarm.

'Yes, yes.' He laughed, placing his hand on Finn's shoulder. 'Don't worry! If it's broken it's broken! We can't change what's written in the stars! And how are you?'

'Yeah,' she croaked, registering warmth on her shoulder, her legs wobbly. She cleared her throat. 'I was helping down at Richard's this morning, then I'll be back for the IEWA circle tonight.'

Finn felt pride rising through her. In all her conversations with Ethann, she'd been trying to find a way to introduce the topic of Invisible Exit Wounds Anonymous, the spiritual circle which Richard had founded.

'Oh, yeah, what's this circle?'

'It's a spiritual group I belong to,' Finn shrugged. 'I help out with therapeutic appointments, you know ...' She trailed off. All words left her, except one.

'Boat.'

'What?'

Finn's face felt hot. 'We meet on a boat,' she blurted.

'In the river or the sea?'

'On the land. On Trusting Lane ...'

Ethann threw back his head and laughed. 'Hey, I'd love to check it out!' His hand was still there. 'It's just I've got this dreaming workshop on Wednesday nights. I'm keeping a journal, and my dream-decision-making-powers are definitely up. But the course finishes in four weeks, so after that I could come down!'

'That would be cool.' Finn smiled, then felt anxious.

She worried about how she looked when smiling. She hoped she didn't appear as she usually did in a photo. Her face always looked scrunched-up, or frumpy, over-eager, squinty, even when she tried her best.

Ethann frowned. 'Well, I'd better go. I'll see you soon!' He finally released his hand.

'Bye!' Finn called as he walked away.

And it took a while for the sensation to fade – a shoulder so pleasantly warmed by touch.

THE BOAT

Once a scrapyard belonging to Richard's great-uncle, the block sat nestled between an auto wrecker and a warehouse specialising in Balinese imports. The address was 21 Trusting Lane. It was the southern pocket of the suburb, where streets were lined with workshops, mechanics and artist studios. The block wasn't officially residential, and nowadays, Richard's dwelling place wouldn't get all the right approvals. But he had been here for over twenty years, and hadn't been moved on yet.

A few weeks ago the earth was green with wintergrass and nasturtiums, creeping through rusted wheel fittings, coiled around tin sheets, climbing over bricks and concrete rubble. Still two months from summer, the grass had now dried to white-yellow, revealing dusty earth beneath.

Just below the topsoil, remnants of scrap were abundant: ceramic fragments, glass, wire, Serbian plum brandy bottles in their dozens. All around were makeshift sheds, made with corrugated iron, wire and old timber. Draped across scrap piles were neon and gnawed styrofoam buoys, Chinese lanterns, solar-powered fairy lights, and fishing lines littered with floaters and sinkers.

The boat sat at the far end of the block. Just in front were several faux-Persian carpets, which became mouldy in winter and dried out in summer. This was where the Circle of IEWA had held outdoor sessions in the past, back when there were more Receivers around. In the west corner of the yard was the sculpture garden, where Richard and August often spent an afternoon, moving around scrap objects, creating what he called 'totem poles'.

Richard was sitting on a chewed-looking vinyl couch, alongside one of August's recent creations; a cluster of wire, ribbons, shells and feathers. She'd called it TALIS-WOMAN.

But he was trying hard not to look at the sculpture. It resembled a dreamcatcher that had become mangled by a nightmare. He shuddered, turning instead in the direction of the boat. That was not an easy sight to take in either, but perhaps it was time. He slowly raised his head. It was hard to look. It was painful to look, because really, there was nothing else. Finally, he took it in, the creaking, sighing mass.

It was a houseboat, the kind that is usually moored on a river. The boat sat high up on stilts, like a stork in its nest. Its bow and stern were mustard with cream trimmings, the paintwork faded and crackled.

Richard's Ark, he'd wanted to call it. *Richard's Ark at the End of the World* was the sign he'd sketched up. Fields swaying, grass lit up in strange sunsets, the ocean hovering somewhere in the distance: this part of the valley brought the end of times to his mind.

His friend Ross had talked him out of the name.

'It sounds too biblical,' he'd said. 'Such a turn-off for anyone seeking a spiritual experience.'

Richard had reluctantly agreed, though he still regarded the boat as his own private ark. Instead, he and Ross had agreed to call the boat *The Little Mother Earth Ship*, and spent hours painting up a sign.

Ross had further protested at calling the ladder up to the boat 'stairs'.

'Rich, it's just not a staircase. It's a ladder,' he said.

'It doesn't seem right, taking a ladder to a therapeutic appointment,' Richard said. 'It sounds too practical, not esoteric enough. There's just a rightness about the word stairs.'

That was years ago. None of the current circle members even knew Ross. And nobody called him 'Rich' anymore. But for Richard, those beginning days felt like yesterday.

Richard had bought the boat from a Croatian boatbuilder, for the cost of moving it. The previous owner had given Richard a tray of vegetables grown in his market garden, which Ross had turned into several fabulous curries.

This was all back when Ross lived in town, before he'd met Rocia and moved to a date farm in Alice. Ross and Richard had met at a full-moon drumming session down at South Beach, and quickly realised they'd both spent much time in India. Richard had recently inherited the block on Trusting Lane, and was looking to set up a healing centre. It seemed like the kind of thing that would fly in Fremantle.

'We built this thing together,' he'd found himself almost sobbing to Ross on the phone recently. He reminded Ross about the nights they'd spent on the roof, drinking in wine and stars after hard days hammering, laying carpets and lino, getting the plumbing and electricity working. Well, Ross had been sorting most of that, while Richard half-heartedly followed orders', providing jokes and other entertainment between jobs.

Richard wasn't exactly sure what he was expecting from Ross, with all these late-night phone calls. Maybe just to come back from Alice, once in a while, to help with upkeep and repairs.

Perhaps Ross had been trying to fob him off when he created the dating profile for Richard. When Richard opened the link in an email about a week back, he'd found a profile of himself already established, with six months access to the website paid up in advance. The site was called 'Divine and Dateless', a portal for conscious dating.

The photo was quite old, and flattering, Richard thought. His hair was not completely grey. His glasses were small and distinguished looking, and his smile was carefree. Richard wondered what had happened to those glasses, and if his smile would ever be like that again.

Then, as he began to search through profiles, a wave of excitement swept through him. Perhaps he could use the site to find Serena.

But there were so many women named Serena! He trawled through hundreds of profiles, with no success. Besides, there was every chance she didn't call herself Serena anymore. Fed up, Richard began to browse through pictures of divine, conscious women. And that's when he found the profile of 'modern day guru' Celestiaa Davinaa.

'See you in 5D!' read her catchline. What really caught Richard's eye though – apart from her cheeky smile, knowing eyes, and long white-blond hair – was that she called herself an 'aggressive healer'.

Richard hit the send good vibes icon, before typing a message.

@RICH_NOT_YET_IN_HEAVEN

Hello there Celestiaa! My name is Richard, and I am a fellow healer! I was intrigued to read that you identify as 'aggressive'. How unusual, and fascinating!

Personally, I consider myself a 'reluctant healer'. It's not that I am reluctant to heal others! It's just I was reluctant, initially, in following this path. It took me a long time to see healing as my true calling. And, well, I suppose that in the context of being 'called', reluctance is not such a foreign concept!

Well, I hope to hear back from you, Celestiaa!

It was three a.m. the previous Friday morning that he first made contact. After Richard hit SEND, he found sleep came easily. On waking the next day, he felt perhaps this was a sign: Celestiaa would be an important person in his life.

However, days passed and Richard's inbox remained empty. Today, after he had removed Eloise's needles, waving to her as she descended the ladder, he felt deflated. Had he done something wrong? Richard decided to sit out in the sculpture garden, hoping to find some clarity by reading over his message in the open air.

Perhaps I didn't show enough interest in her, he thought. He did spend most of the paragraph talking about himself. Or, perhaps she was offended at his suggestion that he was reluctant in his healing work. Maybe she took it as disrespectful, as though he was defying the will of God.

And so, Richard attempted a follow-up message that he hoped was more direct.

@RICH_NOT_YET_IN_HEAVEN
Maybe it would be more appropriate if I called myself a 'reserved healer'. But enough about me! I was wondering Celestiaa, if perhaps you would be interested to talk to me sometime about what it means to be an aggressive healer?
I have all kinds of images running through my mind, and you look like such a light-sprite of a woman. I take it to mean you get results?
Well, I await your reply, with bated breath.
- Richard.

Once he had finished his appointment with Joan – in which he had been haunted by the thought that Light Sprite might be a soft drink – and given her a cup of warmed milk, at the sight of which, she had squirmed, and promptly left – Richard sat in the garden, with his laptop, and found a reply.

Then began an afternoon of gong-alerts, letting Richard know that he had new messages from Celestiaa Davinaa. He felt like Pavlov's dog, panting every time he heard the sound, desperate to be served dinner.

THE DOCTOR

The doctors surgery walls were covered in pictures of people with shingles – landscapes of scars across bodies – advertisements for a dietician, and a series of block-mounted children's artworks. Scratched in pencil were a diplodocus, tyrannosaurus rex, stegosaurus and a raptor. The dinosaurs looked towards a sun, who smiled back.

Finn stared at the picture for a while before realising it was enlarged. The pencil textures were so blurred any enjoyment of the artwork left her. No pencils bore lead that fat. They would be impossible to sharpen, unless you did it with a knife. No-one would let a child sharpen a pencil with a knife. Perhaps the teacher could sharpen the pencil, but that would be too much trouble. Sharps probably aren't allowed on school grounds now anyway.

But then, Finn didn't know anything about schools, about children, about life outside what she called her 'safe zones'.

When the young woman began calling her name, Finn didn't register. She stared back at the short, smiling doctor, who seemed about to bounce out of her office attire.

'Fiona! Please, come this way!'

That's right, Finn's real name was Fiona, and this young doctor-woman was summoning her. An elderly man scowled as she peeled herself off the chair. The doctor waited, shifting weight from foot to foot. She seemed like someone created in the image of productivity, unable to stand still.

'Hello Fiona, I'm Laura, Laura Epstein. Please, this way.'

Inside the consult room, on the large desk, were pictures of Doctor Laura and her husband in the snow, wielding large goggles and skis.

'Hello Fiona, or, did I read that you have a preferred name?'

'Yeah, it's just Finn.'

'Great!' She closed the door. 'So Finn, you don't come here very often, your last appointment was two years ago!'

'I try not to be one of the "worried well".'

Things-sorted-out-Doctor-Laura smiled. 'Well, that's a good approach, although it must be quite easy to be led astray around Fremantle!'

'It certainly is.'

Finn didn't like herself at times, especially when she was reminded how small her world had become. She'd never meant to be one of those Freo types who moves in the world, in a car, from one safe-zone to the next: the healing centre, the organic grocery store, her home she shared with a sound-healer. Going to the doctor was a reminder of the world beyond.

'And so, what brings you here today?'

'I'm just here for a check-up,' Finn said, scratching her arm, resisting the urge to say, 'Because my mum said I should.'

Doctor Laura chuckled. 'Okay, Finn, so thirty-one years old this year. I bet your body is starting to creak and change in some strange places.'

'I do okay, I think,' Finn said. She didn't bother mentioning her ongoing pain and body problems. How picking up a tissue-box could be like lifting five bricks. Another day turning the pages of a book felt like doing origami with sheets of metal. Squatting was easy, squatting was impossible, squatting was possible with light bladder leakage, sneezing whilst squatting would be the cause of heavy bladder leakage. Another day, Finn could walk for three hours, help unpack pallets of dry goods at Pure Source, even attempt a headstand, so long as there was a pile of blankets surrounding her yoga mat. And then, with no warning, the pain would arrive, and keep her awake through the night.

'Now, let's see, when was your last pap smear?'

'I've never had a pap smear.'

'Never had a pap smear?'

'Nup.'

'And when did you last have sex? Are you sexually active at the moment?'

'Oh no, I've never really had sex. Not penetrative sex.' Finn's face began to warm. 'I mean, I've done other things!'

'Don't worry, no need to know about specific exploits here. But tell me why? Why have you not had sex?'

'I mean, I've tried, it just hasn't really worked before. I have wanted to, but it hurts too much.'

Laura's concern sparked discomfort in Finn. It was easier when no-one asked, when no-one seemed interested.

'So, it has been painful. Too painful? Painful without a sense that perhaps pleasure could be at the end of the tunnel?'

'No, it's just one long pain-tunnel.'

'Okay, that's not great! I mean, great you can describe it so well, but not so great at the same time!'

Doctor Laura seemed skilled at typing and talking. Finn wondered if she was creating a direct transcript of their conversation.

'Well, you happen to have come to a doctor with an interest in women's sexual health, so Finn, let's have a look at all this!' She turned to face Finn directly. 'Tell me now, why, exactly, haven't you had sex?'

Finn sighed. 'I haven't had sex because when I have tried, I have found it to be too painful.'

'Can you describe the sensation? Try to be as precise as possible.'

Finn thought for a moment, back to Eric, her boyfriend at university, all those years ago. What they tried to do seemed like the most natural thing in the world to him. For her, it felt like she was the wrong shape, as though they were unable to come together in that way you're supposed to.

Finn sighed. 'It felt like something bumping up against a balloon.'

Laura frowned. 'Do you mean a well-inflated balloon, or a balloon that has gone down slightly?'

'I mean, a really well-inflated balloon.'

Laura swivelled back.

'I've tried, I wanted to do it,' Finn felt embarrassed, as though she was defending herself. 'It just hasn't worked.'

Laura turned, casting a significant look. 'Finn, how do you feel about doing a pap smear? In a way, this doesn't make any sense because a pap smear is really meant for women who have become sexually active. But I think it could be a way for me to at least ascertain if there is a physiological reason for your lacking ability to have sex.'

Laura continued to talk in a calm and considered way. Finn saw herself in a mirror across the room. Her frown lines were very prominent. Perhaps people thought she was always frowning, even though the lines were more likely caused by a lifetime of squinting, being such a light-sensitive creature. Finn pulled her face into a sudden smile, attempting to flatten out her ruffled forehead. Laura halted.

'Finn, are you okay? What's wrong?'

'Nothing, I was just ... Go on.'

'Okay, well, we talk about men's sexual dysfunction quite a lot. It is a very noticeable thing if a man is unable to achieve arousal. However, for women, things are more easily muddled, even in ourselves. But it is very much possible for a woman to experience sexual dysfunction, for reasons that are entirely not her fault, and not at all based on her mental state, or her sexual orientation, or anything you might expect really. So, would you, Finn, allow me, now, to perform a pap smear?'

'Okay.'

'Great!' Pressing the return key sounded like a celebration.

'So first, just hop behind this curtain, take off everything from the top down and lie on this bed.'

It was all happening so quickly; there was no way out. Finn kicked off her shoes and whipped off her pants and underwear. It felt like Doctor Laura's efficiency was rubbing off, but unfortunately there were no gold stars awarded to those who can disrobe quickly.

'Okay, now, no, just lie back for me. And just relax. Take a deep breath, and this will be cold between your legs.'

The prodding was intrusive, uncomfortable, and in no way unfamiliar. After those repeated feelings of physical pain and failure, back in her early twenties, she had decided that sex was probably just not for her. Finn realised how stupid she was, when she was just five minutes younger than her present-self. Just five minutes ago, she had thought the doctor might be a safe-zone, somewhere she felt comfortable to just be herself. It was not a safe-zone. It was a place where she could be freshly reminded of what was raw, pink and wrong with her.

'Just as I thought. Nothing happening here,' Doctor Laura announced. 'I just can't get up there.' She continued investigating all the same. 'You know, even if you were a regular virgin, this wouldn't be so hard for me here. I mean, I wouldn't try to break in here, not if you didn't want me to. Okay, that's all fine, you can get dressed now!' She seemed to shout the news.

'But what's going on? Do you think there's something wrong with me?'

Laura sighed, somehow sounding far from disappointed. 'Well, women are born with a protective, perforated barrier, that, of course, is called the hymen. It is designed to break easily. For some, it is semi-perforate, which can cause very painful sex. For some, it is imperforate. And I mean, usually, this is noticed early in life, when you are a baby, or then, at puberty. But, if it goes unnoticed as long as it has for you, for instance, there is an increased chance of morbidity. It has probably changed the shape of your life in some ways.'

'Morbid ways?'

Laura hesitated. 'Potentially. Morbidity is just what we say. I don't mean to make you feel bad. I mean, even though this probably isn't something you have considered consciously, it's likely to have caused things in your life to happen in a particular way. And things in your life up till now, might have been different. Things still could be different.'

'But what if I don't want things to be different?'

'Finn, I would like you to try something at home.'

She held up her four fingers to me like she was showing a score. Then she pulled them all down, except her index finger.

'Finn I want you to try, gently, to stick one finger up there. Then two. If possible, three. Then if you can get to ...'

She held her four fingers together in a funny squashed way. 'If you can fit four in, like this, that would be roughly the same size as a penis. Just so you can see for yourself.'

'Oh. God.'

'Look, from your examination, I am quite certain that there is a problem! I am going to give you a referral to a specialist.'

Finn sat down again, shrugging into her cardigan, feeling as conspicuous as a tradie stumbling into Pure Source, asking for a pie and choc milk.

'There will be surgery, and basically, you will go in, get put to sleep, have the procedure, and it will all be done. And how are your periods? Do you have any unusual discharge? And what is your arousal fluid like? I mean, sorry, this is a lot to think about.'

'Is the surgery optional?'

Laura screwed up her face. 'Of course. Elective surgery is always elective. But believe me, you will want to have the surgery. It will mean you are able to have sex! Of course, at first it might be difficult. You may need to have genital physiotherapy to help get you started.'

Finn felt suddenly aware of the tight cross of her legs, always pulled in close, as though her body was bound, knotted in on itself. She reflected on the idea of loosening, and realised: she never wanted to hear the words 'genital' and 'physiotherapy' in the same sentence again.

'But here, you know, life begins!' Laura smiled and then looked as though she regretted her words. 'I'm sorry, I meant no disrespect by that. Of course, your life is already happening and you are happy and everything is fine. But this is the chance for, how shall I put it, a whole new range of options!' She turned back to the computer. 'I am writing you a referral. Don't worry, she is female.'

THE BOAT

@CELESTIAA_DAVINAA

Richard! Call me Celeste!

You're not the first person to query me on the title 'aggressive healer'! My girlfriends tell me it rubs people up the wrong way. But you know what? It gets a reaction, and that's saying something!

It's like when you ask someone if they like beetroot. Whatever their reaction is, it will be a strong one.

'Of course I hate beetroot!' 'Of course I love beetroot!'

Why are there these things that divide our opinions? Beetroot is a trigger point, touching our deepest nerves. The term 'aggressive healing' is no different. If you ask people if they are comfortable with it, you will get a firm Yes or No.

I can see that 'aggressive healing' may give an impression of violence, as though a person is being healed against their will. And in a way, this is true to what it is. Of course, a person can only heal if they want to be healed. But sometimes, their inner resistance is so strong, it's truly impossible for them to fight alone.

I am certain that people's firm reactions to my title as an 'aggressive healer' is proof that I am on the right track. This is, absolutely, what Spirit is calling me to do.

And don't get me wrong. I find no pleasure in provoking others. I don't WANT to hurt anyone! It's just, I know I was put on this earth to stir things up. I am here to get things moving, whether people like it or not!

Aggressive healing is all about working with people when they are at breaking point. I only work with those in crisis.

I am really of no use at any other time. I could also be called a 'confrontational healer'; I meet patients in their darkest moments. I reach inside them. I locate slime and terrible darkness. I push and I pull, until I find the core.

Personally, I think we all need to fall apart the right way, in order to be put back together correctly. All I do, is provide the perfect conditions for someone to fall apart. So yes, perhaps I am 'aggressive' because I help my clients break.

What kind of healing work do you do? Do you have a preferred modality? And where do you work? I always love to hear about the processes of my contemporaries!

I look forward to meeting you,

Om Shanti,

Celeste.

@RICH_NOT_YET_IN_HEAVEN

Well hello Celeste! Lovely to hear from you (finally! ☺)

I very much relate to what you're saying. I only enjoy working with clients who have genuine problems. That's how my centre runs really; people come here when they're truly desperate.

I practise from home, and my home is a land-dwelling boat. My healing centre is called Invisible Exit Wounds Anonymous (IEWA). Basically, I work with people who are holding extra-earthly deposits in their bodies. They are called 'Receivers'. A lot of people come here when they find they have been touched, but don't quite fit in to the usual alien experiencer paradigms and support networks.

I tend to get bored listening to people's problems when they're not really big ones. I know the value of a friendly, listening ear. I know there are healers who never earn that title because their work is behind the scenes; they are listening, solving problems, putting things in place and probably preventing crisis. But that's not the work I do. Really, people come to me when they have been suffering bad and nothing else has worked.

@CELESTIAA_DAVINAA

How amazing to connect so quickly on this level! I don't only struggle treating people when their wounds are shallow, I also can't stand talking to people about anything that's not deep and meaningful. It's straight to the heart with me! God just didn't give me the gene for small talk!

So your work is with Receivers! It's so strange to be contacted by you because I've been drawn to that area these past few months. I've been reading Receiver accounts and I understand that there's usually this moment of crisis in their lives.

I experienced a crisis in my late twenties, and from that old life, my new spiritual life was birthed. Since then my path has been breakthrough after breakthrough, but I must admit, that can be tiring ☺ I do enjoy the quiet times, when I am able to rest and recover, from all that time spent Up There.

I have felt called to study several different modalities over the years, and lately, I have really been hearing that expanding to work with Receivers is the next frontier for me. After all, despite our differences, we are all One. I am more familiar with casting out entities rather than deposits though. Do you have any particular thoughts on the similarities between the two?

@RICH_NOT_YET_IN_HEAVEN

Celeste, again, what a pleasure!

Now cleansing entities is not something I would claim to know a lot about.

If I understand correctly, entities are generally living beings, even if they're only partially alive. They are like displaced spirits that attach themselves inappropriately to people. They have yet to either 'pass on', or are just freely moving about the subtle atmosphere with their own private motives, seeking viable hosts.

While I believe that deposits a) each carry a special message for Receivers and b) come from what I believe is a higher vibrational space, they are not in fact living. Deposits do carry purpose and intention, and in that way very much resemble living things. I think of deposits as like seeds; they carry all this incredible information, but require just the right conditions to be activated, to grow with, and beyond the Receiver.

In other words, the deposit is not a living thing on its own, but once planted, it grows together with the Receiver, the living being, and together they are transformed.

I sometimes affectionately call deposits 'Star Seeds'; at once they are small, but hold this wonderful celestial material.

But generally I stick to the term 'deposit'; while perhaps less poetic, it is just easier and more straightforward to explain.

Richard felt a tear coming to his eye as he described his work. Perhaps it had meant something, all these years, all these extractions. Or maybe it just sounded better in words than it did in real life. Or maybe, Richard thought the painful thought, he was able to be impressed with the sound of his own voice.

@CELESTIAA_DAVINAA

Star Seeds! What a beautiful concept! A seed packed with a divine message of love!

@RICH_NOT_YET_IN_HEAVEN

It's funny you say that! I always thought that if every deposit were stripped back, the underlying message would be love. But that word is already surrounded with noise and cultural clatter, so I tend to avoid it.

Well, on Wednesdays we have the Circle of IEWA. Would you like to come sometime? Perhaps you could be a special guest next week, and give us a presentation on one of your preferred healing modalities. Or we could do a coffee. Or a walk at the beach. Or all of the above.

@CELESTIAA_DAVINAA

That sounds almost perfect. The only thing is I have zero-tolerance of caffeine. But I can definitely drink an LSD with you! (Latte Soy Dandelion – my favourite ☺)

I have been asked to write an article explaining Fifth Dimensional and Photonic Energy. Do you want to read it? I would love to know your thoughts. It's for the Esoteric Database Online, but I'll probably put it on my website too.

@RICH_NOT_YET_IN_HEAVEN
Fantastic! Well, if you send over the article, I'll have a look.

@CELESTIAA_DAVINAA
Fantastic! Om Shanti to you xx

'I made cupcakes!' August exclaimed, bumping her way into the yard. She pulled the plastic container from her backpack and thrust it towards Richard, trying to catch her breath. He never said no to a cake. 'There are plenty, so we can have one now!'

She flung her backpack next to her bike, then plucked off her helmet, shaking out her mane of blond hair. August had returned home from work around midday, and baked up a storm for the Circle of IEWA.

'Fabulous!' Richard shouted, flipping his laptop shut, then holding it under his arm, as though it were an envelope with a secret message inside. August felt her face scrunching up. It seemed like Richard hid things from her. Perhaps he saw her as just a kid. Or perhaps it was because she hid things from him too.

'Let's hop aboard and make ourselves some tea!' Richard declared, gazing around the sculpture garden, seeming to frown. 'Although it is looking fantastic out here, August!'

The sculpture garden was where August and Richard had first met. August was riding past on her bike when she noticed the proliferation of scrap: so many colours, shapes and textures. There were springs and rusted cogs, ceramic fragments, tin sheets, parts of old machinery that she would never know the names of, so many mirror shards, and so much wire ... It was back in the beginning of the year, when she dropped her bike to the ground and, still wearing her helmet, began to grab at this piece of metal, pull a pink tile from under that mess of wire, choose from a selection of bricks, stack the bricks and tiles on top of an old tyre, and thus started to create sculptures. Richard came out, smiling and laughing, and joined her. August and Richard shared many hours together, back then, populating the garden with sculptures. Before long, August was coming into the boat, tidying, making tea, vacuuming, hanging artworks, attending the Circle of IEWA, and even assisting in extractions.

'Your enthusiasm is your superpower!' Richard announced, back then. When he said that, it felt like August was being given special permission; it was okay to just be herself. What Richard didn't know was that August had been seeking healing for such a long time, before she chanced upon his scrapyard, and found acceptance there. She had been a part of women's circles, dreaming workshops, dance therapy, experiencer support groups, meditation classes, sound healing and yoga. But with Richard, and IEWA, she finally found a place that made her feel like she once did in church; a place where she could laugh too loud, talk too much, and knock things over without being accused of a lack of spiritual awareness.

Richard climbed up the ladder and August followed, scurrying up into the galley and flicking the kettle on.

'August, you are a gem,' he called out, before he slumped into a chair. 'I am ravenous, and there is nothing besides a mass of beige biscuits in the cupboard.'

He laughed in his smooth, charismatic way, and August joined in. She often found herself laughing hysterically with Richard, never sure if anything in particular was funny. But this didn't really matter, because in a way, all of life was ridiculous and what can you do if you can't laugh?

'It will certainly be nice to eat something that isn't beige,' Richard said, as he plucked up one of the golden cupcakes.

August squealed with delight, becoming slightly breathless. 'Jsun should be bringing some supplies today! Perhaps he will bring foods of many colours!' Suddenly realising how thirsty she was, August took a huge gulp from her pink water bottle, which sparkled as she squeezed it. She pushed her sticky hair away from her face.

'Yes, I have come to depend on Jsun and his supplies lately,' Richard said, taking a bite from the cake and chomping loudly. 'Call me lazy.'

'I would never call you lazy!' August cried, then coughed, thumping her chest.

'Are you okay?'

'Yes,' she choked, coughing again, feeling that blockage inside. 'I think some water went down the wrong pipe.' Richard nodded, a little too significantly. August wasn't sure he was listening properly. Perhaps there were other voices, more important voices, speaking inside his being. He stared out the porthole, drumming his fingers on the table. August looked out the window too, but couldn't see what he could see. The kettle started to boil, and she bounded over to the cupboards to look for cups.

'And what are these delicious bites exactly?' Richard called out, words muffled by food.

'Semolina cakes,' she sang out, finding two floral mugs in the sink. She began rinsing them: 'With orange pulp and sultanas. I think they're alright!'

'I think you've outdone yourself this time!'

'I was actually paying attention while they were in the oven. I usually just forget, and they end up well beyond ready. Tom likes these ones too.'

'When are we going to meet him?'

August laughed, opening cupboards. 'I promise you will meet him one day.' The tea was moving around, she could never find it. 'Have you finally run out of teabags, Richard? I don't think I should have any more coffee, I've had three already today.'

Richard began to swing on his chair and sighed. 'God only knows. I haven't seen any in a while. There should be some leaf tea on the loose somewhere.'

'Aha!' August had opened the lid of a saucepan to find Green Tea with a Hint of Rose. 'Found some!'

'Oh God, not that stuff!' Richard cried. 'Everything is hidden for a reason!'

August watched steam rise from the kettle as she poured water into the mugs. The steam was water, transformed. It was energy that had changed form, because energy never dies. It just takes on new and unexpected shapes. She cupped her hands around one mug, closed her eyes and hummed.

'I hope it doesn't taste the way it smells!' Richard called out.

August's hum broke into a laugh. She carried over the mugs of tea, a scent of potpourri wafting between them. After placing the cups down, August realised she felt too hot, and began flicking her hair. Some hair got caught in her mouth, and she coughed, knocking her tea.

Richard chomped into a cake, nodding. 'It's good, August, actually. Quite moist. Really good!'

'You sound surprised!' August wiped tea from the table with her shirt, thankful Richard wasn't observant enough to notice her clumsiness. She pulled herself into a cross-legged position on the chair.

Richard shook his head, speaking through mouthfuls. 'I didn't mean it like that! I'm not surprised it is good, I am just impressed!'

'Thank you. Also, there are crumbs all through your beard.'

'But there are no crumbs on the floor,' Richard said. 'A beard is a preventative broom, sweeping up the food before it falls far.'

He squashed more into his mouth, causing more crumbling. 'YUM!'

August snorted with laughter. His cake-eating was truly grotesque, and she loved to watch. He had a careless abandon that was like a form of enlightenment. 'Richard, you are the best!'

'Oh yeah,' he chuckled through mouthfuls. 'Maybe you could go shout that out to all of Fremantle. IEWA could use some new clients.'

August nodded sweetly. 'I can shout it out as loud as I can.'

'Well then! Do you think we should have an IEWA committee meeting soon?'

'Oh please, go for it.'

Richard was motioning towards the cakes.

'The tea tastes dusty rather than rosy,' August mused, staring at a hole in the wall. 'I licked the spoon. And the bowl. So I'm not too hungry ...' She began carefully denuding her cupcake of its biodegradable patty pan.

'Oh thank you. And that was great, the last meeting,' Richard said. 'We must do that again soon. With the hats, mind you.'

'Richard, I don't know what you're talking about.'

'Our last IEWA committee meeting. With you and Finn? And we all wore hats!'

'Oh, the hats! I liked the hats. I don't know that Finn liked it.'

'You have a meeting, you discuss serious matters, but everyone wears a funny hat. I love it. I had the jester hat and you ...'

'I had my owl hat!' cried August. 'And Finn, she didn't have a funny hat.'

'Oh that's right! I mummified her head with a scarf.'

Richard chomped down the last chunk of cake.

'I was afraid, I suppose, that Finn didn't like the hats. Or maybe she didn't like any of it, the meeting.' August looked down at her arm, and began to scratch the skin around her elbow. It was hard to raise the topic with Richard. She didn't want to create any discord within the group. But sometimes it felt like Finn didn't like her at all. August felt like a bounding puppy, while Finn was an older cat, ready to swipe. 'I was concerned, perhaps, that in the meeting I was too domineering?'

'Nonsense! Finn just takes things too seriously. She once told me that she never dresses up. Not at school, at parties, and if she was invited to a dress-up party, she would come dressed normally. I don't understand, you would stand out more, not dressed up, be uncomfortable.'

'I think some people just don't dress up.'

'We are sticking with the hats. Next meeting, hats, if I have to buy Finn a silly hat myself.' Richard leaned back and patted his belly. 'Well, thank you dearly, August my dear. I think, now, I need to have a bit of a rest before people start arriving.'

'Oh sorry, yes, of course, I hope I haven't bothered you.'

'Don't ever apologise, not for anything!'

'Oops ...' August trailed off, trying desperately not to say sorry again. 'Well, I was thinking I might spend some time with the scrap.'

'Don't overdo it.' Richard's eye looked crooked, behind his crooked finger pointing. 'You need to take care of yourself.'

'I'm sorry, I make you worry.' August frowned, collecting the plates, then laughed. 'I'm sorry I said sorry again. Let me just get this place cleaned up. But I just realised something, Richard. We both live in forms of transport! You live in a boat and I live in a caravan!'

Richard belted out a laugh, and swung back on his chair, as August collected the plates, took them to the sink, and then skipped over to the ladder, excited to spend some time in the garden.

The evening sky glowed like toffee. August scraped her way off the ladder, past chicken-wire fencing, tin sheets and forty-four-gallon drums, out to the sculpture garden. She looked up to the recent piece she'd spray-painted. It was a giant plywood board, with the neon-green outline of an alien. The being's legs were crossed, eyes closed, hands held together in prayer position. Above were the words: FIND YOUR INNER ALIEN.

August looked up to the boat. She could just make out Richard's face, a shadow in the golden light of the porthole. His head moved, jerkily, and occasionally she heard him laugh. He seemed excited about something.

She turned to the configurations of brick, rubble, rusted cogs, wooden slats, pieces of ceramic and coloured glass. She looked at the sculptures that she and Richard had constructed, that the wind had deconstructed, that they had built again.

Here in the garden, Richard had once spoken of preordained negative spaces. There were spaces ready, assigned for shapes to neatly lock into. A smooth river stone slid perfectly down the neck of a bottle. Three clay bricks were wedged into a wooden shipping crate, making the sound of rubbing earth as they touched. Some negative spaces shifted and changed, their needs adjusting over time. Other remained waiting, unfilled for what seemed like an eternity, waiting for the perfect object to provide wholeness.

August kneeled in the dirt, eyeing the scrap. Squelching her hands into the dirt, enjoying the coolness of deeper earth, she began to scope for those empty nooks where junk-items might be accepted – where lost, unwanted things might be welcome. And that's when she found the pipe. It was just a small section, but heavy, like it might have once been used by olden-day plumbers, or as a murder weapon. It was caked with dirt, but August didn't bother to dust it down. Instead, she held the pipe in her lap, as if inviting it to speak.

The pipeline snaked underground, across farms, above rivers, from the coast to the goldfields, carrying water in its belly. They walked along it in the silver moonlight; climbing carefully over fences, creeping by paddocks, shouting over hills. They were a league of adolescents, swinging torches, discussing why the word 'booshwa' isn't spelt the way it sounds. When Dean – the kid with big lips and drag queen impersonations – fell into some collapsed gums, he laughed, and who knows how many others laughed. But maybe it wasn't funny. Maybe he was hurt, and maybe his drag queening wasn't comedy, but maybe he was practising for who he might one day become.

Amongst dangling torchlights, clopping feet, voices rising out of the darkness, along a giant cement snake rising up and over the land, that is where August met Tom the second time.

The first time was in art class. He was a year older, but not many people did art, so the year eleven and twelve art class was combined. When she walked through the door, Tom was standing there, like a porter.

He said, 'Welcome to art class, August,' and who knows how he knew her name. Tom had long blond curly hair, tied up in a ponytail. He had a ski-jump nose, and a lisp, and wore purple Doc Martens. His fingernails were painted, some blue, some red, some orange. He painted the bush and women playing guitars wearing rainbow beanies. Everybody knew he would get the art prize, but he was so sad sometimes. It made him sad that he was good at art and nothing else, even though that wasn't true. He was also good at accounting. One afternoon, August overheard him talking to Dayna – the girl who would be runner-up in art – about the youth group, where he went on Friday nights. August knew the group he was talking about. There wasn't much for young people to do in town, especially at night. A local church ran a group where fifty or so kids went and hung out. She'd tried it a couple of times, but always found herself stuck on the sidelines; of loud sporting activities, of the loud throwing of flour and water at each other, of loud playing the limbo, or the loud cheering on someone as they shoved endless marshmallows into their mouth, at intervals trying to say 'chubby bunny'. It's not that she didn't like the loudness, the brightness, the excitement of it all. She actually craved to be a part of it. But it's like this was a loudness and brightness that didn't belong to her. She couldn't find a way in, and found herself always watching, always trying to smile, while feeling lost.

But when she followed Tom there in year eleven, things seemed different. Some kids were there for the Christianity. Others were there for the running, jumping, kicking, high-fiving, climbing walls and shovelling cake and chips into mouths. But then some kids stood on the sidelines, and didn't seem like they were missing out. It seemed like they were having their own version of youth group, a more private one, which had its own language, its own secret codes. Maybe these sideline-kids were 'dorky' or 'weird' or 'misfits' or 'not good at sport'. But Dean would make jokes and the sideliners would all laugh, but be laughing with him, not at him. Kelly, who at school was 'the overweight girl', smiled over at Jenton – 'the one who was good with computers' – her hand giving his a squeeze. Jessica, who was 'the girl who always wore the backwards cap', slipped a letter into Ada's back pocket, and it looked like she had done it a thousand times. All the sideliners listened politely to the 'devotions' when kids from easy homes told everyone why Jesus was the way. But on that first night, walking along the pipeline, there were no sidelines. Everyone was moving together.

'I've been saved. It's weird.' Tom's voice floated along behind him, as he stepped along the grey, into the night. He chuckled: 'being saved' seemed like something he was shy about it, but it also seemed very important.

He hadn't meant for it to happen, he said, over his shoulder. It was one of those big rallies in the city. The youth leaders took the teenagers up on a bus.

Dean had asked if they would go, because he thought it would be funny. But then there was singing, lights, electric guitars and smoke machines, and all these emotions rising up, and some other thing being smoked out of him.

And the man with the microphone started to say, 'If you feel it ... If you feel it now, come to the front. Come to the front now.'

Tom found his feet, while Dean's mouth formed a perfect O. Tom's feet walked him up, and he was taken backstage by a team of women with white-blond hair. Out the back, people were shaking and falling over, and a man put his hand on Tom's forehead and asked, 'Do you know Jesus?'

'I do now,' Tom said.

Next Tom was seated at a small desk and a man told him he needed to get baptised as soon as possible, that he must also sign this form, but from the moment of baptism, his pain should be washed away. That's the story he told August, that first night, walking alone the pipeline. Then he began to laugh too, and say how it was all very strange.

It had been months since he'd been saved, Tom said. He wasn't on a high anymore. It's as though his brain, body and soul were all washed clear, but he was still a bit directionless. The church elders and youth leaders said he just needed to get right with God. He just needed to get washed, properly, in the spirit. He needed to be baptised in-house. But Tom didn't feel ready, then he felt guilty for feeling sad, because he wasn't supposed to feel sad; all that pain should've been washed away when he was saved. What difference would baptism make?

It had started to get cold at the bottom of the garden on Trusting Lane. August's arms were covered in goosebumps, and the sky was no longer glowing. She dusted down the piece of pipe, rubbing it against her jeans, which were already covered in paint marks, torn in places, patched up with pink love hearts, flowers, peace signs and celestial figures drawn in coloured fabric marker. She gently placed the pipe down in the centre of a cement slab.

❁

Richard, I finished my article super-quick in the end. You can check it out on my website! www.celestialbeamsoflight.com xxx

Celestiaa Davinaa Welcomes You!
Celestial - Divine
Celestial Beams of Light
Celeste, She Beams Light
Aggressive Healer - Modern Day Guru - Violet Flame Worker - Theta Expert - PLR Therapist - Fifth Dimension Advocate -

**How do we heal? What should we put in our mouths?
Will vitamins help us? Magnesium relaxes muscles, B12 reduces stress, but what else can we do to facilitate repair?
How do we create sound spiritual health?
Our subtle selves are crying out at a cellular level. They are crying out for the Triple C - 'Complete Cellular Calmness'
CU in 5D!**

**Upgrade your DNA now!
Unlock codes from ancestors and past lives!
Find the genes to defeat inner Resistance!
Switch off Cancer Genes!**

Davinaa's Daily Thought

Everything happens for a reason. I'm sorry to break it to you. There is spirit and intention in all things. Nothing can escape that. But what is motion without intent? I trip over on my way to the dinner table. What is that telling me? Maybe I've got a vitamin deficiency, blocked ears, an awareness problem, or something else entirely. What was that experience trying to teach me? Was the table saying, 'I'm here, I'm closer than you think'?

Was Spirit saying, 'Look around. Be present. It is time to be aware of your surroundings'?

What message do I take on? *I should watch where I am going. It is right to be consciously connected, in perfect harmony with my surroundings.*

Yes, that's awareness. It is okay to move quickly, but we must be careful to avoid motion without intent. Movement becomes mere activity rather than action. It is right that when I am cold, I put on a jumper. It is right that when I am uncomfortable, I adjust the cushion on my seat. Yes, our actions, our reactions, have causes. They mean something.

What is your meaning?

CU in 5D!

Recent articles

The Right Kind of Regression – PLR Therapy Today

Waterwise versus Water Wisdom

From Pain Bodies to Light Bodies; The Photonic Future

The Great Shift Process is upon us. The purple edge of the photon belt has touched the earth's atmosphere. For some Lightworkers, our internal vibration counters are jumping and blipping all over the place. Our Vibrational States are ready to shift. For others it is a release, what has been prayed for, like welcome rain. For others, little strange things are starting to happen.

Maybe we are beginning to experience Ascension Symptoms, physical pains, parts of our pain bodies not feeling ready, sabotaging the movement into a Light Body.

I have talked to many Lightworkers who used to be Christians, leaving the church because the doctrines failed to accommodate their open spirituality. But I've heard from them, again and again – 'I always knew we would be the generation who would see Jesus.'

Watch the progression of awareness through recent generations. In the sixties, there was a new knowledge about war, environmental issues, the treatment of women. There was a raised awareness about these broad issues, but now, so many young people have become aware on a deeper level – of their own spirituality. Veganism is not so much popular now because of animal rights, but because of the diet's sentience, because so many young people are devoted to Spiritual Self Evolution.

Yes, these are all signs, the Great Shift Process is here.

Even think about colours. What colours are you drawn to? Has this changed in recent years? Photon Belt energy, which is Fifth Dimensional (5D), or Holographic Energy, translates as light, pastel colours. Even hyper-colours, bright pink and green – that is the intensity in this Energy – not deep and heavy, earthy reds and browns. And look around you in clothing stores, they are the colours that everyone is drawn to.

Everyone is affected by the pull of the Photon Belt. Photonic energy is our future; it will replace electricity. It will alter our communication because it will enable Instant Manifestation.

We will think thoughts, we will desire things, then be able to manifest them instantly. The gap is closing, between human abilities and powers of the divine.

But I know, it won't all be like this, and it won't be easy for everyone. I strongly believe that everyone will be better off with the increased presence of Photonic Energy in the earth's atmosphere.

But as you know, powers of good are capable of wreaking havoc as well. Because those amongst us in the darkness, they are going to react against the light. People don't want to change. Some have been stuck in the same, lightless realities, lifetimes, over and over again. Yes, even for them, there will be Ascension Symptoms.

At first, Photonic Energy will be like manic depression; it will make every beautiful moment seem brighter, more clear and pure, more real. But it will make dark and terrible moments feel all the more fierce, inescapable.

Knowing this, Lightworkers need to be careful where they put their energetic focus. For different Lightworkers are called to work with people at all different stages in their Path to Enlightenment.

Me, I work well with people in crisis mode, because that's when my powers as an aggressive healer can really speak freely. When people are at their lowest, that is often when they can really take confrontation. But that is not for everyone – that is a heavy Burden.

Some believe that the best place for most Lightworkers to vibrate is around 5. The Photonic Energy is up around 9, but that is really for monks living in solitude, and you can feel the energy from their good thoughts radiating miles away. Most people are vibrating down at a 2, but if Lightworkers try to stay around 5, that will work well.

So what is there for us to do?

Call out to the Energy.

Ask for it, ask it into your life. Every morning, every night. Allow it to transform you. Cover your walls with the colours of the Fifth Dimension. Allow yourself to be Transported, At Night, Any Time.

Know sometimes it is time to rest because we all know how tiring it can be, endless travelling Up There.

We are all in this together. This is the future of our Beautiful Earth Ship Planet. Thanks be to Spirit!

❀

Richard finished reading and looked around the walls of his room. They were definitely not the colours of the fifth dimension. To call it a room was perhaps an overstatement. 'The sleep cabin', Ross had named it. There was just a small porthole, and the walls were old pine panelling which could really use a varnish. He had gone for such a long time not seeing the faults in the boat like this. The thoughts weren't plaguing him all the time, now, but there were moments when the inadequacy of the boat just lurched up in front of him. Yes, we are on a 'Beautiful Earth Ship Planet' as Celestiaa called it, but wouldn't it be nice if our homes were vessels equal in loveliness?

He looked back down at the screen, at some of Celestiaa's wonderful phrases, like 'call out to the Energy', 'there is spirit and intention in all things', 'the Great Shift Process is upon us'. He couldn't quite follow what she was talking about – vibrational states and Lightworkers were not really a part of his healing vocabulary – but what he did read was her enthusiasm. What he did read was that she wasn't spent. In this way, she felt fundamentally different from him. Was he past it?

There were still fifteen minutes until the circle members arrived. Richard decided: it was time. He wanted to find out if he still had a passion for all this. Maybe by speaking, by slipping back into his preacher mode, he could rediscover, recreate that passion. Maybe that's what was missing.

'Love is like bread, it needs to be baked fresh every day,' he said aloud.

Maybe the love for the self, the love for the self's own projects, works like this too. Maybe he didn't need to devote daily loving attention to IEWA.

He took a while, finding the way to open the camera on the computer.

Ross had been encouraging Richard to try to make a video-blog for a while now. Maybe it was just his way of fobbing Richard off again. When Richard had complained – the waning numbers of appointments, the lack of interest in IEWA, the way it felt like the place was falling apart – Ross seemed dismissive.

'You've got to get your name out there, tell your story,' Ross kept saying.

Richard was half-listening, dreading that moment when Rocia's body, shiny with sweat, would come up alongside Ross, pressing that cool glass of white wine into his face, a gesture which said, again, *come to bed*, followed by the flicker in Ross's eyes, his attention caught by something bigger and more important than Richard.

'Even if you talk and talk and don't get anything useable for your website, it could just be good for you, yourself, talking it all out.'

'Oh yeah, "Hi, I'm Richard and this is my story, gather round, folk ..."'

'It's not weird, Richard, everyone's doing it now. You've just got to talk to the computer, look into the camera like you're looking inside a person's soul.'

Richard removed his glasses, and his head fell in his hands. There was a story he wanted to tell, but that story was difficult to tell. Maybe it wasn't even a story really, but dread; a sense of an end closing in.

THE CIRCLE OF IEWA

There was a picture of her on the wall. Black and white, thick dark fringe, hoop earrings. One leg bent, left hand clasping a straw hat. She was on a bustling Asian city street somewhere, smiling up at a confusion of signs. People in pyramid hats rode past fruit vendors. A man sat cross-legged on the ground, painting.

When Finn arrived, Richard's bedroom door was closed, August's chatter drifting up from the sculpture garden. She could be on the phone. But it could be that August was talking to someone who wasn't there at all: August was the kind of person who might be 'in touch' with beings, or spirits, or entities, from other places.

The photograph wanted to be looked at. Sitting on the couch, you were helpless to it. Perhaps the eyes drew you in. Or was it that portraits like this with candles nearby evoked the words *rest in peace*?

Finn felt a wave of anger. She was tempted to fling the photograph off the shelf, and let it shatter across the room.

'She was just too young.'

It happened often, back in the beginning, that Richard mentioned Serena. He made mournful comments in passing that seemed like invitations for condolences.

Beneath the picture a litter of tea-light candles often glowed, and a Buddha-shaped incense burner, though Richard was not a Buddhist.

'She burned so bright,' was another thing he always said.

Back in the beginning, Richard told Finn that this was Serena, who was once his wife. She had 'disappeared' when they were travelling, back in India in the seventies. Finn imagined there were drugs involved, sitars too, streaming shapes and all that Oneness. But she couldn't resist. Finn knew it was not helpful, how curious she could be at times.

'Was her body ever found? Were you questioned by the Indian authorities?'

'What are you talking about?' Richard had laughed in that slightly manic way. 'Serena's not dead! Our marriage ended,' he clicked his fingers, 'just like that! We were too young!'

'I don't know what to say,' Finn had stammered. Back then, she hadn't known Richard long enough to get angry. But she was certain he'd wilfully misled her. She was sure that his passing comments implied something tragic had come of her. Then again, in Richard's mind, it *was* pure tragedy. His wife left him.

'People don't ever really disappear though,' Richard's speech had quickened. 'Even when they will their own disappearance. There are still particles of her all over me. I have her bacteria on my skin, inside my digestive tract. Every hair on my head knows Serena, better than God knows me.'

Richard had grabbed fistfuls of hair, pulling tight at the roots. Finn felt her body tense, feeling a wrench at her own scalp.

'Gah! She's still here! The DNA I had telling me to be Richard is producing new messages, telling me to be the Richard who once knew Serena, and this is all because of the way she touched me!'

Finn wondered about letting go when Richard said all this. The natural urge for elimination that comes in the morning. Her own sense of celebration, resisting the urge to applaud at a bountiful morning poo.

'Does it feel good, remembering her like this?'

As soon as Finn finished the question, she knew she had

gone too far. He didn't need a solution here, he only wanted the problem to be heard. Theoretically, that was okay.

'Nope!' He'd reached over and grabbed a bottle of soda water. It hissed open, liquid erupting down the sides.

'Sorry, I dropped that earlier. I should have said.'

Richard just stared, bubbly water pooling on the coffee table. It seemed very hot in the room.

'No,' he sighed. 'It doesn't feel good. Not now, not ever. I think I'm still hanging on to some rope, thinking if I just reel it in, there will be some answers tied to the end. But who knows, maybe hope is just a habit designed to avoid pain. I know it's a cliché, but when she left, a part of me left too. I'm carrying her around with me, but I have lost something as well. People say that because it's true. I'm an incomplete person.'

Now Finn breathed deep, hoping a calm would wash over her. She sat down, in the place where Richard always sat, and looked at Serena. Something began to flutter inside her. She felt something like excitement for his departed wife. She closed her eyes and saw Serena – a turning wheel, spinning wild and free over the blue earth.

The sound of gamelans flooded the boat as Richard emerged from his room, a small cabin which housed a single bed and a very large stereo. He looked past tired, despite his bustling.

'Hey, my Finn! What did the doctor say, an apple a day?'

'Why are you shouting? You look terrible.'

He laughed, bopping out of time. 'Sorry, got to get myself into a crowd-pleasing mood. How was it?'

'She thinks I have an unbreakable hymen.'

Richard's face changed colour.

Dammit, the knee-jerk overshare.

'Sorry. I probably didn't need to tell you that. Richard, you've gone red.'

'I'm red? You're red!' Richard was now cross-legged on the floor, looking up at Finn. She felt irked at how this positioned her – a storyteller, or Jesus, ready to share a moral tale.

I don't have all the answers! She wanted to climb onto the roof of the boat, and shout this at Richard, at the universe.

'We don't have to talk about this. I'll figure it out.'

'But surely, my Finn, this isn't material for a "figuring it out" kind of spectrum? It's more a one-off by the sounds.'

'I hope it's a one-off, one-snip-fix-all. What if it's like getting your ears pierced – if you don't wear earrings regularly the holes just close over?'

The gamelans had switched into double-time, Richard's face turning once more.

'I'll turn that down,' he shouted, dancing back to the bedroom.

'I know how to be strong,' Finn called. 'I'll deal with it.'

Settle for the shit end of the stick. Learn how not to be special. Become exceptional for all the wrong reasons.

The image of Doctor Laura's jab-happy wand flew into Finn's mind. Something trying to force its way into her body, something unwanted. Now she was here, inside, in a place she always regarded as safe. But was she happy? And anyway, what would it be like – really – to go to a hospital, to have doctors fiddle with her body, after all this time pursuing healing only with Richard and IEWA?

'I can't believe you're shouting about this!' he called back, apparently struggling with the controls. The music increased to a banging before cutting out. A new smooth sound emerged, which Finn recognised from *Harmonium Drones for Healing*. She felt a pleasant resonance inside her chest. It seemed the shapes were settling.

Flopping onto the couch, Richard cast his arm around Finn's shoulder, hauling her in.

At times, Finn still felt troubled by his blurred sense of personal space. Richard tended to stand too close in a way that didn't seem opportunistic – the brush of shoulders giving the gift of non-consensual intimacy – just unaware. He would rest his palm on a stranger's shoulder, providing comfort and propping himself up at once. He would pick strange moments to offer massages, during discussions on water hygiene, or the mercury content in vaccines.

Whilst this unnecessary touch was alarming at first – and more than once Finn had to tell him, 'No, I do not feel like a shoulder rub'– she now and then looked forward to these snatches of intimacy. A close-up of Richard's face – his grey wiry beard, big brown glasses, the garlic smell of his breath – was something Finn came to associate with secret-sharing, because Richard had become her closest friend. It wasn't that she was physically attracted to him, but that when he held her, it meant that she, just for that moment, had a home.

But Finn worried too, that her potential future partners may not be comfortable with the relaxed boundaries between Richard and her. Ethann – if and when he visited IEWA – might find it confronting. Perhaps Ethann and Richard would fight over her, resolving to sling an arm around one shoulder each.

She knew that things would have to change, eventually. Also, there were those times when Richard's touch just zapped her of energy. She knew he didn't mean to do it, but that didn't change the fact. It's as though he used human touch as a way of fuelling his own spirits.

Then why doesn't he realise, Finn wondered, that when he is fuelling himself, he is depleting someone else?

Finn crossed her arms, and her legs, finding herself in that tight bind again. An image of a CLOSED sign, slung around her neck, came into her mind.

'I worry about your saintly qualities, my Finn,' Richard broke her thoughts. 'Do you know the "burnt chop syndrome"?'

'I always thought my mum had that,' Finn cocked her head to the side, reflecting. 'Then I realised she liked burnt chops. Gnawing at them, sucking the marrow from dry, salty bones.'

Richard grimaced. 'That's gruesome! Well of course, we can develop a taste for it – not getting what we want. It takes some highs and lows out of life. You know – "Smile, expect nothing, and you won't be disappointed". I think the Dalai Lama said that.'

'Why are you quoting the Dalai Lama? I thought you weren't a Buddhist.'

Richard rolled his eyes. 'Finn, here's a challenge. Every day, first just ten minutes, I just want you to sit and try to believe that you deserve something great in life.'

'I've been set enough personal challenges today.'

'But you *deserve* it!'

'I deserve to be challenged?'

'God, you can be facetious!'

Oh I'm God now, am I? Finn didn't say.

'Listen to me! There are three kinds of people in this world. There are the ones driven by an inner child, screaming "I'm not good enough!" Then there are the ones who get angry when any little thing goes wrong. They scream and shout "I don't deserve this!" And then there are the ones who just get up, and piss all over life,' Richard was standing – hands on hips – gyrating to his diatribe, 'like they're able to just check out, be exempt from all this!'

He was still now, arms pointing rigid towards the floor. The room fell silent a moment, before harmonium again spewed forth. Finn pulled her cardigan close, although it was quite stuffy.

A mosquito buzzed close to her nose. 'How was the rest of your day?'

Richard sat down, frowning. 'I read your story.'

'You didn't like it.'

'It just made me wonder, are you okay, Finn?' He placed his palm like a starfish over her head.

'I'm fine.' She closed her eyes, enjoying the feeling of pressure on her scalp. 'I'm always fine. Did the treatments go okay in the end?'

'Well, Joan didn't like the warmed milk. She said she

knew it had been microwaved. She could tell the molecular structure had been altered. "Tampered with" I believe are the words she used. She said she didn't mind if orange juice was heated because that's so heavily processed anyway. "Not ideal" she said, but more manageable than the milk.'

'Well that makes no sense.'

Richard shrugged. 'What does make sense?' Footsteps thumped on the ladder, and Eve's face appeared at the door to the main cabin, her mouth open wide. Her talking was like howling – her hideous day, which involved work as a marketing assistant, and volunteering as a medical intuit. After her, the face of Rhodda popped up – a face always smiling, atop three chins and a large mole. Eve must be talking to Rhodda, Finn realised. Her shoulders relaxed; she wasn't expected to be following the tangled threads of conversation.

Rhodda wasn't a Receiver, but she was a true listener, and Finn wondered sometimes if that was a more profound thing. Rhodda worked as a psychic and accompanied her partner Jsun to the circle. His face appeared next, a tiny, skinny face, brown teeth. Always wearing at least two watches, he worked at a local tyre-fitter and a supermarket and was responsible for the circle's supply of tea and biscuits. August materialised after Jsun, eager and wide-eyed, as though afraid she might miss something. The whole boat began to creak with the weight of everyone.

Looking around at the motley Circle of IEWA, Finn wondered, as she had done often lately, what on earth she was doing here. She had never seen a Grey alien – or a 'Zeta Reticulan' as Jsun called them. She had never heard the sweet voice of a Pleiadian as she lay down to sleep. Her car radio had never experienced unexplained interference during a long drive at night. As a child, she spent afternoons imagining what lay beyond the powerlines, wondering at what point the sky stopped being blue and became space. But she had never seen any strange lights, had no memory loss, and no peculiar scarring on her body. And in spite of all this, Finn had always known that her shapes were from somewhere else. And that they were special.

Finn recalled her original visits to the alien-experiencer support group. It was about ten years ago, when Finn was in her early twenties, still at university and living in share-houses around the city. The group met on Wednesday nights in a Greek Orthodox church hall. The experiencers were mainly older women, sitting on folding chairs, drinking milky tea, sharing plant cuttings and offering Finn plastic bags full of frozen pies. Finn was welcomed warmly, but something didn't feel quite right. The grandmas smiled and nodded when she told her story.

Finn had been acquainted with the shapes for as long as she could remember. When she was little she called them her 'floating blocks'. At night, they were luminous red and blue forms hovering above her bed. Sometimes they resembled coral plankton, things lit up in the deep. Tendrils that swayed, touching each other. Gaps between light beams formed more shapes – triangles, webs, tiny faces tucked into leaves, between the cracks of snail shells.

Each morning she would call them back. There were many ways to get in: through the ear, mouth or nose. And the shapes were able to enter, as they could exit, straight through the skin.

Back then, the shapes moved freely and easily, inside and outside her body. If Finn's body were an aquarium and the shapes were goldfish, they were able to swim out of the water, flit about in the open air, then return to safety, behind the glass. They were particles of matter moving between her and everything else. Finn did not begin or end anywhere. She was one with all.

Once Finn hit adolescence, the pain-experience began. Her mum swayed in at night, clutching a glass of port, showing her the foetal position.

'This is just the way it is for us women.'

When she was thirteen, the words started. Dyspepsia. Irritable bowel syndrome. Period pain. Painful ovulation. Crohn's disease. Fibroids.

Also when she was thirteen, the shapes changed. Finn needed to go to bed early. She would lie there quietly, gradually breathing them out. Sometimes they didn't exit at all, no matter what Finn did. She would fall asleep, exhausted in the extraction process, only to be woken at two a.m., the shapes moving wildly about her abdomen.

There were times when the release came so suddenly, her bedside shuddered. Glasses of water were knocked over, toys fell off the bed. As soon as they had exited, the pain would leave, sometimes slowly, sometimes instantly. Either way, the process was exhausting. And that's the way things were for Finn, from when she was thirteen, and into adulthood.

The women at the experiencer support group smiled and nodded at the story. Smiles and nods said they had seen it all, knew it all, but they didn't have any advice to offer.

And for once, Finn wanted advice.

She had found Richard's flyer – years later – wedged amongst other strange advertisements on the Pure Source noticeboard.

...Do you feel ALIEN amongst ALIEN EXPERIENCERS?
DO YOU have.... UNEXPLAINED, RECURRING PAIN?
...Feel like it's TRYING to TEACH U SOMETHIN?........
Want to LEARN more about DEPOSITS THEORY????....
Need aSSISTANCE in HEALING from EXTRA-EARTHLY
DEPOSITS....LIVING IN U 2DAY???? YES!!!!.............
Phone 92429080, or come to....................
——IEWA—INVISIBLE EXIT WOUNDS ANONYMOUS!
————At the LITTLE MOTHER EARTH SHIP ——
Aka RICHARD's WORLD's END, 21 Trusting Lane!!!!———
2nd WED each MONTH - INFO NITE 5-6pm—————-
——EVERY WEDNESDAY 6.30-8pm CIRCLE of IEWA——
—Don't LeT This DIVINE MESSAGE CALCIFY!!-
CALL 2 DAY!

A few of Finn's co-workers took photos and posted on social media, with comments like 'alien grammar', 'wacko!', 'Pure Source classic', or 'are these extended ellipses trying to teach me something about the universe?'

Finn laughed like everyone else, but secretly stuffed the advert into her back pocket during the monthly noticeboard clear out.

To her, the poster read: *you are not alone.*

Richard cupped hands around his mouth, shouting, 'Time to start!'

August dashed to the kitchen and switched off the lights so that candlelight patterned their faces.

Rhodda and Jsun were squashed together on the couch, the remaining circle members sitting with crossed legs on the floor.

'Lord of all,' Richard began, 'we give thanks and praise, to the creators of all matter: divine, human, living, decaying, burning, earthly and unbridled. To all energy and floating matter, light and stars, to the gas, the galaxies beyond all knowledge, the galaxies within.'

Eve began to move and shake. 'Ooohh, Richard, you're sending shivers down my spine!'

Gentle laughter rippled through the circle; Richard just smiled and nodded. He was 'Serious Richard' now.

'Time to share. Jsun, do you want to go first?'

Jsun opened his backpack and unfolded a small woven, Peruvian-looking mat. On that, he laid out several crystals, causing Eve and August to gasp.

'This morning I had a pain in my chest, a heart-pain. Rhodda gave me a little rub, then out came this stream of light.'

'I couldn't see it but I knew what was happening,' Rhodda chuckled, grinning proudly at her partner.

'I followed the beam, out in the backyard. It changed direction a bit at first, zigzagged about, as though the light was making sure I was following. Then it stopped by the frangipani. The beam started to pour into the ground, just like a rainbow marking the pot of gold. Rhodda was sighing away in her dressing gown.'

Rhodda shook her head. 'Once I saw him on his hands and knees, beginning to dig ...'

'She went and found me a trowel.'

'And I made the tea.'

'I knew it was telling me to dig. I had to pull out a few rocks. Then my heart skipped. Beautiful crystals, such clear and light energy.'

'He was running out the door, I had to chase him with his teacup.'

'I packed them into my bag, along with some juice boxes.'

'Juice boxes have too much packaging!' Eve called out.

Jsun nodded patiently. 'Yes, but everyone likes juice, and the packaging means it's all hygienic.'

Eve's face remained scrunched up. She didn't seem happy with this answer, but let Jsun continue with his story. Too often the circle became the 'Eve Show', as Finn called it in her head.

'Then I let the crystals direct me around town, to where they were most needed. They showed me to three different groups of people living on the street. I sat with those folk, got the crystals out, and anyone who wanted to could hold one for as long as they needed. I shared out the juice too. That's what I'm grateful for – the chance to share love with the world.'

Eve and August gushed at Jsun's story. Richard nodded at the crystals.

'That's really incredible.'

Jsun was beaming. 'Please, everyone. Take a look.'

Eve and August swooped for the crystals.

'Thank you, Jsun. Eve? How are you travelling?'

Eve, holding a large pink quartz, pressing it hard between her palms, sighed heavily. 'My week has been bullshit really. I'm working way too much and haven't had time for my medical intuition assignments. Well, I was at the hospital for a few hours on Monday. I saw this patient whose throat was literally on fire. I knew it was throat cancer, from a calcification; her message was about speaking up for herself. But when I went and talked to her, all she said was that she "wasn't interested in spirity things". "Well, just because you're not interested in the spirit world doesn't mean it's not interested in you!" I said back. She looked seriously offended and walked off. It's just so hard sometimes, being an empath, feeling so clearly when no-one cares. What is the point in my "gift"? Spirit wants me to unburden others, but all that's happening is I'm feeling their burden while they still suffer. It's like, a problem shared is a problem multiplied.'

Rhodda laid her hand on Eve's forearm. She fell quiet.

'What would I do without your healing hands, Rhodda?' Her eyes were red behind glasses.

'Eve, I am really sorry to hear of your troubles,' Richard said. 'I will make a special prayer for you every day until Saturday.'

Eve looked up, tears like stars glistening.

'Thank you, Richard! I don't know what I'd do without you, without this place.'

Richard nodded and turned to August. Finn's thoughts turned to Ethann. She imagined him sitting cross-legged amongst the Circle of IEWA, his knee gently brushing against hers.

August drew her index fingers and thumbs together, forming a wonky oval-shape. She began to hum. Everyone joined in, wavering around the same note, before August raised her hum gradually up into a squeal, then a yawn.

After laughter and applause, August shouted, 'THANK YOU EVERYBODY!'

Richard's gaze found Finn. She couldn't help but compare it to the Eye of Sauron. The warmth of Ethann's imagined knee dissipated.

'And? Finn, how was your day?'

'Well, today I am grateful for the basics,' she began, not really thinking about what she should say. 'I've really got the bottom levels of Maslow's hierarchy sorted. Food. Today I ate good food, really wholesome and nutritious food at work. And I didn't have pain in the night, though I guess I'm grateful for the pain too and the things it teaches me.'

Richard looked across the circle. *Will you tell us about the other thing?* his eyes said.

No way, Finn's glare replied.

'Whose turn is it tonight?' called Jsun.

'What? Oh, Finn! It's my Finn's turn!'

She had forgotten all about the presentation. The printed pages were crumpled in her backpack. Everyone began to clap as she rummaged. Richard reached over to the bookshelf, handing her the copy of 'Solitude' she'd lent him earlier.

'Here, Finn. Read from this. And stop panicking!'

'I'm not panicking!' Finn hissed.

Nursing a leg that had fallen asleep, she slumped up against the wall, by the portrait of Serena. Indian tapestry was her backdrop, scratchy against her elbows.

'Okay. I wrote something. Surprise, surprise.'

Everyone chuckled.

'You're my favourite writer!' August squealed, hands cupped around her mouth.

'So,' Finn was thrown by the enthusiasm. 'Here we go.'

She drew a deep breath, her palms sweaty on the paper, and began to read.

There once was a house by the sea. Here lived Lonely and Content, sharing together in a peculiar two-handed solitaire. There was nothing left to do but get along. There were many games played to pass the time. Sometimes Lonely won over, other times it was Content. There was an old dog who visited every third night. A grey and hairy beast, a scavenger from some lost world whose carer had departed.

Lonely and Content were certain this dog did the rounds

at many different houses, perhaps all situated on verges, or cusps, or the edge of the sea like this one. He was a lost wanderer, only ever seeming to emerge from a blur in the distance.

But as you stare down the shoreline, it is very difficult to discern whether another place ever begins or ends, whether this is our world we share with other beings. Only Lonely and Content appeared to dwell in this one, although anything could be possible beyond their shared field of view. And so it would appear the dog didn't speak a language common to these beings. Lonely and Content themselves did not share words, but general impressions; thoughts became imprinted on each other's minds. These imprints appeared of their own volition, and each being would know on some innate level, that this thought was not original to themselves, but had its awakening in the other.

However, Lonely and Content each tried to convey much more to each other than they were able to interpret. For them, common ground was limited. The dog wore a loosely woven rope about its neck. Not like a shackle, more like a decoration, of red and orange thread. On this thread hung a bronze bell, which had become tarnished and rusted, though still merrily announced the dog's arrival at the deep purple of dusk. Lonely and Content shared with the dog their supper, which always consisted of a bread made by fine, earth-coloured flour. The dog, nourished, would sleep on the floor by the hearth for some time. A fire crackled in the home every night, tended usually by Lonely as Content curled its toes out towards the flames in pleasure.

And so life went on. Day in, day out. The shoreline and waves began to move closer and closer to their fence at night. But life went on.

The dog eventually became more and more ragged. One day he arrived without his bell. His sad eyes conveyed to

Lonely that soon his visits would cease.

And that day came. Still Lonely and Content lived, and shared, lighting a fire every afternoon, baking the bread, which they broke together.

There is a glowing light on the distant shore, and sometimes I wonder if I could see further, I might see more glowing lights. A constellation, a series of lanterns dangling about in black space.

The room was blank faces, before some nodding and clapping.

'I can't love it enough!' August shrieked in laughter.

'What does this mean?' Eve asked.

'I was trying to show solitude as an interplay between loneliness and contentment,' Finn said confidently, though in truth she had no idea what the story was about.

Eve frowned at that answer.

'I want to change their names though. Maybe to Sholoch and Nezbah.'

'What do those names mean?'

Finn shrugged. 'I don't know they mean anything. I just thought, maybe it was too obvious otherwise.'

'You shouldn't use names if you don't know what they mean. You don't know what you'd be inviting into the story.'

Jsun nodded. 'I get it. Sometimes when Rhodda's away I'm happy as Larry. Doing my projects in the shed, or cooking up a storm.'

Rhodda chuckled. 'He always cooks the stuff I can't stand when I'm away. All that rich Italian food.'

'But then sometimes I can't stand that she's not around.' Jsun shook his head. 'I have no idea why, and I don't know which way it's gonna go until she's out the door.'

'I always do a quick cleansing before I leave. Doesn't seem to make much difference.'

'I think I'm happier when I'm not in relationships,' exclaimed Eve, arms crossed, one leg crossed over the other.

Face cross. 'Doesn't stop me wanting one though. I still dream of meeting someone called Adam. Is that what the story's about?'

'Yeah, I think so,' Finn lied, betraying none of her own boredom with the story. She didn't like to bring more recent stories, as they were too close to her heart, and painful to share.

At the IEWA gatherings, Richard would select a theme, and would ask a member to do a presentation on that theme. Interpretations were broad, and presentations could be anything – a group dance, an exercise, drawing, a tarot reading, poem writing.

Last week, Eve had everyone moving about the room, taking turns, staring deep into each other's eyes. The staring-couples would lock gazes for one minute. Finn found it difficult and stressful, and wondered if that was perhaps the point. Everyone else seemed to get past the difficulty and find the experience enlightening.

The week before, Jsun asked everyone to close their eyes, then let an animal walk into their mind.

'That is your spirit animal,' he'd said. August was a dolphin, Finn was a deer, Eve a monkey. Rhodda was a panda, Richard a donkey, though he claimed this was a mistake. If he knew the exercise was about finding our spirit animal, he would have chosen a frog. Jsun already knew his: an otter.

When Finn was eventually able to look up from her story, she found August's face beaming at her. Cross-legged, hands on knees, she resembled a preschooler. She was rocking gently, forward then back, seeming about to burst with enthusiasm.

'And now, let us recite the IEWA creed. Does everyone have that up on their devices now or should I get the sheets?'

'I know it by heart!' shouted August, while everyone else pulled out their phones. And then the voices began to rise all around.

Inviting the experience; it's
Not for everyone, but we are
Visionaries, Prophets –
In this together, because
Seeing isn't all there is to believing.
It's true that
Beauty is in all things, we can
Love things
Everywhere – **we love with ease.**
Each of us, though,
X-tend ourselves, past loving the easily loved,
In the interests of **spiritual growth**, and
The greater good.
We are all in this together;
Otherworldly worlds are here, around
Us, which is why we
Never Give Up!
Doubts come and doubts go, it is our inner
Strength that holds us, as we hold hands,
As we each hold the world, in our hands,
Never forgetting
Our place in the stars,
Never forgetting the flight of our great **Mother-Earth-Ship**.

Eve shrieked. 'AWESOME!'

'Right! Beautiful people! Beautiful, beautiful people!' Less
Serious Richard was re-emerging.

Ecstatic laughter whooshed through the boat. Eve started
dancing. Finn felt like sinking into the ground. She needed to
hide, and there was only one hiding place in the boat. It was
the only place where Richard didn't burn incense – an unholy
place. This always seemed strange to Finn, as it seemed like
the one place that could really use some freshening.

On her way to the loo, August jumped in Finn's path.

'Finn! Hi!'

'Hello.' Finn registered a flatness in her voice, feeling guilty she couldn't mirror August's enthusiasm.

August's face fell. 'Are you okay? I loved your story!'

'I'm fine. Thanks! I'm just, sorry, I need to …' She motioned towards the toilet.

'Oh! Sorry!'

Finn sidled past to the unholy place. No incense required there. No spiritual cleansing necessary. Just leave the toilet be, where we drop away parts of ourselves, parts of us that hold us back. In the tiny space, Finn stretched into a forward bench, fingertips touching the lino. The shapes had been like two large moths, all day, one tucked under each shoulder blade. She felt heavy and sore, but sensed they were resting, and would exit easily tonight.

As she passed Richard's bedroom, she heard something that sounded like a gong, and saw his computer screen light up. She glanced into the room.

In giant letters on the screen were the words 'DIVINE AND DATELESS: THE NUMBER ONE CONSCIOUS DATING WEBSITE!'

A flashing icon on the screen indicated that Richard had one new message.

THE HOUSE

It always caused distress when Finn remembered she lived with another person. Like kids who only know parallel play, she and Danielle lived side by side, with a respectful lack of interest in each other's lives. Occasionally Danielle became excited with Finn, declaring 'We are so in sync!' after they both mentioned going to the beach, a walk around the lake, or seeing a willie wagtail.

But when Finn came home with her fried chicken, seeing Danielle's car in the driveway, hearing her 'spiritual vocal improvisation' erupting from the studio, her shoulders would become tense. Finn felt like a spider, furtively dragging dinner back to her web as she slunk into her room. Quietly, protective of her secret fondness for grease, not wanting to wrinkle wrappers, wanting to hide the sound, the dense smell of packaged chicken, cheese, meat, bread, fat. Finn wanted to hide her casual disregard for God's plans for her and all humans, God's plans for her life, and the kind of food she should put in her body.

By eating the fried chicken, the fat salty yellow chips, she was drawing a line between Danielle and herself, saying 'Let me be alone'.

Danielle worked in Fremantle as a cleaner and sound healer. Finn could feel Danielle's eyes as she talked about the relationship between awareness and cleaning, about 'raising your awareness of when it is time to clean'.

It was never 'time to clean' for Finn. There must have been

things that, at different moments in time, were not clean in the house. But these things were never dirty enough for Finn to notice.

She was aware of the sighing in the night though. Danielle sighed as she swept up the partial contents of a probiotic sachet Finn spilt on the kitchen floor – one of her nocturnal attempts at pain relief. Danielle again sighed as she mopped water off the floor – water Finn had spilled from a hot-water bottle in the hallway and left, thinking the puddle would dry up soon enough.

Finn did not like the fact that Danielle cleaned up after her. She tried to do as little damage-by-dirt as possible. She never cooked. She brought home leftovers and out-of-code stock from work. She ate from one of her three bowls. After eating, she stowed the bowl under the couch, until all three were there, and she would then do a quick wash-up.

She created so little mess that she told herself it was okay to do little cleaning, even though she knew that wasn't true. Her skin cells fell off here and there. She brought sand and dust home in her hair. Her laundry basket smelled distinctive after a week of work. The grout between the bathroom tiles gradually blackened, thanks to the grime under her fingernails as well as Danielle's. But the grout never seemed black enough to actually clean, before it was suddenly white again.

Finn knew it wasn't fair to say 'Danielle likes cleaning'. The only solution was to engage in nominal cleaning – to clean what was already clean. So, Finn occasionally scrubbed white walls, swept the shiny floor, vacuumed the spotless bathroom, making sure Danielle saw or heard some evidence of cleaning.

Sometimes Finn genuinely looked up to Danielle. She was able to prepare nourishing meals for one. Buckwheat porridge for breakfast, with dates, rice malt syrup and flaxseed. Carrot and coriander soup or pumpkin and adzuki bake for lunch, kitchari with lentils and asafoetida for dinner.

For a quick snack, Danielle might sit and peel a zucchini,

then eat it whole, gazing out to her edible-flower beds. She did not believe in non-sentient foods like onion, mushroom and garlic, preferring to keep herself light for the night-time, when she travelled up there, at night.

Danielle believed in preparing and eating food with pure intentions. She never ate meat, believing that people who did took on the anger felt by beasts before they were slaughtered. That anger was translated to the cooked flesh, to the raised fork, to the soul of the person raising that fork. Even vegetarian meals, she believed, if prepared in an anxious way, in an angry way, would retain that unpleasant vibration.

Danielle trusted only herself and her own intentions with food. Thus she kept her relationship with food a closed circle. She was careful to know the source of her Himalayan pink salt, to not buy bleached garlic from China, and to eat lettuce that had been planted in alignment with the moon's phases. Then in her own preparations, it was always simple: food not overcooked, seasoned with organic olive oil and tamari, herbs from the garden, nigella seeds to replace onion, dulse flakes only if she didn't sense a strong radiation from the packet. Danielle often encouraged Finn, telling her that intuitive eating could really help with her sense of spiritual lightness.

What she didn't know was how much Finn liked to feel heavy, close to the earth. How she lay in the bath after pulling the plug. The water drained, her body sucked onto the ceramic tub, her body drawing close to the ground. And in this heavy slowness, this sense of becoming part of the earth, Finn remembered herself.

When she arrived home to an empty house after the circle, Finn felt a surge of relief. She opened the fridge without worrying to close it quickly. She went to the toilet with the door open, enjoying staring at the laundry trough, like it was a luxury view. She found some hash browns in the freezer and put them in the oven, after boiling the kettle for some instant soup. Danielle would be home by ten at the latest; she never upset her circadian rhythm too much.

Finn brought her laptop out to the kitchen. As she hunched over the computer, the shapes began to flutter.

She typed in the words DIVINE AND DATELESS.

Divine and Dateless!
The No. 1 Dating Site for Conscious Individuals!

Conscious and Lonely?
Devoted to Intimacy with God, but still want someone to hold at night?
Want to fast-track your way to a soul-connection, where you learn those tough life-lessons?
You've come to the right place!
D & D is dedicated to connecting the conscious around the world!

We already know each other in the collective unconscious,
So let's start a conscious collective already!

What's your deal?
Advancement of the Soul

Casual times

Friend-Ship; the vessel of life

Hey, I think we've met before! [Past life connections]

Let's learn from each other! [Soul mates]

I believe in Monogamy!

Open Plan Living

Tantra and the Beyond

Interested in
Women

Men

Gender doesn't matter, it's the SPIRIT I'm attracted to

Choose your deal

Add keywords to describe yourself
And our team of intuitive programmers
Will help match you with others!

This is Me! Keywords to describe Yourself

Activist

Alien-Experiencer

Astral Traveller

Colours of the Fifth Dimension

Cutting Connection Cords - Changing Destinies by Healing
Past Lives

Indigenous Eyes - Seeing the world through the eyes of the
Earth's original inhabitants

I See Dead Peeps!

Let's Talk About Sex!

Lightworker

Lucid Dreamer

Out of Body Experiencer

Purple and Prophetic

PRTD - Post Religious Traumatic Disorder

Psychic by Impression

Self-employed Healer

Sound Healer

Skinny-dipping by Moonlight

Spiritual Journalling

TCM – Human, Animals and Nation States

'They all die the same way' - Veganism and Animal Rights

We Are What We Eat

D & D

Scrolling to the bottom of the page, Finn saw a picture of the 'member of the month' called Yann, his tagline shouting 'READ MY SHIRT!' His profile picture showed a smiling man with a large moustache and a shirt reading 'HEAVILY MEDITATED'. After years spent in the Himalayas, then 'monastery-hopping' through Nepal and spending time with wolves, Yann had returned home to Germany and was 'eager to form conscious connections with spiritual women'.

Part of Finn wanted to laugh, but there was an undercurrent of sincerity on the site she found appealing. The graphics were dated in a charming way, featuring word art and spinning logos.

She began to create a profile, careful to be somewhat true to herself, while still hoping to be placed on Ethann's radar. Having his interest in broccoli sprouts and dreams to go by, she selected 'we are what we eat', 'lucid dreaming', then just for herself, added 'alien experiencer' and 'spiritual journalling'. And just to appear like a person she was definitely not, but would perhaps like to become, she chose 'skinny-dipping by moonlight'.

For a tagline, purely to catch Ethann's attention, if he was there, she wrote 'FREO DREAMER'.

Once Finn hit 'Create Profile', and charged $17.99 to her credit card, she was able to search other profiles. And there he was. A photo of him, wearing a green singlet with a large red parrot print. He had his arm around a pretty girl, who was laughing in an 'I'm great' kind of way. Finn's shapes rose to her throat.

His tagline read 'MAKE ME, BREAK ME, SHAPE ME!'

Act now. Act now, or you'll see reason, think about it so much, write him a message that sounds wooden, over-thought, not casual and carefree. Act now and ride this incidental tone – you have just stumbled across Ethann on a dating site, that is a truth; just roll with that truth.

Finn rushed a quick message, 'HEY! Fancy seeing you here!!! I just joined, what an awesome site!'

She felt dishonest saying this, as the site was quite bizarre.

'Well, maybe we oughta catch up soon. I can give you the run-down on the IEWA circle, so you can decide if you want to come visit us weirdos. WELL OK, You can see my number now, so feel free to text BYE!'

Finn hit SEND before she could talk herself out of it. A wave of regret swept over her, following by silly, nervous excitement.

The shapes whizzed about her abdomen. Finn closed her laptop and switched off the light. Then she pressed a point on the right side of her lumbar spine, an index finger above the sacrum. This was a special point; pressing it usually resulted in instant release.

The shapes flashed up her throat. She fell onto the cool wooden floor, a gushing exhale. The balls of light flooded, floating up to the ceiling. Finn lay still, watching them bob and glow.

THE ART SHOP

August sat at the counter of The Heart of Art, sketchbook in hand. It was a quiet morning: she had unpacked boxes of cartridge paper, paints, oil pastels and craft glue, beautified the shelves, rearranged the display of easels and tried to sweep up a tub of glitter that a kid dropped on the floor.

Her boss, Emerald, was writing on the shop's vision board, a large blackboard they propped in the window to 'reach out to customers'. August was looking forward to the day when she might write on the board. Emerald chose words like 'CREATE, RE-IMAGINE, SKETCH, PAINT, DRAW', but August longed to write phrases like 'THERE'S NO HEART WITHOUT ART; INHALE POSSIBILITY, EXHALE CREATIVITY; FOLLOW YOUR BLISS; I'M GLAD YOU EXIST!'

August dug her phone from her pocket, which was covered in glitter – as were various parts of the shop, and probably August's face, since the kid's spillage. She flicked past all the messages from her mum and dad in the inbox. They were always checking up on her. They cared and worried too much. And besides, their messages were boring. They were always short, like *call us, we love you, let us know if you need anything.* Messages from Tom were more elaborate and interesting. She opened up their conversation, which went back years, which felt endless. There were so many special phrases in the messages from him. And he brought out the best words in her too. Their conversations read like a flood of inspiration.

After a few moments, August found the words that she

knew were right. She flipped open the sketchbook, closed her eyes and hummed, allowing her pencil to meet the page, allowing long, flowing lines to pour, from the tip of the pencil, across the white open space. This was her receiving, this was how she opened up to the universe. Emerald didn't seem to mind her doodling while things were quiet in the shop.

August listened as a car rolled by. A couple walked past the shop, shouting at each other. The scratching of Emerald's chalk was louder than anything else.

She looked back at her phone. 'They say a big bang created the universe,' August read in a hushed tone. 'But for us, it wasn't a bang, or any kind of explosion. It was just a little moment where we brushed up against each other, but we created a universe too.'

'What was that?' Emerald called out.

'Sorry!' August jumped, knocking her phone off the bench. 'Just talking to myself again.'

Emerald laughed. 'I've just had my ears candled. It's amazing how much clearer everything is!'

'That's great!' August called out, jumping to the ground to pick up her phone. There were no new cracks, just the usual ones.

Emerald began to sing 'Fever' in her 'sultry Lena Horne kind of voice' – as she once described her style to a customer – and August began to hum. She began to see the words across the page, surrounded by flowers, lightning strikes, puffs of clouds and stars.

They say a big bang created the universe. But this wasn't a bang, or any kind of explosion. It was a moment where two people brushed against each other. But they created a universe too.

Everyone could see that a new universe had been created. August and Tom stood a little too close to each other, but didn't hold hands. A kid wearing a shirt that read

'WARNING – EXPOSURE TO THE SON MAY PREVENT BURNING!' ran up and squashed them into each other, shouting, 'Come on! God wants you to be together!' The elders chuckled, 'You two are doing it the *right* way.' Because the others were doing it the wrong way – where a lot of rubbing with clothes on happens, and marriage and babies happen a couple of years later. 'For you two, it's all about patience,' they said. 'It'll all happen, in God's time.' Really, it was just August trying desperately hard to be patient, while Tom was trying to figure things out.

Even though they weren't actually a couple, Tom and August developed the secret language of their universe. It was garbled sounds, hysterical laughter, throwing grass seeds at girls striding past, looks in their faces, reading each other's looks and making more noises, always knowing what each other meant, most of the time, at least.

Tom had dreams about being caught in his old life, on the wrong side of the river. He couldn't cross the water, he couldn't find his way to her. August knew this was it, she knew it was love. She couldn't understand why Tom needed all this time, but she also knew – and had always been told – she needed to learn to be more patient. Maybe this was her chance to learn.

And so, in the absence of getting closer to Tom – in a rubbing through clothes kind of way – August got closer to God. And that was the first time she had a friendship with a middle-aged man. Some people at the time thought it was strange, how close they became. But Terry just smiled at August from another pew one day. She smiled back at him, and then they both burst into tears.

'I know your spirit,' he said, hugging August, and from then, they were close friends.

Terry drove a four-wheel drive. He'd pick her up on a Sunday morning, worship music or country music or country-style worship music blaring on the stereo. They'd go to the top of the hill to pray over the town. On that hill they could survey all below, like it was a kingdom and they were all-knowing. August felt strong, and it was seven a.m. They stood together and cried out to the breaking sky, to the Lord. She looked up for a burst cloud, for the heavens to open up, but it was just bright white. Still, August knew this was ecstasy. She knew ecstasy. She knew God.

'God is moving! God is moving! Can you hear the sounds of revival?'

They shouted and called out, and Terry was so excited when he said to August, 'Can you feel that? Can you feel it? I really believe we are the generation who will see Jesus!'

Terry was the most beautiful and sincere man – apart from Tom – she had ever met. She sang and he played guitar with her. She performed in church sometimes, songs she'd written, about knowing she will learn to fly on Judgement Day.

Some clapped after their performance, and some hesitated. Some didn't clap at all. They didn't want to give praise, because really they were there to praise God. August wasn't asking for praise, or for the spotlight, but just sometimes, Terry talked her into singing. But it was okay that no-one clapped, because Tom would smile at her, he would make the sounds from their secret language. But the smile and the sounds were still all about not being ready.

And so, August was still waiting. Waiting for his hand to linger. Waiting, when they sat after church and played 'piano duets' that sounded 'a bit experimental', as one of the elders said, giving a pained smile. She longed for him to lean up close. She felt that warmth of shoulders touching, as they tinkered on the keys. She knew, if he didn't want to be close to her, he didn't have to sit right up by her like that.

But she just couldn't ask him. She couldn't say the words in the English language, 'Do you like me?' All she could use was the secret language; making a garbled sound with a rising inflection. He would answer, an equally garbled sound, but she knew it was an answer. She knew the answer was, 'Yes, of course I love you, but I don't know anything more.'

August had already been baptised, when she was a kid. Her parents went to a different church in town, one where they didn't have guitars and drum kits and waving praise-hands, but they did have an organ, stained-glass windows and thick red carpet.

There, she had been baptised *and* confirmed, but August wasn't sure this translated in her new church.

The moment when she accepted the Lord into her heart was confusing. It was another youth rally in the city, where they all went up on a bus. August was called backstage, where they asked, 'Do you know Jesus?'

'Yes?' August said, wishing she sounded more certain.

The girl wore glasses, a furrowed brow and tried to confirm, 'But do you have a personal relationship with Jesus?'

'Oh yeah. I mean, yes!'

'Are you sure? Why did you come up for the altar call if you're already right with God? Look, have you given your heart to the Lord? Have you been washed in the blood of the lamb, have you been forgiven, set free, you know, has *your* stone been rolled away?'

August began to feel less sure of her convictions. But by then the girl's hand was on her shoulder and she was praying and giving August's heart to the Lord for her, but August couldn't blame her for rushing because there was a whole line of kids waiting to be saved.

Things did feel different after that. No, despite all her private prayers and visions, despite the water on baby skull and first communion at her parents' church, August couldn't be sure that she'd actually *given her heart to the Lord*, not until the moment that girl gave it up for her, amongst loud singing of 'mountains trembling', bright lights and electric guitars, and waving hands and hot-rolled curls and tumbling people, shaking and rolling on the floor, strange noises coming from their mouths.

After that moment, things were different. August tore up her old journals and sketchbooks. She threw out CDs. That was all from her old life, before she was born again.

Finally, she was baptised in a lake, and was jumping with excitement as they prayed over her. Afterwards she and Tom swam across the deep dark water that was full of leeches and laughed all the way. She'd always been afraid of the lake, but not now.

Not after she'd been ducked underwater by those large, special hands, and came up to everyone clapping and a voice on a microphone that seemed unnecessary, praising God, praising August.

She framed a photograph of herself, head down in prayer, hands, many hands reaching out touching her body. Many hands praying over her, many hands ready to catch her if she fell. A small smile played on August's lips, as she prayed for herself, and for Tom, and the amazing future that God had in store for them.

But still, Tom wasn't baptised. She was going ahead of him.

August was scared. What if he didn't make it to where she was? She was scared of being lonely, and of him being lonely too. All her old school friends had fallen away, as she'd forgotten how to talk to anyone who wasn't Christian.

It was lonely up there, where she'd chosen to be. And so she sat up there and tried to learn patience. She sat and waited for Tom to be ready.

'Wow that's amazing!'

August looked up from the page, shocked from her thoughts. The page was covered in colour, rainbows surging from the words 'WE CREATED A UNIVERSE TOO!' The pencil, she realised, she was gripping very tightly. It was blunt and her hand hurt. There was a face, close to the art, peering over at it, the face of a boy. Where had he come from?

'It is so bright and pretty, Mummy!' The boy called over to a young woman with red hair and a nose-ring.

August smiled brightly. 'Thank you!' she cried, noticing the woman flinch a little. Was she being too much, too loud?

'Why is your face sparkly?' The kid was now staring up into August's face.

She took a deep breath, and pressed her palm against her cheek.

'Oh no!' she said. 'Are they red sparkles?'

The boy nodded and laughed.

'I think that's because there was a red fairy in here before! She kissed me on the cheek when she said goodbye, and must have left some fairy dust!'

The boy and his mum began to laugh.

'There might still be some fairy dust around the store, if you want to look for it.' She nodded at the woman, who smiled at August, as the boy began to look around for any sparkling on the floor.

THE BOAT

'Hello everyone, and welcome to Invisible Exit Wounds Anonymous. Yes, there is a real Richard, and that is me!' Richard spoke enthusiastically at the camera, feeling like he was dying inside. But he must keep going. He took a deep breath. 'IEWA is a therapy centre for people experiencing spiritual awakening as a result of the deposit of extra-earthly substances into their bodies. Some prefer the term "extraterrestrial", some like "extra-dimensional" or "interdimensional". The problem with these terms is they can exclude each other, or at the very least imply different things.'

Richard began to stroke his beard thoughtfully, and looked out the porthole. 'There is much debate and controversy as to where these substances have come from. I like "extra-earthly" because we all know that divine matter is not of this world; really, that is the whole point of it. "It", or "they", whatever you want to say, is here to show us something we don't know, to teach us a lesson. What is the learning we most need?

'I come from a long line of Anglican ministers but, to the dismay of my parents, I moved over to the Pentecostal camp with the Assemblies of God. There I met a ravishingly beautiful woman, but my parents didn't approve of the inter-denominational match. So I eloped with her: this was the seventies; we were in our early twenties, and we went off to Indonesia and India.

'I don't like to talk about that time much, but suffice to say that I was lost. I was once confirmed, twice baptised – once water on my skull as a baby, once in a lake of my own volition –

but it was here in India that I truly found God. Again! There in a small village in the south I met a holy man. I was still committed to the church, although the seeds of a much deeper experience were now taking root.

'When I returned to Australia, I began my training at a bible college. I became a student-preacher. I was quite good at it actually, and gained a reputation as a "beat preacher". I was well on the way to leading a fairly conventional life, if you call the life of a Church of Christ preacher man conventional!

'I really thought my life had stopped changing. But there, in the light of the Lord, and in the spotlight of the church, my problems began. At first it was terrible pains in my right forearm that made me rub my skin. And then a shape appeared in front of me. I felt like Aladdin, rubbing the dusty old lamp when thus appeared a genie. It wasn't a really clear form, just light and faint, like incense smoke that fades quickly. That first time, as the shape left me, the pain faded too.

'But it returned again, in different places. When I rubbed the pain-places, I began to sense this thing erupting from my body was a loving presence, though not quite a "being". I couldn't tell anyone. My enthusiasm for the church waned; its teachings were unable to account for these experiences.

'I was listening to Radio National one night, to a program all about alien-experiencers. And that's when I knew. I was being touched, as though touched by angels. I began to learn that there are people who remember existing as liquid forms in test tubes – now that's a different kind of test-tube baby! They recall living peacefully in these receptacles, until they were wailing in dry need, thrust into the bodies of noisy, red-faced, desperate human babies. These beings are not people, they are creatures from other worlds, trapped in human form. So what does that mean? It means that these higher beings who walk among us, dressed like you and I, are like Jesus and the other holy people. They are here to enlighten us.'

Richard leaned over and pressed pause on the webcam. He

buried his face in his hands, wishing he could just sleep. That was his 'origin story', as Ross called it. The story of how Richard got to where he is now. But it probably wasn't enough. He probably needed to let people know what IEWA was actually about, and what kind of healing he was able to perform. He hit the red button again, and resumed his intellectual tone, cocking his head to one side, holding his palms in his lap, swivelling his chair from side to side.

'Now, this may come as a shock, but my therapy centre, while open and loving to all, is not specifically directed at alien-experiencers, and these higher beings who walk among us. The work, that I believe is my calling, is to work with those, like me, who have been touched and left with a special gift.

'There are a few different names for these special gifts. And for some, they are certainly viewed not as gifts, but as pains in the neck, literally! I like to think of them as "deposits", just the way you get a deposit in your bank account. Cha-ching, you're in the money! If you have received an "extra-earthly deposit", there is something in that deposit for you. There is a real, tangible message, though it may take some time, and self-inquiry, to establish that meaning.

'People come to me because of pain in joints, backs, feet, necks, noses, eyes, fingers. They want to get rid of their deposit. My role is to help them grasp the deposit's associated message, rather than just cast it from their bodies like an unwanted demon. I'm not an exorcist! And it's not my job to administer Panadol!

'So luckily for you, I have spent years learning the skills necessary to extract deposits, while keeping their accompanying messages intact. Since leaving the church I have trained in traditional Chinese medicine, acupuncture, and body-reading. I can now sense the anatomy of the spirit, I can feel the sites of pain by hovering my hand over a patient, and sensing energetic states. I believe that the places where the extra-earthly beings choose to lodge the deposits – sometimes called the "pain-places", or the "planting site", the "site of seed" – are very important.'

Richard considered touching upon the significance of the meridians, but thought that might be too detailed for an introduction. He looked at his watch and realised it was probably time to wrap things up.

'For many, the experience of a deposit is a one-off. Others return, experiencing deposits over and over again. Some miss their deposit terribly when it is gone, describing it as like a special friend.

'But what if the deposit and its accompanying message are left locked up in the body? Here there are real health risks: when we hold on, the body clenches, stiffens, and we get sclerosis, oedema, calcification, stagnation, decreased blood and energy flow. Either a deposit must be released, or it must be accepted in a spiritually sound way.'

Richard had no idea what he meant by those final words. But it was too late and complicated to try to explain. He hit END on the webcam, his face snapping to nothing.

THE CARAVAN

'That's enough now. Let's leave Aunty August alone,' Kaye called out, clapping her hands behind Seb and Beatrice.

Beatrice was sitting on August's back, holding onto her hair, like a mane. August neighed and laughed, while Seb pointed at the girl on her horse, shouting, 'Alakazam! Now you're both frogs!'

Seb now turned to his mum, 'No! You will be a frog too!'

Beatrice giggled as August squealed, 'I'm happy to be a frog! Then I can hop and swim all day!'

'Yes!' Bea cried, and jumped onto the grass, next to August. 'Riddup! Riddup!' They sounded loudly, squatting, fingertips touching the grass.

'Finally!' Seb cackled like an evil wizard. 'My work is done!'

'Good, I'm glad you're all done. Now guys, Daddy is home ...'

'Yay!!!!!' Both the kids tore inside, Seb's purple cape trailing behind him.

The sun was setting, the garden pink and peach in the light. The sea breeze was in, but it was still warm; there had been so many hot days lately. Kaye squinted, hands in the pockets of her jeans, her long curly hair falling round her face. August felt the heaviness within, knowing what was coming.

'How you doing there, August? You good?' Kaye was stepping across lawn towards her. August felt her shoulders tighten, but smiled brightly.

'I'm doing great!' Her shoulders relaxed a little. Sometimes words were enough. Sometimes saying something makes it real.

'Yeah?' Kaye stepped closer. 'It's been a bit hot lately. It feels like summer's coming way too early.'

August looked down at the grass, feeling an urge to tear it up, to push her hands into the earth, and dig until she found that cool wetness. To keep digging until there was change. She took a deep breath, and looked up, giving her biggest smile. 'Really, I'm doing great!'

'Okay.' Kaye stepped back. 'No worries. But let me know if there are any problems, or if you need anything, anything at all. Okay?'

August nodded again, watching Kaye sashay away, smiling back at August as the screen door clanged. There was something wrong, but August didn't want to say. She didn't want to tell Kaye and Dave about the black dots. It seemed so silly, and they were so small.

August jumped up from the lawn, something fluttering too fast in her chest. She took a deep breath, and muttered the three steps under her breath. Walk into the caravan, fill the kettle, place the kettle on the stove.

Inside, she began to flick alight the stovetop, humming to herself. Then she exhaled, looked around, knowing the dots would still be there.

The black dots arrived months ago. First a cluster on the ceiling, resembling the seven sisters. Next was behind the rubbish bin, the dots forming the face of a seal pup. Above August's bed was where the largest constellation appeared. The black dots encircled inspirational words like 'LIVE! PRAY! JUST BE!' The dots crept behind the syngonium plant, which was still draped with tinsel from three Christmases ago.

It was just mould, August thought. And for some people, the mould would create the mental response: clean it. Now. Some would ignore the dots, hoping they would soon resolve into the walls. For August, the mould was confusing. Why was it here? Was it from the trees? Should the caravan be aired out more thoroughly? Had a bad spirit been allowed in? Was it God trying to tell her she needed to do things differently this time?

Generally, she kept the space neat and tidy, at least to a standard she found practical. It was also important to be able to relax, to be comfortable in one's home.

But the way she saw it, people either a) believe in God and universal order, thus by being more neat and tidy, they may draw closer to him, as CLEANLINESS IS GODLINESS, or b) see the universe as inherently chaotic, rambling and wild, thus by allowing messiness, they are just being honest about the nature of things – allowing chaos to take over.

Always wanting to keep on the one true path, August sometimes struggled to get out of bed. Getting out of bed meant making the bed, which was difficult as she couldn't get around its perimeter to tuck the sheets in properly. Making the bed properly was actually impossible.

But to not even try would be giving in to chaos. That would be admitting spiritual defeat. An unmade bed would cast a bad feeling over the whole day, and possibly into future days of beds made in fear of rebuke, because who knows how long God and the universe might take to forgive that one, single aberration?

If you really couldn't fathom making your bed on a certain day, it made more sense to not get out of bed at all.

When the mould first came, she scrubbed with vinegar, imagining the fungi as Pac-Men, gobbling up the vinegar, only for it to dissolve their insides and destroy them. But then the mould reappeared, then again, and again. After mould crept over a sign she'd painted in red, green and purple – 'YOU CAN HEAL YOUR LIFE!' – she decided it was time to take the sign down.

Could the mould be a teacher, she wondered? What lessons might be learned? And what if you can't heal your life? What if the saying was meant to be 'You Can Fuck Up Your Life'?

August tried hard to limit cleaning to just one day a week – 'Wednesday Cleanse Day'. If she didn't impose some restrictions, and specifically set timers for herself, she could go on cleaning well into the afterlife. Maybe she could work as a cleaner in heaven.

But what if a nuclear apocalypse happened? Someone clad like a spaceman with a blipping Geiger counter would find her. In a desolate landscape of burnt-out houses and trees turned to dust, they would creak open the caravan door, to find August's wide eyes and relentless hands, scrubbing the walls to nothing.

So one day, she decided to stop fighting, because, although August liked to create an easy division between clean/ unclean, holy/unholy, godly/non-believer, she found it hard to consistently feel good in herself. When she fell, she fell hard, and she wanted to avoid this at all costs. So, one day she got out of bed and left the sheets in a tangled mess. She resolved to let the black dots be.

Maybe it was mentally healthy to let go like this. Maybe the right thing would be to never make a bed again. She walked away from ruffled sheets, feeling a similar excitement to the one time she took a drag on a cigarette in high school. And then she surveyed the mould.

It was seeing things in a new light. The mould wasn't threatening anymore. It had become beautiful. The patterns close-up recalled fossils, snowflakes, things from an old world, lost, recovered, preserved.

'You've got to pick your battles, not your scabs,' her mum always said.

After she gave up on bed-making and mould-cleaning, August sometimes panicked, that this might be a kind of spiritual sleepwalking. Maybe she was succumbing to the universal untruth of chaos, dirt and godlessness – an ocean of rubbish, stinking waves, ready to swallow her up.

But contemplating the mould came to bring her stillness of mind. And so she took a deep breath, she began to see the division of cells: the easy dividing, and easy conquering. The cells divided, all across the walls, across every surface, across August's vision, as the kettle rose to a whistle.

THE BEACH

'I'm so afraid of being creepy,' Finn announced.

'Creepy?'

'Yeah. It's my worst fear.'

Finn and Gloria, her buddy from university, were walking along South Freo Dog Beach. There was something satisfying about watching dogs, although Finn didn't like to come here alone. Being alone without a dog at the dog beach, she had a feeling that all eyes were on her. Finn was that suspicious vehicle, driving too slow through the school zone. It didn't feel so predatory to be checking out dogs with company.

A tanned woman was flicking her hair, her breasts dangling openly. Finn tried not to look.

'Hmmm...' Gloria considered. 'I don't think I'm afraid of being creepy. Maybe that's because I've been with girls.'

'Yes,' Finn mused, trying to push away the image of the breasts. 'I often wonder if all my anxiety will go away when I finally take that step.'

'Well, I've taken that step, but this still makes me anxious,' said Gloria. 'There's a girl at the gym, and she just does something to me. I can't let myself near her. It really gets me afraid, but as soon as she's not around, I'm fine. I love John. Although, he's said he would be totally okay if I was with girls. He wouldn't handle it if I had a thing with a guy, but girls are fine.'

'That's so weird. Don't guys realise girls can be just as much of a threat?'

Gloria giggled. 'Or more of a threat! I guess it's like there's some secret, quiet enjoyment that his girl likes girls.'

'Well, for me, I'll meet a new girl, at work usually, and there'll be the tights and everything, and I'll think, "How in hell am I going to work around her?" I'll start from day one with this huge, full-blown crush, and then I'll get to know her more, and the crush will just disappear.'

'That's so interesting. Have you done the Kinsey scale lately?'

'Yeah, I still come up as more than incidentally attracted to women, yet predominantly emotionally attracted to men.' Finn always found herself falling into this intellectual tone with Gloria.

'I wonder if it's really that you've objectified women to an extreme point, so now you are only attracted to them physically. Maybe you hate what you desire.'

'Am I the original female misogynist?' Finn laughed, though her shoulders felt tense. *If I hate what I desire, isn't this exactly what I am?*

'It's so easy to be hard on yourself! Wasn't this sexuality issue one of the things you planned to figure out when you moved to Fremantle?'

'I suppose I knew I was going to be occupying a more liminal space here,' said Finn, trying to shake away that searing self-loathing. 'What about being in Melbourne?'

'It was strange moving to such a big city with John. I think the move made us grow, but sometimes I wonder if we are growing in different directions, even in tiny increments, and one day we will turn around and realise we're very far apart. It's a terrifying possibility.'

'Hey, is everything okay?' Finn rested her palm awkwardly on Gloria's shoulder.

Gloria shrugged it off, squinting. 'It's fine and it's not. We've hit rock bottom a few times. Sometimes I say, "Look I'm not feeling it," and he says, "I'm not feeling it either," then we spring back to life again! What about you, what's happening with this Harry High Pants character?'

Finn laughed. 'I'm really attracted to him. He is a bit unusual, which sometimes worries me, like maybe a motherly part of me looks at him as a creature in need of nurture? And I'm aware I should really have experienced being with a woman by now. But then he has long hair and no beard, and he shaves his legs because he cycles, and I wonder whether we'd just have one of those heterosexual relationships where each partner plays out an inverted gender role. I'm weird, he's weird. But then I see him get nervous around the girls at work, and I get scared that he's just a strange-looking guy who still goes for conventional kinds of beauty.'

A small terrier was tearing away from his owner. The large man wobbled after the dog, shouting, 'BARRY!'

After university, Gloria had moved over east. That was years ago. Once a year the two caught up and resumed their ongoing conversation, which now largely seemed to be around sexual anxiety. The whole time they'd walked, Finn had been silently comparing their legs. Whose were bigger and whiter? Both pairs display the little red dots, telltale signs of lactose intolerance. Finn thought Gloria's were a more pleasant pale, with a pink undertone. Finn's own seemed slightly yellow.

'I read an article recently that viewed sexual anxieties through the lens of obsessive-compulsive disorder,' Gloria reliably continued on the topic.

'I always knew I was the obsessive, perfectionist type,' said Finn, feeling anxious that she was making this 'all about her'.

'Me too. We're high achievers.'

'Except I'm not a high achiever.' It seemed important, after so much indulgent self-focused talk, to bring herself down a few notches. 'I'm a high achiever that hasn't achieved.'

'Don't be silly, Finn! You're just figuring things out. You're the most honest person I know.'

Finn snorted. 'I'm not sure that's a good thing.'

'But being here in such an alternative place must give you a new frame of reference for your sexuality?'

'Definitely. But the last time I went to the psychologist, which was ages ago, she told me my head is full of rocks. And when I told her all about my sexual panics, she just looked really frustrated and was like, "Why don't you just say you're bisexual?" I have tried to repeat a "My name is Finn and I'm bisexual" mantra to myself. It's not like I feel it's not true. I just don't know that the contentment I am looking for can be found in a label.' Finn looked out at the ocean where a cargo ship was shrinking into the horizon. 'But I feel scared, that bisexuality excludes me from monogamy. Like I can never maintain a long-term relationship with a guy because there's always the chance I could fall in love with a girl, and vice versa.'

Gloria smiled and caught Finn's eye. They'd never mentioned the time, years ago, at Connections Nightclub, when their friend Mike left the table, and the silence between them drew out that little bit too long, but they both knew; they were both wondering if they might kiss.

'In a way,' said Gloria, 'it's like anyone being in any relationship. If there's a hetero guy in a long-term relationship, it doesn't mean he's going to stop being attracted to other women. He'll probably have his types, and you have your types too, they're just spread across different sexes.'

'That's probably true,' Finn began to laugh. 'Why haven't I thought of it like that?'

But would it be like all the other solutions Finn had ever thought of to this problem? One minute, these 'solutions' seemed like the keys that unlocked everything. The next minute, they seemed like old thoughts, propositions quickly disproved.

Finn groaned. 'Will we always be like this? Crushing and burning?'

'I think it's okay to crush and burn; it's a sign of a generous heart and whimsical nature.'

'I miss you. I miss study. I miss having someone to talk to like this.'

'Why don't you move over east?'

'I'll never find another Richard. Although he does seem a bit odd lately.'

'How do you mean?'

'Oh I don't know. Richard is always odd. He does seem distracted though.'

Two labradors were twisting and slipping, a barking golden mass.

Finn considered telling Gloria: *I might have found out the truth about my weird body. I always thought there was something wrong with me, and I was right.*

'There are just so many layers for us to shed!' Gloria cried, her hands raised to the sky. 'I think the best antidote would be living in Berlin for a year. So many Australians wind up there, I think it's to undo all the bullshit we've inherited here.'

And that's when Finn saw her. Dressed in flimsy white pants and a flowing shirt, she was frolicking in the sand after Richard. He had his metal detector out, to Finn's surprise; she hadn't seen him detecting in at least a year.

The woman had blond hair, maybe grey beneath, but it didn't matter. She looked like a retired model, or somebody's hot mum. Richard looked up and pointed at Finn and Gloria.

'Who are those guys?' asked Gloria.

'That's Richard and some lady.'

'Get out, the famous Richard?'

Richard's wave was reminiscent of semaphore. 'Ahoy there, weary travellers!' The blond lady was giggling. As they approached, he called in a singsong voice. 'FINN! YO-MY-FINN!!!'

Richard continued shouting, Finn and Gloria heaving their way through the sand. As they arrived by the dunes, the blond lady held out a large, smooth stone.

'What the hell? Richard, did you find that with your detector?'

'Oh God no, I don't find proper things like this!'

The blond woman laughed and locked eyes with Richard like they shared a secret.

'I was wandering in the dunes, and sensed something calling me. Then I found this stone. And holding it in my hand, judging by the feel, the weight, the way my hand takes to it, fits into it, like a glove, I'd say it is an ancient sharpening stone. See.'

She passed the large grey stone over to Finn, guiding her fingers to hold it correctly. Finn's hand grew tingly.

'Can you feel that?'

'It's very smooth.'

'But can you sense a deeper knowledge in the stone?'

Finn closed her eyes, unsure of what the woman expected of her.

'Does it feel like your fingers are in just the right place? Like your hand was made to hold this stone?'

'Well, yeah, there is something that seems really natural about holding it.'

'That's right. I'd say this stone has been held over and over, for generations. It belongs in someone's hand. An ancient tool, this is a piece of wisdom.'

Finn felt her face turning to a frown, unconvinced that it was appropriate to be judging the stone's qualities.

Richard broke her thoughts with a loud belly laugh.

'Oh Finn, this is really strange! I was just talking about you to Celeste. Finn, this is Celeste!'

She held out her hand and looked into Finn's eyes. 'I think I began to sense that. When you were shouting the name "Finn" across the beach.'

The giddy pair laughed again, before she turned to deal Finn a firm, eye-contact-heavy handshake.

'Celestiaa Davinaa.'

Finn caught a small giggle from Gloria before her friend thrust her hand forward too.

'Gloria. Pleased to meet you.'

Finn was always a touch jealous of Gloria's extrovert nature, the ease with which she met new people.

'This is serendipitous,' Richard was nearly shouting, 'because I was just telling Celeste about you earlier! I was telling her about, you know, the thing!'

'What's the thing?' Gloria squinted, sunlight bursting off her glasses.

The image of a female reproductive system, blowing in the breeze on a washing line, came to Finn's mind.

'Gloria, I was just about to tell you. It's a little health situation. I'll tell you later.'

'I have been very much looking forward to meeting you,' said Celeste.

'There is no such thing as *co*-incidence, only *God*-incidence!' Richard shouted, metal detector now slung over his shoulder.

'I would love to chat sometime, Finn,' said Celeste. 'Will you be coming to the circle tomorrow night?'

'Of course, I'm always there.' Finn heard her tone as dejected, hoping no-one else did.

Richard turned to Gloria. 'And you, the lovely Francesca?'

'Where the hell did you get that name from?' Finn found herself sounding too forceful. Richard frowned.

Gloria's face scrunched up again, then she burst out laughing. 'It's Gloria! Well, Richard, I have heard so much about your famous circle and boat.'

'But why are you laughing?' asked Richard.

'I always laugh at the wrong times,' said Gloria.

Finn registered her face feeling hot. But they had been in the sun for a long time.

'Alas, I have a family dinner tomorrow, I think my family would be disappointed if I turned them down on my last night in town,' Gloria smiled.

Before parting, Celeste gave Finn another handshake. 'I very much look forward to meeting you again,' she said, looking deep into her eyes.

Finn felt her palms tingle, and stepped back quickly. 'Yeah, me too,' she smiled, feeling inadequate, much less whole around this person.

As they trudged towards the bus stop, Finn was relieved that Gloria forgot to ask about the health problem. The time was taken up discussing Richard, Celeste, and Divine and Dateless.

THE CARAVAN

'You're here! Finally!'

'You're so not awake.' Tucking a strand of hair behind August's ear, Tom gave her a peck. She was in bed, cocooned in doona.

'GGGRRRRRMMM!' Squeezed together, there was his soft sweet smell mixed with sweat.

'Why did you wait up with all the lights on?'

'I know, it's not very circadian of me,' August mumbled, rubbing her eyes. 'I just really felt like a good enzyme-cuddle.'

Tom sighed and crouched by the bed. 'I suppose I wouldn't have known you needed a lock-and-key-hug if you were in a deep sleep.'

He began slipping off workboots. White dust rose in the air. 'Look at that floating stuff,' said Tom. 'What is it?'

'Star matter.'

'Or plaster. Or dust. God knows. It scares me if I think too much about what we work with.' Tom heaved a sigh. 'I'm so tired! I watch the other guys at work, and I'm not convinced it's sapping their energy in the same way.'

'But you're as strong as anyone. And country people are the hardest workers, that's what everyone always says.'

'I know, it's not that. I'm strong. I'm fast. It's just I don't get what the hell those guys talk about all day. This guy Merle today was asking everyone if they think McDonald's tastes better in Bali or Australia.'

August hooted. 'That's terrible! What did you say?'

'I just laughed in his face. By accident. It was so embarrassing.

He probably thinks I'm fucked in the head.'

'Are you hungry?' August yawned, rubbing her eyes.

'Tom followed her yawn. 'I'm getting there. What did you make?'

'Some kind of curry. It's still in the pot.'

'Some kind of curry? Sounds promising. Do you know what kind of curry it is?'

'Not really.'

Tom chuckled. 'Well just look out, August, that's actually my favourite kind of curry!'

'Hey, no making fun! It's a really good thing you know, knowing how to cook. It can save a lot of money.'

'I know, I've eaten lots of tasty things made by you, it's just, I think maybe the creative approach to cooking...'

'I know! Shhhh! You don't need to tell me. It's the same with photography. Everyone thinks it's an art form when really it's also applied science. I just need to remember to switch on my methodical brain, but I just really like zoning out, getting carried away.'

'Curried away?'

'Stop! No puns. Unless they're mine. I find them pun-ful to listen to if I don't think of them.'

'Maybe you just have pun envy.'

'Or maybe hearing other people's puns is repulsive in the same way that other people's farts are. That's a medical thing you know.'

'You've told me that so many times!'

August shrieked with laughter.

'What about it makes it a curry?' Tom had sidled over to the stove and was clanking open the pot. A smell of cabbage, potato and turmeric wafted into space. 'Maybe you could call it a stew.'

'Look at it, it's yellow! I put Malaysian curry powder in it. I went to this shop in town today where there were all different kinds of curry powder. I liked the colour of this one the best.'

'Oh I take it back, definitely a curry then!'

'Hey!'

'Oh, I'm sorry!'

Tom came back over to the bed, unpeeling some of August from her cocoon. She climbed into his lap, squeezing his shoulders.

'You smell. Sweaty. Sweetie.'

'Yeah, it smells a bit in here too.'

'It always smells like microwaved food in a hospital when I cook.'

Tom leaned over August and began pushing open the window. 'So you went out today?'

'Yeah, just into town to do some shopping. I can't believe how quickly the money disappears! But this curry should last a few days, and Kaye said we can come and eat dinner with them tomorrow night.'

'Well that sounds good.'

August nodded. Tom dropped like an anchor on the bed.

'We fit together like slime in a glob,' she said, pressing against his chest.

'Or corn on the cob.'

'Or a door with a knob.'

'A face and a vase.'

'That's different, Tom. I think it's a different concept, but it also doesn't rhyme.'

'Well, some of yours were only near rhymes. Like penis and anus.'

'Venus and canus.'

'That's great, a dog planet. That would be the best.'

Lying down, Tom rested his head on August's shoulder. It all felt wrong, shapes and sizes not interlocking.

'I want to be the little one!'

'Can't I be the little one sometimes?'

'Yeah, but I'm automatically the little one aren't I? Maybe you need to ask permission to be the little one.'

'Yes, well I could ask.' Tom sighed. 'But being small sometimes is important for me too.'

'Okay, but can I always call you my falconer?'

'Yes.'

Tom squeezed her in close, allowing August to become as small as she desired. He pressed his hands heavily over her eyes. Her pulse slowed, shoulders relaxed. Everything else faded, slow, wispy shapes appearing in the black.

'You've melted like a hypnotised chicken. And look, I can do this when I'm being the small one. You don't need to worry about ever losing your place as the falcon, I won't ever share your special requirement for regular sensory deprivation. I just need general comforting sometimes.'

'We could probably do this to each other at the same time.'

'But then who will keep a lookout?'

'Your phone's flashing.' Tom looked over and began to laugh. 'August, are you recording us? I feel so invaded right now!'

'Oh shit.' August sat up slowly. 'Sorry, I should have asked!' She began rapidly twisting a strand of hair around her finger.

Tom laughed. 'What's going on, what are you doing?'

'It's just, I have this idea that I want to start using words in artworks, but when I sit down to start, I can't think of the right words. So I've been talking to myself and videoing it, but I thought, maybe I should start recording us talking. We talk about much better stuff than I do when I'm alone. And I love being able to record things!'

August rested her head on his chest. He ran his fingers through her hair.

'I wish I was hanging out in here, talking to myself and drawing all day,' he said.

'Don't be jealous! You get to work with maths and accounts most days, and every other day you get to build walls and compare and contrast different McDonald's!'

Tom laughed. 'I know, how can I complain?'

She reached over and hit the red button.

❇

It was becoming dark. August was lying on her bed, watching videos of her and Tom. They were videos from the beginning, when they first moved to the city together. She was excited about being able to record herself, record him, record every detail about their new life. The caravan seemed far less cramped then; August hadn't discovered op-shopping yet, so shelves weren't jammed with stuffed toys, odds and ends. The walls weren't covered in words, or mould.

She flicked through the phone, reading back on recent messages from him. The messages usually came later at night, when the work of the day was over, when there was more time and space for words to float between them.

You have nothing to worry about, he'd written to her, when she'd told him about Finn, again. *If she doesn't like you, if she doesn't want to be friends with you, she's the one missing out. BIG TIME! Xx*

August smiled and closed her eyes. Soon, she could see it all, a canopy of stars in the roof of her caravan. The planets aligning. The whooshing of spirits, and long-haired Pleiadians, floating and smiling down at her. Wind rose through the trees, a branch scratching at her window. The tabby cat from next door miaowed outside her window. She held the phone on her chest. Tom would message her and then everything would be okay.

THE ART SHOP

'August, I think it's time.' Emerald's voice sounded from behind the shelves of paintbrushes. 'I'm going to take my break, but I've got a few errands to run.'

'No worries!' August smiled.

'But I'm going to be a while, so I thought, while I'm out, do you think you'd like to do up some words on the vision board?'

'I'd love to!' August tried to curb her enthusiasm, to stop the flow of it from drowning everything. She coughed a little, took in a breath. 'Sure. Sure thing, if that's what you want.'

'Wonderful,' Emerald clicked some perfume on her wrist and began rubbing them together. It all smelled very grown-up, something August didn't feel yet and wondered if she ever would.

Emerald raised her eyebrows. 'I've got to go to the post office, but then I'm having lunch with someone special. Wish me luck, not that I'll need it!'

'Have fun!' August called out, as Emerald's heels tapped along the floor.

'No, you have fun!' Emerald turned and pointed back at August, before throwing her head back in laughter as she stepped outside.

August felt it, the fluttering and pumping, spinning and rising up in her chest. She took a deep breath and picked up a piece of chalk. The vision board was cleaned and clear, a wide-open space. It made her think of Tom's family's farm, the endless possibility, the many places you could walk, ride, run. August didn't know what to write, where to start, and so she began in the right-hand corner, and traced a long, winding line. It was the pipeline, that wove across the land, connecting her old life to her new, the pipeline that carried water, and the possibility of renewal.

The pipeline crossed over Tom's family farm. While his brother tore around on a quad bike, Tom and August skipped along the pipe, jumping off whenever they reached a dugite sunning across their path. They would look for skins, scaly and thin, shed by the snakes.

'Maybe I can shed my skin one day, when I'm finally away from this place,' Tom said once.

Another day they found a dead mouse near two halves of a brown snake. A dog must have got to the snake, which had got to the mouse, which looked wet and sleeping, waiting to be digested.

Tom's dad was always somewhere in the background, though August rarely saw him. He would be far away, in the sun, in the golden paddocks, in one of the silver sheds, somewhere that required you to call if you needed him. Nobody dared do that though, unless there was an emergency, or if dinner was ready. That was the way it often was with the farmers. They seemed far away, even when they were near. Their pink faces were hidden beneath wide-brimmed hats. All you could see were their hands, large, tanned and cracked like the earth in summer.

Tom's brother Joe was older, and would stride about in shorts, singlets, showing off his long tanned legs. His work-boots were topped by frill-necks that made August think of ballerinas first and lizards second. Tom said they were protective covers to keep chaff from getting in socks. A serious-eyed kelpie always followed Joe and his friends as they entered the shed, switching on loud metal – machinery or music.

There was always wheat in a vase on the kitchen table whenever August visited. Tom's mum explained all the parts of it to her – stalks, tillers, spikes. She told August how the wheat can be too yellow, or too green. Not enough rain, and the wheat will shrivel before it grows much. Late rain and the crops will be waterlogged, unable to be dried and rolled properly, mouldy and ruined. Sometimes when it was so green, bright and waving, people sent their praises too early. Maybe God punishes people for assuming to know the way things are.

Up on the hill on Sunday mornings, Terry and August never prayed for rain. They prayed for God to fill the church with new faces, ones that would be loved and accepted by the old faces. August did love everyone at church, and never meant to judge Mrs Finnegan, who saw shop signs as Bible verses, then turned away from her sister for having relations with another woman. But Mrs Finnegan didn't even know that her son tried to rub girls between the legs, or that her other son talked about shotguns and wanted to join the army because, 'It's okay to commit murder: it's between them and God whether they're right with Jesus.'

Yes, it's true, there were people at the church who did and said things August felt uncomfortable with. But there was the music, and the singing, and the hands waving in the air, and August was regularly carried away in this sea of love.

She didn't mean to stray from the one true path. Tom and August hadn't meant to run away together. That's just how it came across. It was the end of school. August got into uni, studying art. Shirley arranged for August to stay with Kaye, and Tom came along too. It all happened so quickly.

But maybe it was that her love for Tom was bigger than her love of God. Maybe she got deeper and deeper in with church because she couldn't find the love of Tom at first. Maybe if they were close straight away, she wouldn't have become this budding youth-leader-evangelist who was baptised in a lake and singing Christian songs to a non-applauding congregation.

'Sometimes when I can't sleep, I just get up and walk, down the dirt roads, through the fields,' Tom had said, that day. 'Just me and the moon. I was walking last night, and finally, I knew what I wanted. I just didn't know what I wanted at first. I'm sorry it took me so long.'

He had come to August's house, late on a Friday afternoon, before youth group. Tom had finished school already, and had been working on the farm for the past year. He had become tanned too, but his face was not all unknowable, like the farmers. He had agreed with his dad that he would move to the city the following year and study accounting.

It was sticky and hot, crickets clicking, and August knew her armpits were sweaty, but it didn't matter. Shirley brought them each out a glass of lemonade, and they sat on the verandah. He was slow and quiet and gentle, and he was large and tall and held her, finally, in that safe way. And he kissed August.

If it was the creation of a universe the first time they touched, now this was when the universe moved from chaos to order. All the flitting little molecules of uncertainty and painful excitement, and August finally knew, it was safe to say: we are together. And that long, long story was their creation story.

Maybe love was the only thing that would ever have made August stray from the church. Because what she felt in church was so real. It was ecstasy. If Tom was grounding, and making her safe and secure, the church was bright lights and noises and sparks and stars and her feet rising off the ground in joy and elation. Maybe some lightness is about meaninglessness, and floating off into space because one is small and insignificant, but some lightness is about pure, clear joy, all burdens removed. And maybe that was transcendence, even if to transcend was really being taken away from the present.

'Backslidden.'
    'You've changed.'
    'Have you found a new church?'

'Where are you worshipping now?'

'Oh how the mighty fall.'

When August and Tom came home to visit their parents, that's what they heard. They didn't tell anybody in particular that they had moved in together, but everybody knew anyway. What all the church people didn't know was that there was never anything happening that might cause pregnancy. But August and Tom held each other at night. They slept in the same bed. They shared the medicine of body warmth. And they made a home.

August and Tom bought mismatched crockery and blankets from op shops and tried to make life as bright as possible. Whenever August went home to her parents, she was excited to bake a cake. To bake, otherwise, would be too expensive, using beaters, eggs, butter, a stockpile of dry goods like flours and baking powder. She would gaze at her mum's full pantry and fridge, full of pickles and sauce jars. Not necessarily delicious food, but at least an abundance of options. She would bring back jars of peanut butter and baked treats.

It was a simple life, but it worked. Kaye and Dave brought over rescued food. August and Tom lived off tinned beans, pasta, packet noodles, cheese toasties, steamed cabbage, stir-fries and curries.

There was the syngonium in the caravan that always stayed alive somehow. A month before Christmas – just before Tom went home to help with the harvest – they adorned the plant with tinsel, handmade stars and toilet-roll angels.

Maybe life would have been easier for them if they'd managed to go home every weekend. They could have gone to church and sung praises and felt like everything was okay now. Time at home, and at church, might have replenished them, giving the energy to return to the city for another week. But Tom and August only went home now and then, and on every visit they got the looks and whispers, and some people even came and said to their faces: 'Backslidden. You've changed.'

Even if they didn't go to the church on weekends at home, it was hard to avoid being seen by members of the congregation. Even going to the supermarket, August would see someone. She once saw Mrs Watson, the tambourine lady, who couldn't even make eye contact with August. Mrs Watson stopped to speak to Mrs Hines – who'd flagged down August in the tinned food aisle – about the need for intercession prayer for a kid who had fallen from his motorbike, 'head cracked open like a paddymelon'. But she didn't even talk to August. She looked straight past her. She wanted Mrs Hines to pray for the boy. It wasn't too late for him to say yes to Jesus. But by not looking August in the eye, August began to wonder if the tambourine lady thought it was too late for her.

What if she'd wanted to come back, one day? Did her act of leaving burn a bridge, a bridge disappearing in flames behind her as she blundered on, trying desperately not to look back? What if she just couldn't handle being in two places at once? Maybe the problem was God that was watching – her and Tom – when they lived together with that syngonium. God sees all. Maybe that's what happened; they were too guilty and scared to dishonour him, to touch the wrong way.

In the end, Tom went home for the summer, to fill his socks with cut chaff and his pockets with enough money to fill his car with petrol. He was planning on saving enough money so he and August could rent their own place together. But still, he wasn't sure, she wasn't sure. Was that the right thing to do?

'August, what on earth is going on here?'

Emerald had returned, and was wide-eyed, her eyebrows like jagged mountains. August looked up at the vision board. Her heart was beating too fast. She hadn't stopped before now, to take it all in. The vision board was covered in words, tiny words.

Emerald stepped close, squinting, trying to read the words. But the words were scrawl that fed into other scrawl. The board was covered in messages that might be inspiring, but they were not readable. August placed the chalk down and held her head in her hands. Her face was burning, she realised. The fan was on, but she was sticky underneath her arms.

'I feel too hot. I think I'm actually not feeling too well.'

Emerald rested her hand on August's shoulder. 'August, it's okay. I think perhaps you should go home.'

THE BOAT

Who do you find attractive?
I'm attracted to people of both sexes.
Who do you have sexual fantasies about?
I don't have many sexual fantasies.
With whom do you form strong emotional bonds?
I don't really form strong attachments.

'My Finn! Fancy seeing you here!'

Since when did August call her 'My Finn'? That was a Richard-ism. Finn shoved her phone into her pocket. She had done the Kinsey quiz not so long ago, but after meeting Celeste she fell into a panic, and decided to test herself again. The attraction was so strong.

Various bells jangled as August stepped off the bike. A strand of fairy lights wove and blinked around the frame. Finn felt her toes curl up tight as she tried to smile.

They were both early for the circle, but Richard wasn't home. August and Finn both knew how to 'break in' through Richard's window – by climbing on top of a stack of milk crates – but neither much enjoyed doing it. It was fine, sitting in the sculpture garden, waiting.

August had emptied the contents of her backpack onto the ground and was rummaging through the scatter. Her blond hair flailed in all directions, and it didn't seem fair to Finn. How could someone be conventionally beautiful – with her long hair and doe eyes – and also extremely weird, extremely young, and have a stable boyfriend? In some bizarre way, August seemed to have it all. And how old was she anyway?

Probably ten years younger, maybe twenty-one or twenty-two, Finn guessed. Her bubble of self-confidence had not yet been burst.

'Your bike looks like a disco,' said Finn.

August snorted with laughter. She seemed to find what she was looking for, and began dragging belongings, like caught prey, back to the bag.

After wiping her forehead, she flopped down by Finn. There was a wooden park bench in the garden now – though nobody knew where it came from.

'God provides,' Richard had chuckled when he saw it.

August had been quick to paint it pink and purple.

She was still wearing her pink helmet, and panting heavily. 'I like this spot for thinking too, it's my favourite spot. I wish I could write the way you write, but all I do is talk to myself.'

She sucked on her sipper bottle while Finn looked on, vaguely worried. She thought about asking August if she was okay, but felt strange about it. This just wasn't something Finn did. Instead she blurted the next thing that came into her head.

'Is your hair naturally blond?'

August smiled and giggled. 'Of course! I can't be bothered much with hair care. My mum thinks I should get it cut more often.'

'Sorry,' Finn said, sitting on her hands, wondering why she'd even asked. 'It just seems like a lot of spiritual people dye their hair blond. Maybe it's because they want to feel "light" and "pure",' she air-quoted, shaking her head.

'I know! August exclaimed. 'I used to go to church, and lots of worship leaders had dyed-blond hair. I never understood it.' She shrugged and sat next to Finn. 'If spirituality's about what's inside, why should hair colour matter? And if God loves every hair on our heads, why should we change them? Our hair is already perfect, whatever way it is.'

Finn nodded, and smiled, not sure what else to say.

'It was hot today wasn't it?' said August. 'I think I overheated.

I got sent home early from work and just lay in bed till now. I'm not ready for summer.'

'It's more humid than hot I think,' Finn said, wondering why she felt a perpetual need to disagree with August.

'And maybe I'm overdone, it's hard to know, hard to say. What are you up to? Do you have an interesting hat?'

'Oh not really anything significant,' said Finn. She remembered she had her journal in her bag, and pulled it out, crossing one leg over the other. 'I was just about to start reading over a story I'm working on.'

'You must be so patient,' panted August. 'Writing. It's so slow.'

'It can be fast.'

'And talking can be slow, for some people I think.' August squeezed, shooting water into her mouth. 'Not for me!' she gurgled.

Finn shrugged and reopened her journal. August took a few more sips, then ventured out into the scrap. And then the clanking, the scraping as she began to move objects around. Finn opened her journal and tried to interpret her mountainous scrawl.

❀

'Joan! Where have you been all my life!' Eve dug into an embrace. A red glittery headband pushed Joan's fine grey hair off her face. It was the first thing Finn saw as she climbed up the ladder, Joan's eyes closed, surrounded by sparkling red. Eve had done the 'break-in', and was letting the crowd pile into the boat.

'My Finn,' Joan called out, then gave a deep guttural laugh.

It didn't seem quite as painful when Joan mimicked Richard.

'How are you?' Finn said.

'It was so warm today, my joints are feeling very relaxed.' She kissed Finn's cheek. 'I felt quite alright about taking the "stairs" tonight. It might just be that winters are too much for me.'

'It's so great to see you again, Joan,' called out Jsun. 'Richard will be stoked.'

'Hmmm,' Joan folded arms across her chest. 'I was thinking it seemed a bit quiet in here and, of course.' She clicked her fingers. 'No Richard. Terrible. I noticed his absence only because it felt so peaceful.'

Everyone laughed. Finn wondered if she went away and reappeared like this, would everyone care so much?

'So what have you been up to Joan? Tell us everything!' Eve demanded.

August put on *Deep Sounds for DNA Repair*, an ominous hum moving through the boat. It seemed to fall as a strange soundtrack for Joan's tales: her trip to India booked, her Friday morning seniors' yoga, conscious counselling sessions, the art therapy workshops.

It was already dark outside when a bright, pixie-like face appeared at the top of the ladder. All eyes were drawn away from Joan and her red glittery headband. Celeste waved to all, making eye contact with Finn, as Richard barrelled up behind her, metal detector slung over his shoulder.

'HELLO! HELLO all you BEAUTIFUL PEOPLE!'

Richard always spoke loudly when he turned up late. Everyone laughed and he began his large wave again, waving like it was an important signal, a message, and everyone laughed more, waving back.

'Richard's so awesome,' Jsun murmured to Joan, who did not look impressed. She was eyeing off Celeste.

After waving a while longer, Richard sat down on the couch.

'Right everyone, tonight's going to be easy. Different. New. AMAZING! This is,' and Richard stood up, thrusting his hands towards his showpiece. 'Ta-da! This is Celeste! Celeste, over to you!'

'What, now?' Celeste had just sat down in the most elegant cross-legged position Finn had ever seen.

'Okay,' she smiled, with that look of ease and laughter in her eyes. When she stood up, it was prance-like.

But just as she started to talk, there was the sound of rain. A collective groan sounded.

August hopped up. 'I'll get the saucepans!'

She was followed by Finn, and the two began opening cupboards under the sink. They each found four pots, and began to move about the boat, placing one on the bench, two on the kitchen floor, one on the top of the bookshelf in the living room, two in the bedroom, and two in the toilet.

'Oh God, I hope the power doesn't go out,' Richard groaned.

'It's okay!' August called out. She magically produced a headlamp from somewhere in the kitchen, snapping the band around her forehead. 'If it does, I'll go out to the fuse box.'

Richard's laughter boomed as he looked around at the group. 'Ah, what would I do without these girls?'

As Finn and August sat back down, there was the sound of water moving through the drainpipes. It sounded like a stream running overhead.

Eve had closed her eyes and was tearing up. 'The earth is crying,' she whispered, then began to smile, looking to Celeste. 'We are ready for change.'

Celeste looked back at her with firm eyes. 'I am happy to be the instigator of that.' She looked around at the group, smiled and waved. 'My name is Celestiaa Davinaa, or Celeste for short. Yes, Celestial is a nickname, but Celeste is the easiest. Okay, so ...'

Everybody laughed, the sort of laugh that kind crowds deliver to empty spaces. Finn couldn't be sure whether Celeste had created that space, wanting the kindness of the laughter, wanting to be encouraged.

She flicked her hair again, and mouthed to Richard, *now?*

'Yes, now, darling, go for it. Hang on, everyone,' Richard looked up at the circle. He was barefoot, looking relaxed, right leg crossed over the left, right hand pressed onto his scalp. 'Everyone, I have asked Celeste to talk to us tonight, to lead our circle, telling her story. Celeste is a healer, and yeah, I think we are probably all interested in what she has to say. So let's give her a round of applause.'

Everyone clapped but Joan, who sat quietly, seeming vacant.

'So, Richard has asked me to talk to you tonight,' she cocked her head to one side, 'and say a bit about my story and what I do. I haven't actually come through an encounter group, and I am relatively new to the world of Receivers. I am a local healer and I run my own business ... Well, I do two things. I make raw chocolate treats and bliss balls for local cafés, and I also conduct healing sessions.

'I suppose you could call me an inter-modal practitioner. I usually have no idea what is going to happen with a client until the moment they walk through my door. It's all about feeling, or intuitive therapy if you like. I've studied Past Life Regression Therapy, Feldenkrais, Violet Flame Therapy, Craniosacral Analysis, TCM, Body Reading, Network Spinal Analysis, it's almost a case of you name it! So, tonight, I think, I will just go by feeling too, the way I always do, and tell you a bit about myself. Does that suit you, Richard?' She spoke in a teasing tone.

He returned a sweet smile and gave a thumbs up. 'Shall I turn down the lights?'

'Please. Oh, also, Richard, could we have some different music?'

Celeste reached down to her bag and pulled out a CD that Finn saw was called *Pythagorean Harmonics*. 'I find this usually helps take me on a journey with my story.'

An unpleasant buzzing sound created a kind of friction in the room. Finn wanted to block her ears, but no-one else looked bothered. Celeste drew her gaze in, towards her tiny feet. Now there was just candle glow on her face. When she looked up again, it was like she had collected up a different part of herself.

She swayed gently from side to side, then began to speak in

an even, hypnotic tone. 'I always knew I would be childless. That was a strange thing for my mother to hear. Having children was passing on knowledge, ensuring we go on living. It was removing uncertainty from our lives. We leave school, we go to work, we get married, we have children, and so when we are old and dying, we are not alone. Also, I always knew I was not afraid of dying. For me, there is the risk of dying alone. Is this sad? I don't believe so. I am never really alone. But what else is this conversation about? I said before, I believe that by having children, we are passing on our ways of being. We are ensuring we go on living. This has never been a concern for me. And this is why also I have never been afraid of dying. Because I know that we go on living.

'I was in the backseat of my family's car when I remembered the last time I died. It was in a car crash, and I was a young woman. Memories of past lives have come to me in flashes, many times, throughout this lifetime, before I understood my gift. Now I know the way past-life memories are stored at points all over my body. I have before, deep in meditation, felt my subtle body drawn completely into my knee. There I've seen in dream-speed, my life as shoemaker, a dear and naive man, in a European city during the Middle Ages. Happily married, poor, with many children, my life came to a swift end when a mob, of some political persuasion I believe, set my modest shop, and the rest of the town square, on fire. And that is how it is. Memories are stored in different points across my body. Deep in my elbow, I've been a woman who died young, unable to say goodbye to her loving parents, who were flower farmers.

'Our lives are not played out on a level field. We would all like to believe they are. In fact, this is exactly the opposite to the structure of the universe. The righteous are rewarded. We grow stronger and stronger, we ascend further and further along our paths. We are not all equal here. We all want to be happy, but how do each of us go about it?

'Happiness involves some serious work. If we look at our

lives, we will be able to see some patterns. Resistance. Weak points. Ways in which we are holding back, holding ourselves back, being held back by others, holding back others. We inspect closely, and we will start to see the past lives we've lived and shared with those around us.

'We begin each life with a very small Soul Circle. What I mean by a Soul Circle is the group of souls with whom you travel from lifetime to lifetime. It is not just husband and wife. One lifetime, you may have a wife who was previously your father, a daughter who was your mother, a boyfriend who was once your child. And don't we all know about that one! Have you ever had a relationship and fallen into a dynamic so quickly that you felt utterly powerless to it? Well, that is the powers that be, the powers of spirit history taking over.'

Everyone in the circle was quiet, drawn in by Celeste's words. Even Joan seemed transfixed, Finn noticed. She felt that feeling between her legs again, but didn't know what it meant, and certainly didn't trust it.

'Before I became a healer, I worked in the world of media and marketing, for major financial institutions. I knew it was banks and big business that ruled the world, but I was sure of my own place in that reality. I had a good enough life, a fiancé who was a lawyer, we had an apartment overlooking the ocean, and we had the things we wanted.'

Celeste swayed, speaking with her eyes closed. Finn couldn't help feeling such broad and confusing things towards this small, swaying woman. She began to feel like a shepherd, trying to get her flock of feelings to move in the same direction. There was her heart pounding, the shapes fluttering in her chest, her feet shifting, and what was happening down there. Finn suddenly felt too open and exposed. She didn't want to be sitting cross-legged. She didn't want to be a chain in this circle. She wanted to be closed up in her own circle, and so drew her knees in towards her chest, clasping hands around her legs, her body like a clenched fist.

'*There must be more to life than this*,' Celeste continued. 'That's what I began to think. My fiancé was ready for marriage and kids and tried to convince me that's what I needed to make me happy! And that's when we began to grow distant: he grew smaller to me, as I grew bigger and stronger inside.

'Many people believe that we all have this ability; we all have intuition, instinct, the power of foresight. There are thought-forms surrounding each of us. Run your hand through the air, and you will feel the changes in temperature. You will sense the subtle shifts in air density, as the thought-forms float like clouds, from one person to the next.'

Celeste paused, and moved her hands slowly through the air, fluttering her eyelids. Eve and August raised their hands too, tracing patterns through space as Celeste nodded and smiled.

'But I don't believe that all of us can sense these forms. I think by saying that, we are dumbing down spirituality. We are selling spiritual skills, like "learn how to be a psychic", or "we can all be clairvoyants". But was everyone a sage, a soothsayer, a medicine man in a traditional society? No, healers were and still are in the minority. We are different. We are more advanced souls.

'I believe all of you – just by virtue of being here – are advanced souls. Firstly, you are special to be touched in this way, and secondly, you ask to be touched again! Do you have any idea how many people are scared off from spiritual awakening? Maybe they found a teaching dream was too frightening, or saw a ghostly form once and were so afraid, their clairsentient skills halted before they even had a chance.

'It is rare to be here, in a place like this. It is rare to feel this higher vibration. But of course, we are healers, yet we are still here, on this earth. There is still work to be done. Remember how easily I said it is for thought-forms to attach themselves, from the thinker to a passer-by? Know that the same goes for spiritual entities. SET – Spiritual Entity Transference – can happen via your DNA. It is a spiritual transference of memories, knowledge and pain across lifetimes. But it can be much simpler than that. It can come through the pores of your skin. Tiny, like bacteria, it can come through touch. It can come through feeling. Entities will be attracted to you if they deem you a good home. You will begin something like a host-parasite relationship. SET can happen in relationships with partners, siblings, friends. It can happen when someone serves your groceries.'

Finn looked over to Richard. His eyes were closed, scrunched lines of skin behind his glasses. His teeth were clenched too, and mouth slightly open. 'You are clearly holding tension in your face,' a yoga teacher would probably say. It was a pained expression she had never understood: was it deep listening, concentration, or something else?

'What have you asked into your life? What did you do wrong in your past lives? If you're experiencing hardship though, don't look at it as retribution. We have the chance to ask the question: what can I learn from this experience? How I can help is, I can flush people of spiritual entities that are holding them back. And that is, really, my specialisation.

'Sometimes when I see clients, I say, "You've brought this on yourself. You've done it again." And people get really upset, really angry. "I didn't choose this," they say. "This is not my fault. I wouldn't do this to myself and my family." That is what they say at first, but soon they come round.

'So what is it we need to do? Well, we need to remember that happiness comes with hard work. But remember also, there is always help at hand. Oh, and also, it's not all bad news! Sometimes higher entities will attach themselves. Sometimes people are protected, for instance, by the spirit of a passed-over brother. Higher entities will guide, keep you again from danger. They will be presences to talk to. They will be voices that keep people sane. This is more rare, and it's not for me to judge openly. If someone comes to me looking for help and clarification, I am able to do that. Sometimes it is an entity that requires flushing, and sometimes it is not. It has actually been very fortuitous meeting Richard, and you all. You can probably hear from my story, the similarities between my healing work, and the work of Richard.'

Celeste leaned close over the candle, shadows crossing her face. 'I look forward to getting to know each of you, and beginning to understand this new system of knowledge. Well, new to me at least! I am really interested to bring the two together, somehow, and see if we can make something new. Exciting times ahead. Well, thank you, that's me for tonight.'

Finn was slower to stand than the other circle members, who stood suddenly and clapped. She had a strange feeling coming over her, one of maybe dread, or discomfort. Something wasn't right. August's clapping seemed particularly loud and hurried, but it ended abruptly, as she dashed towards the toilet.

※

'Something like this was always gonna happen,' Jsun said, his voice muffled through the wall. 'Someone was bound to be called, to rally us together. You know, Australia has the most Lightworkers in the world. The west has the most Lightworkers in Australia. And I reckon here in Fremantle, there are the most Lightworkers in the west. Now that can only mean one thing.'

'Freo has the most Lightworkers in the world!' Eve screeched.

August was in the toilet, holding her head in her hands. Her chest felt warm and soothed, tucked up against her thighs. She was looking down at her feet, her toenails, which she'd tried to paint to calm herself this afternoon. But she couldn't sit still long enough to let the paint dry. The pink was smudged, uneven, and spread on some of her skin. She began to pick at her toes, trying to slow her breath.

'Do you know how many patients come here to deal with

the grief of losing their deposit?' August heard Eve fire the question. 'They're not all extractions, Richard's appointments. For some, they were young and foolish at first contact. Scared of the pain. Some of them feel they've lost their whole life source. And I wouldn't be surprised if that's true.'

'It's called *Devotional Jukebox*,' Richard shouted. August smiled, listening to the thumps of his footsteps. She pictured him dance-strutting around the kitchen.

'Oh there are plenty of interdimensional beings around here. See them all the time. Dwarves, elves,' Jsun explained to someone. 'Yesterday a guy came to pick up new tyres. He had a real feel of the giant about him.'

'I have always been this way, since I can remember. It's only the last few years it's got out of hand.' August imagined Eve leaning in towards Rhodda as she spilled her testimony. 'First it was pure psychic sensation. Now I experience terrible physical pains, anywhere from my shoulder, to my neck, back and feet. I will walk down the street and it's too much. In a crowd, points everywhere. A woman will walk past me, and we brush shoulders. Her left breast throbs. Mine begins to throb also, and I know it's cancer. Once the top of a man's head was literally on fire. A glowing crown of flames. He frightened me, a meek, bald man with glasses. He stopped and asked, "Are you okay?" What could I say to him? What do I do with this information? "Your deposit has calcified! Come see Richard!"'

'Eve, if someone was already in that state, I'm not sure what I'd be able to do,' Richard called.

'I know, I know! I just, BRRRRRMMMMMMM, whhhooop! Shake it off, shake it off! It's just – what do I do? God's given me a gift but he doesn't seem quite so clear about the steps I need to take to actually help people.'

'I just need to call on the angels,' Eve said.

August slowly lifted her head, hoping her heart would steady. But it was still thudding too fast. She looked around at the walls of the toilet. They were pine panelling, covered in small knots. The knots usually reminded August of stars, floating in the galaxy. But today they were faces, tight with pain, mouths wide, screaming.

'Angels aren't real, Eve!' Richard called out again.

'What?' Eve cried.

'They're not real!' he shouted. 'Well, they're real because they're part of the human experience. They are just as real as anything else for the people who convene with them. But they are not actually real. Or you could say, they are real, because we made them up.'

'Richard, you are my guru,' Eve called out. 'But that is not something we are going to agree on.'

'I honestly believe that photonic light exposure can unlock DNA memories, change behaviour patterns, and ultimately upgrade your DNA,' said someone. 'And what if these deposits are actually little tight bundles of photonic energy? Some of us are willing to receive that kind of love, some of us aren't.'

'We are animal, we are vegetable. Look at the gourd, look at the sea cucumber. Their insides are the same, but one is full of seeds, the other is full of intestines. Scrape them clean and make either into a curry.'

Conversations were threads unravelling. August sat and tried to focus, but was unable to pick the right strands.

'Did you know Jesus spent time in India? He was just another holy man.'

'I asked, "What did you do in Thailand?" He said, "I found God."'

'This morning my colleague came in complaining about stomach aches and I said, "I dreamt about your digestive system last night! I've already made you a peppy tea!"'

'Sometimes I need to remind myself that chlorophyll isn't chloroform.'

'I always get Paleo confused with polio.'

'It was like a spiky bauble, desperate to get out, but I didn't know if I wanted that straight away. Was there a way I could soften the spikes before passing, like, gently blanching them?'

'The time has come for a more democratic spirituality.'

'I have been meaning to create a photonic energy forecast chart! You know, it will amplify both fear and love.'

'I like to call it my "pain brain".'

'I always wear three watches. Time just isn't that steady. I read three times and pick the middle. I can never put faith in just one clock.'

'Love is the message after all. Simple, unboxed love.'

August pulled out her phone and began to message Tom. *My love. I've just listened to the most amazing words from this wise woman healer. Her name is Celestiaa. I think she might be able to help me, but I'm scared! I've had a weird day. I'm not really sure what to do, but I think there's something big and wrong inside me and it needs to go away, or I'm not going to make it xox*

She pressed send, then flushed the toilet, stepping back into the main cabin. Finn looked up at her. Was she frowning, or was that the flicker of a smile? August could never tell.

'Richard, what is this huge tin of Milo?' Celeste had entered the kitchen, and was taking in the state of the pantry.

'Oh, sound spiritual health overrides any need for concern about the food I put in my body.'

'Whatever happened to "you are what you eat?" We take on the energetic frequencies of the foods we consume!'

'It's not relevant. Not if we're spiritually robust enough, surely!'

'Well, I suppose "organic" as a label doesn't make sense anyway.'

'Why not?'

'Because we can change the molecular structure of water through prayer. Bless the water, cleanse the water. Bless the food, cleanse the food. You know that's what the Hare Krishnas do. They don't use organic at all. Absolutely no need.'

The room could be spinning. Maybe the boat hit water

somehow. But August wasn't sure if it was sea legs or true north she needed more.

Celeste was leaning in towards Finn as August approached, trying to get her legs to do what she needed them to. Finn looked rigid. Eve was washing mugs, clearing away instant coffee and chocolate wrappers. August didn't want to disturb but she knew she needed to do it, she needed to make the first move.

'Hi Celestiaa!' But Celestiaa didn't seem to hear her.

'Hey August,' said Finn.

'Hi Finn! How are you?'

Finn seemed to shrink back at the sound of August's voice. It reminded her of a turtle's head, retreating back into its shell.

'Sorry, did I just greet you too loudly?'

'What?' Finn seemed confused.

'Too loud? Am I too loud?' August felt herself turning painfully red.

Something in Finn's face changed; it seemed she registered August's stress.

'It's okay, you're not loud. Who am I to judge anyone by their volume?'

August shrieked in laughter, knowing her eyes were probably maniacally wide. The laughter finally broke into Celeste's attention.

'Hello Celeste! I wanted to introduce myself.' August thrust out her arm.

'Hello there, was it April?' Celeste gave a tired look.

'Just a few months away!' she shrieked again, Celeste jumping at August's voice.

'Yes! Hi! I just wanted to say how much I enjoyed the talk and how much it spoke to me. Also, can I book in for an appointment?'

'Shhh-ure...' Celeste sighed, uncrossing her legs, and reaching down to her bag. 'Let me just get my diary...'

Celeste began to flick through a small book, which was

black and executive-looking, like one a lawyer might have. She flipped open to a page, then looked up at August. She stared, which elicited August's nervous trait, her wild, unstoppable blinking.

Stop blinking! she shouted inside. The sound echoed, reverberating through her body like it was a hollow, empty chamber. And the blinking continued.

With a somewhat unsatisfied look, which August interpreted as *God help me with this one*, Celeste looked back to her diary, tracing her finger across a page.

'I am all booked out for the next few weeks.' The book closed. 'You could give me a call, say at the end of the month, and I'll see if I can fit you in in the near future.'

'Great!' August's face hurt from smiling when she didn't mean to. 'Perfect!'

'I'll give you my card. It has my address.'

She flicked out the shiny pink, flecked with gold stars, a wisp of glittery river. 'Celeste, She Beams.'

Why won't she beam for me?

When August climbed down the ladder, she looked over at her bike. It was leaning against a makeshift brick wall, covered in morning glory. The creeper was sending its green strands in all directions. It looked like the bike would soon be tangled and trapped within the green. The bike could be consumed, it would be gone. August began to panic, and pull her bike up away, grabbing at twists of flowers and leaves, pulling stems and flinging them to the ground. She dumped her backpack in the basket, but before she hopped on, she closed her eyes, and held the phone in her hand.

And then, there was a ding: there was a new message from Tom. She read the words *I'm coming to see you. I'll be there as soon as I can xox*

✿

Richard felt the chipboard base digging into his right buttock. He was surprised that Celeste hasn't commented on the quality of the couch. He'd retrieved it from a verge collection years ago. The inner springs had rusted to crumpled coils. Richard had placed a piece of chipboard beneath the cushions, which made it uncomfortable in a different way. He often thought of chopping the couch up, until it became a collection of wire, fabric, stuffing and wood, then setting fire to it. This seemed like the only way to get rid of it now.

But the couch was too much to think about. He looked up to the photo of Serena, to what both made sense and made no sense at all.

'What's wrong?' Celeste asked. 'Don't you think that went well?'

'Sorry?' Richard tried to snap out of his thoughts.

She followed his gaze. Celeste didn't ask about the woman in the photograph. It was as though she knew all about her already. And perhaps she did. It was likely that 'psychic' was another item on the long list of Celeste's spiritual talents.

She smiled again, then climbed on top of him. Her legs were wide, crotch crushing towards his. Her hair fell to one side, eyes meeting his. This whole movement blocked his view. Apparently the couch wasn't figuring in her thoughts at all.

'What are you thinking about now?' Her voice was lower, purr-like.

There's a right and a wrong answer, were the words behind her words.

He smiled, then spoke more nervously than he meant to. 'You. I'm thinking about you, of course.' Richard rested hands on her thighs, rubbing them gently. But he knew, his hands didn't have that special electrical charge. There was a noticeable lack of warmth. Could she feel that absence? Feel that nothing-special-vibe radiating through his palms?

'This, I'm here,' he laughed oddly. 'I'm in the now. I'm all yours.'

She pulled off her jumper. Underneath, white flesh.

Chest-plate.

Ross once said the chest-plate is his favourite part of a woman's body.

Chest-plate. Chest-nut-plate. An awkward sexual position. Pleasurable for men in particular.

'Richard?' She was waving her hand across his face. 'You're wandering,' she held his chin, glaring.

Is she angry?

She launched, attack-like. Gentle kiss first, coaxing.

Something's not firing.

She pulled back, removing his glasses. 'You okay?'

'I can't see.'

'Well you can feel me.'

Seductive lips. Stretching forward, into him.

She's really quite flexible.

Guiding hands, hers leading his. He imagined her hands saying to his hands, *Come on, don't be shy. Come closer. Come up, towards this place.*

No, here! No no, not there ... Here!

His hands stopped moving. *No,* they replied.

She pushed. *Wrong answer,* her hands said.

Don't everyone's hands have their own answers?

The tongue was insistent: *Come on, come on.* Like rubbing two sticks together.

The fire. Smoke all around. *Who can see? Sometimes when there's smoke, there's no fire.*

A sigh rose in the air. 'This just isn't working for me.'

She climbed off. Pulled the jumper on. Pulled a coat over. Pulled a handbag over her shoulder. Richard pulled his glasses back on, pushing the plastic over the bridge of his nose. Pulling and pushing things that should be easy to move. Hands, tongue, clothing, heart.

She began to adjust her collar, then fluff her hair, lost in thought. 'Just a small rearranging of fibres – clothing, hair – you know, can amount to a rearranging of energies inside you.'

'I'm sorry.'

'It's okay, it's just me. That just wasn't working for me. I should be the one who says sorry, but ...' Celeste gave a tired smile. 'I don't do sorry. Goodbye Richard.'

She moved towards the door.

'Oh, how did you enjoy tonight?'

'The circle is great.' Celeste's eyes shifted in quality, seeming clearer, more awake. 'August is on the waitlist for a session with me, and I'm meeting up with Finn for a drink. Really, you've done well here.'

'Why, thank you,' Richard began to chuckle. 'Are you really going, just like that?'

She smiled – glassy eyes looking up from the ladder. 'Bye.' Her face disappeared into the night.

THE CARAVAN

She heard the footsteps outside, the sound of him slipping off his boots. Tom always took off his boots when he came inside; he didn't like mess and sand on the floor. The door creaked open, but he didn't switch on the light. And then, his body was heavy, warm and sweet next to hers. She gripped Tom tight, and he began to rock her in his arms.

'I got your message. I was worried,' he sighed. 'Are you okay?'

'No. Maybe. I'm not sure,' August's eyes were closed, but her mind moved quickly. 'You must be tired of me. I am so sick of myself. I've been rushing around and not sure why. Or I'm excited, and nervousness comes along for the ride. Then I go from being happy and excited, to happy and anxious, barely holding myself together ...'

'August ...'

'I don't know if I'll ever be able to stop peeing in the shower now that I've started.'

Tom was silent a moment, stroking her hair. 'I had no idea you'd started peeing in the shower.'

'I just can't help thinking, what if I have been corrupted from within? What if all the wrong messages are being sent through my body? Is that why I am stuck like this? Wrong messages are flitting through me, and eventually my coding will change and I'll have different fingerprints. I've been meaning to find out, are toeprints as unique as fingerprints?'

Tom didn't answer, and August felt annoyed. She sat up in bed, peering out the window. Everything looked too crisp and clear. The moon was a white disc in the sky. Wind whistled through the tamarisk tree, and the neighbour's cat sat beneath, looking up at the waving branches. Her heart sank a little. Was the cat hunting? She opened the window and hissed, the cat prancing away.

'I don't even know who I am anymore,' she mumbled, but it didn't matter because Tom would understand; he always understood. 'We are covered in millions of bacteria, all over our bodies and inside our bodies. And then there is the mould. The spores could be all through my lungs. Have you heard of Spiritual Energy Transference? Do you know how easy it is for thought-forms to migrate from one self to another?'

She began to stroke his hair, which was falling long, down his sides. 'Why is your hair out?'

He smiled and shrugged, and she thumped his chest, sighing.

'Part of me is terrified that I could already be someone else without knowing,' August went on, and on, and had no idea how to stop. 'Another part of me is relieved; eventually my little self-particles will fly away, like dust in a sandstorm, reducing me to nothing. Lot's wife, the pillar of salt reduced to rubble. But what was her reincarnation? Did she fly off as a bird? I can be made again, all these new tiny cells coming together to create me anew.'

'August, let's try to get some rest.' Tom was like gravity, his hand on her shoulder, trying to pull her down to sleep.

'I'm sorry! I should have worked myself out of this state before you arrived. I want to be my best self for you but I never seem to manage it.'

'It's okay, I'm here now. I'm glad I'm here. I can help, come on. Just close your eyes.'

'But I'm a burden, and you're so reasonable, and I don't want to be a burden. It's just, sometimes when I need you, you're not here. Then sometimes when I think I need company, when I need to be shown clearly where I begin and end, I absolutely can't stand company. That's when I know, I am at my worst, but I need to find my own shape, for myself, because if I wait for you to give it to me, I won't ever really have it. Because as soon as your body is not pressed up against me, as soon as you leave, I am not clearly defined anymore.'

Tom was quiet for a moment. 'August, you are yourself whether I'm here or not.'

'Is that true though? What about ticks? When you try to pull them out of your skin, their head gets stuck, burrowing in like the head is its own self. You need to get a match, drive it out with fire, and burn a bigger hole in your skin in the process. But what if you don't get the whole tick-head out? Will it become a part of you?'

'Oh, so I'm just a tick now?' Tom laughed.

'I heard a horrible story when I was a kid about a woman with this grotesque pimple. Eventually it burst and all these spiders ran all over her face. There had actually been a spider's egg buried in her skin.'

'August …'

'But I don't want to know all this.'

Tom pulled August close into his chest. The shape of him became the outline of her, enclosing all the wildness and leaking, pressing August back into her own skin. 'It's okay.'

'Is it though?' Her voice was muffled by his body. 'I don't know the way forward. Should I let the world know? Should I keep a secret secret? I've asked for an appointment with a healer. I want to be opened up, put back together again. But I don't want to lose what I know, because then, I'll have nothing to hold me down. I'm just scared, I'll grow and I'll lose.'

She pulled herself up from his chest and took in his face. Tom's eyes should be blue, but you couldn't see that in the dark. They shone just a little, catching the porchlight from the neighbour's yard.

'I'm afraid I'll grow into a different shape, and we won't be the right shape together anymore. I'm afraid I'll lose you.'

August sat up next to him, and Tom turned on his side, looking up at her. 'I suppose that's always the risk, isn't it?

With any change? If what we have is keeping you scared of growing, that's bad. If what we have is letting you grow, that's good, right?'

August found herself nodding, like a small injured bird. 'I suppose you're right.'

The cat from next door was miaowing loud. August looked up and saw the eyes at the window. Many eyes, smiling eyes. They were the Pleiadians, coming to let her know, all would be well. Tom looked over and saw them too, then chuckled.

'There's always someone watching over you, August.'

He placed his hands over her eyes, and August felt herself falling, thrust into that deep, dark, pink and new world.

When August woke, he was gone. She picked up her phone and found a new message.

Don't be afraid. Going to see a new healer sounds like a good idea. I know, you've seen so many healers, and maybe you think you are permanently broken, but you're not. This is a hard time, but trust me, you can get through this. You can be okay. You just need to open up and let the light in. I love you xox

August replied, *There will be a wait anyway. I've got time to sit and think about it. I've been getting anxious early this year. There's still time for this to all come together.*

She pressed her phone to her chest and began to hum.

THE BAR

'I love your necklace! What a gorgeous example of moldavite.'

'Thanks, I got it from the op shop,' said Finn, plopping into a chair across from Celeste.

The sound of bass, didgeridoo and throat-singing thumped through the room. Finn and Celeste had arranged to meet up at Kombu Bar, Fremantle's first kombucha-only establishment.

'Oh, so it's pre-worn. How does it feel?'

'It's really smooth, here ...' Finn leaned forward, Celeste taking the stone in her hands. It felt for a moment like Finn was on a leash, Celeste pulling her in. There was something terrible and wonderful about the feeling.

'Hmmm ... I see. But how does it feel to wear it? Energetically?'

'Oh, okay,' Finn fumbled for words. 'I can't wear it for very long to be honest. It's kind of irritating.'

'How so?'

'It's like a slight pressure on my chest.'

'Let me see properly.'

Finn sat back down in her chair, then removed the chain, passing it to Celeste. Her hands were warm, and Finn tingled all over.

'Yes, that is, phew, that certainly carries some weight! Would you like me to cleanse it for you?'

'Sure!'

Why do I agree to things so quickly when I am just confused?

'I mean, what will that involve exactly?'

'Well, we all know that crystals are very sensitive to the vibration of their owners. Or stewards, I should say; no-one ever really owns a crystal. And crystals are very, very sensitive. I could see straight away that this piece wasn't resonating with your spiritual frequency. By cleansing it, I'm wiping the hard drive. You will find it feels much lighter.'

'So you're overthrowing the crystal's government?' Finn drummed fingertips on the table, aware that what she'd just said was a bit odd.

Celeste slipped the necklace into her handbag, not seeming to register the question. 'Of course, moldavite isn't a crystal though. It comes from meteors. But the same principle applies.'

A young waiter brought menus. Celeste ordered a Galaxy, while Finn chose the Digestive. They glanced over the food menu.

'Well, everything looks good. I think I'll get a Primal Plate,' said Celeste.

'Oh, I assumed you were a vegetarian for some reason.'

'Well, I usually maintain a sentient diet, but anything pre-agricultural is fine. Purity is my priority. I just can't stand processed, packaged foods. Thank you,' she said, handing back the menu to the young man.

'Well, I think I'll get a Primal Plate too then,' said Finn, patting her tummy. 'I love to eat meat, but I wasn't sure if I'd offend you.'

'Our bodies tell us what we need. You should always follow your cravings. But now, the reason I wanted to meet is I feel the need to speak to you about your situation. It's good to see a doctor initially of course, to rule out any serious medical issues. Also, seeing a medical intuitive can make things quicker and easier. I'm assuming you've already spoken to Eve?'

'Are you talking about the hymen thing?'

Celeste burst into laughter. 'Yes, Finn! I'm talking about the hymen thing!'

'Oh, okay. No, I haven't talked to Eve. I've considered it. Richard suggested that too, but I don't really want to presume on her for free advice.'

And also she's a crazy bitch, thought Finn, going red, realising her discomfort with such raging thoughts.

'Yes,' Celeste looked up, seeming reflective. 'Sometimes it's nice to keep these things separate. She's a member of your spiritual circle.'

Celeste gave a slightly glazed-over smile. Finn had observed at the Circle of IEWA, Celeste often placed a hand on a person's shoulder when saying something significant. Sometimes her eye contact lingered too. This evening, it seemed like everything Celeste had to say was significant, because almost every word she spoke, she reached over and touched Finn's forearm. At every touch, Finn felt a sensation between her legs. The sensation was a strange mix of hardening and softening, cracking open and becoming solid.

'Finn, are you okay? Are you too hot?'

Finn fanned her face with the bamboo menu. 'Yes, it's very warm in here.'

'Really? I'm cold.' Celeste pulled her jacket closer in a knowingly cute, pixie-like way. 'Interesting. So your body is prone to heat. I'm quite prone to a low body temperature myself. Well look, I'm so glad you are going to a professional.'

How did she know about this, Finn wondered. 'Did Richard tell you about it?'

Celeste nodded, her arms folded across her chest. 'Is the gynaecologist female?'

'Yes, thank God. I'm booked in for next week. Apparently I might need an operation too.'

'Good, that's a start. But be careful. Don't forget Spirit.'

'Well, I have been pretty afraid. What if my body feels weird after the operation?'

'I wasn't thinking about that. I just mean, when we are sick, we have invited that sickness. It doesn't mean we are weak or bad. It just means we are human.'

Finn flinched, and Celeste began to speak hurriedly. 'I don't mean for you to hear "this is your fault". I mean for you to hear

"this problem is bigger than you and your current lifetime".
Connect with that. Ultimately, this is not your fault. It is the
fault of dark spirit matter, entities that have attached to you,
lifetimes and lifetimes over. Violence begets violence, mess
begets mess, bad spirits beget bad spirits. But how did I get
here?'

Finn coughed. 'You mentioned inviting sickness.'

'Oh Finn!' Celeste giggled. 'I've gone off in the wrong
direction. Yes, I'm glad you're off to the doctor. We all need to
find the treatments that speak to us. But Finn, let me put this
to you. What if your, abnormality, let's say, is not unwanted.
Let's say, perhaps it is a gift from God. What lesson might it
teach you?'

Finn shifted in her chair. 'I see what you mean. I've had a
lot of pain in my life, and I've always tried to see if I can "get
something out of it". Otherwise the pain would drive me more
crazy than I already am. If I didn't try to see pain as offering
me something, I'm not sure where I'd be, or if I'd even be here
at all.'

'But now you're talking about self-preservation. You're still
thinking of this in a negative sense. Maybe I've confused things
by calling it an abnormality. I mean, what if this is purely a
good thing?'

'Well ... it *is* the whole reason I've never had sex.'

'So you've never actually had sex?'

Finn twirled her empty kombucha glass. A stiff drink was
needed now.

'Shall I order us some oolong? This is my shout. I know this
conversation could be heard as invasive. But there are some
things I need to tell you. So, where were we?'

'Well, I had this boyfriend. Eric. We studied together. We
were young and inexperienced. There was all this pain and the
sex just never worked. We tried. Then it's like all we shared
was embarrassment. Embarrassment became really big, while
the relationship became really small. We ended things, and

then one day I saw him. He had his arm around another girl. So I thought, the problem must be with me.'

'Finn, thank you for sharing. Look, let me speak from my heart. Just briefly. Do I have your permission?'

Finn nodded and Celeste closed her eyes. When they opened, they were gazing beyond her surroundings. 'Finn, there is something of sexlessness about you. There is a goodness in you, as though you are above the sexes.'

Ding! Celeste's phone lit up.

'Did you hear that? I have this agreement with Spirit, that when I get an alert tone, it's spiritual confirmation. So I'm going ahead with this. Finn, you wear your hair short, yet there is something very fine and feminine in your features. Even now, tonight you chose to wear a skirt with pants and boots. You walk heavily on the ground, but wear such a delicate blouse, and have very shapely breasts.'

Finn knocked her waterglass. It began to fall, but she steadied it in time. Celeste smiled in a way that seemed flirtatious. Finn pulled her hands under her legs and sat on them.

'Nicely played,' Celeste purred.

'I have the reflexes of someone used to nearly knocking everything over,' Finn muttered.

Celeste's eyes were hazy as she smiled at Finn. 'It is such a pure and holy place to be,' she said. 'In your past lifetimes, I see you, again and again, as spiritual and female. A nun. A teacher, a leader to other women. I see your spirit, but it is partly hidden. It is strong but it also speaks of great suffering.' Celeste closed her eyes again, bent her head forward and clasped at the back of her neck. 'Gosh, even your posture – the way you hold your shoulders gives me pain. I can see your sex has been assaulted lifetimes and lifetimes over. God planted this in you, a biological chastity belt. Just a moment.'

Celeste grabbed a notebook and pen from her bag, rushed it open to a new page and began tracing a circle, over and over, humming. After half a minute she looked up at Finn. A waiter arrived with the bubbly oolong kombucha, slices of cucumber and dill fronds floating in the glass. Like a small and sombre conga line, two more waiters stood behind him, each carrying what looked like the Primal Plate.

Once they left, Celeste let out a loud breath. 'Phew! Woah! Has the pain in your shoulders relieved somewhat?'

Finn readjusted in her chair. 'Oh, there is a lightness actually ... I do feel less tense.'

'Did you even mention any postural pain to me?'

'No, actually. But I am often in pain. In my back, neck, shoulders, my tummy and around my lower back. Even my legs.'

'Gosh! Well, I was sensing pain close to your head because of the weight of your thoughts, and your difficulty in being disconnected from the divine, but this is all over your body!'

'I don't think I've ever had a headache actually. And my feet never hurt.'

'Well, I am pleased to have eased some discomfort!' Celeste seemed dishevelled all of a sudden, and Finn wondered if being a guru was tiring. She thrust the notepad back in her bag, combed back some flyaway hair and gulped down some oolong. 'I was just cutting some connection cords. These cords are like puppet strings, and entities – past lives, habits, dead relationships – they are the puppet masters, yanking us around. I was calling for the powerful ones up there, to cut some of your cords. So drink plenty of water this evening, and I'll make sure you have a good night's sleep.' She began fanning her face. 'Wow, I'm hot now!'

Finn giggled. 'But Celeste, I thought you said you were a low body temperature sort of person.'

Celeste was still fanning. 'Look, when Richard told me about you, my brain started whirring. I have evolved into a sexual being. I don't want that part of myself to be revealed to every person I meet, but it will always be there. We all have the potential to become sexual, and maybe some of us fail to come to grips with that part of us, although it is always within our power.

'But you know, you just can't take back carnal knowledge once it is imparted. And really, there could be the chance for a very spiritual life if one remained asexual.'

'To be honest,' Finn cleared her throat, 'I've always been afraid of being too attractive. I've tried to make myself less desirable because I'm scared of men. It's like, we are all love but some of us are taller and stronger than others, and that concerns me. Maybe some small people relish the condescension of their taller loved ones, for the feeling of safety that tallness provides. "Trust him, he knows what he's doing. He looks like someone who could build a house."'

Celeste was making hums of assent, while Finn felt confounded by the words gushing from her mouth.

'Who do they think they are, those tall people?!' Finn felt her volume rising, reminding herself horribly of Richard, but didn't know how to make it stop. 'Do they think they are gods?!'

Celeste flinched at Finn's sudden shouting, then pumped her fist on the table.

'Exactly! Well, by being less kind of "wow" looking, you are actually protecting yourself, and likely enabling a growth that hasn't been available to other women. But look, what really, really interested me was when Richard told me about your ... Well look, he told me two things about you. He told me you're his Boomerang Girl, the only person he ever met who has the power to call their deposits, or Star Seeds as I like to call them, in and out of their body.'

'Star Seeds?'

'Yes, Star Seeds are another name for deposits. I have a feeling that in the future, everyone will be calling them Star Seeds!' Celeste raised her hands at that, as though casting a spell, then began to smile and laugh.

'But Finn, no matter what words we use, do you know how amazing this is? The greatest contradiction of human existence is that we at once have all the power and no power at all. Spirit writes the story of our life, but somehow we have the power to choose our own path as well. Where does the Spirit plan end and our choices begin? She has written our names in the stars, then we write her name back. We have the power to create our own realities, but only if we really man up and use that power! And that is you! A powerhouse! Really, you are so advanced!'

The platters of curled cured meats were untouched. Finn heaved a sigh. 'That's what Richard tells me, but I am not comfortable with the idea of being above others. It doesn't feel right. I like to think we're all equal.'

· 'And that modesty is what makes you better again! I hear what you are saying though. There is a risk of growing arrogant, and that risk is ever-present there for people like us. It is possible to go up, up, up, then to get to a point of stagnation – where you are actually not growing anymore, but you still feel better than others. I know your heart doesn't carry those intentions. But Finn, what I'm getting at, and the real reason I got you here tonight is ...'

Celeste's eyes fell onto Finn's hands. Her right abdomen had become sore, and Finn was pushing gently in the place, creating warmth. Celeste's eyes lit up.

'Finn, why are you so scared of your future!' she cried. 'Look at your hands! You hold them so close to your sacred site, your creative potential! This is not about child-bearing, it is about your life-purpose as a healer! You should not be afraid of your innate power to create, to make things whole again!'

Celeste trailed off, closing her eyes in something like meditation. Finn took the opportunity to change the cross of her legs, knocking the table as she did. With a thud and clatter of cutlery, Celeste's eyes flicked open. Finn laughed in a weirdly deep way; a laugh that belonged to a teenage boy.

Celeste giggled too. 'Come on, Finn, awareness! A spiritual being such as yourself shouldn't be confused about the distance between your own legs and the legs of a table in space!'

Finn laughed as Celeste broke into a grin, though she wasn't sure if this were a cutting insult or a joke. Their awkward laughter died down, and Celeste resumed her questioning.

'I am just curious, have you wondered if there is a connection between your special powers and this abnormality?'

'Well yeah,' Finn twiddled with her fork, hoping not to catapult it across the room in a moment of spiritual vagueness. 'I thought, maybe this is some kind of blockage and it's harder for the shapes to get out. Maybe that's why it's so painful and drawn out when I expel them.'

'Do they come out through your woman-place?'

'Sometimes. They come out wherever they feel really.'

'Hmmm ... So you think perhaps there is some kind of associated energetic blockage with your ... abnormality?'

'You can just call it an unbreakable hymen,' Finn blurted. 'That's what I do. But it's not like I've mentioned it more than three times.'

Celeste laughed. 'Well, that's what it is, isn't it!' She looked serious again all of a sudden. 'You like to call it like it is, don't you, Finn?'

'I hope so.'

'Okay. Well, the problem with your blockage theory is, Finn, it explains why the shapes are hard to get out, but not why they stay around and why, more importantly, you are able to draw them back in. What I wonder is, perhaps your protected, sexless state is keeping you vibrating at this higher frequency.

'Don't frown, I know you're up there. Yes, it is like there's a plug, a good plug, keeping you full of Spirit. Consequently, your higher vibration has enabled your special ability with Star Seeds. Now they are like a whole flock of guardian angels, perched all around you. Or a giant dreamcatcher, watching over you every night.

'You have called them into your life. You! That is truly incredible. Well, that's the idea that's been eating away at me. I just couldn't get the words out in a straight line! Please forgive my permeable mind. I'm just always half-receiving these messages, and it does make for convoluted conversation.'

'It wasn't too bad actually.'

'I love it! I love your straight talking.'

'Does that mean, do you think my shapes will change when I have the surgery? Maybe I will lose them?'

'Well look, all I'm saying is, that's a possibility, a serious one. It's worth considering the possibility. I'm sure you have a bright future ahead of you as a healer.'

'Me? A healer?' Finn had never even considered this career path, but there was something validating about being told she could be capable of helping others.

'Isn't that your ambition?'

'Oh, I don't really have an ambition. It was always to write, to manage pain, to be in less pain, and to enjoy life. So yeah, I guess I could see myself one day teaching others, sharing what I know. But I'm just not sure. I don't have any answers now, and can't imagine having any in the near future.'

'Do you want kids?'

'I've never thought of it.'

'No, it doesn't strike me as the reason you were put on earth. And if you really were desperate to have kids, I wouldn't be nearly as forceful with you. I know this is a lot to take in.' Celeste put her hand on Finn's. 'You take what you want from this discussion. But I really think it would be good for you to do something special. Soon.'

There were butterflies, somersaults, backflips going on down there. A whole gymnasium, teeming with acrobatic activity.

'Like what, Celeste?' Finn spoke in that gruff, teenage-boy voice again.

'Okay. Well this will sound mad. But I'd like to see you make a man go crazy. Get him on his knees. I think that would be good for you. Because at the moment your sexlessness feels like perhaps it has just occurred without your input. Sexlessness hasn't been your choice even if you're clearly not too bothered by it. I just want to see you put some real power into you sexlessness!'

Every time Finn heard the word 'sexless', she felt a little more beaten down. Guilty. This was her fault. She was lacking something. Finn wasn't exactly sure if Celeste meant 'sexless' as in a virgin, or as in 'asexual' or as in not clearly a man or a woman. All she knew was Celeste's physical presence was able to incite a feeling in her that ran like a river under the tired and old world.

'I think it would be good if you really drew power from a man when he's on his knees like that. I mean, it's half the reason I ever date men. It is so empowering. It doesn't even need to specifically be a man, but I think it should be masculine energy because it should be external and strong.'

'Well that sounds terrifying.'

'You don't need to deliver the goods, you just need to soak up the power. It's the talking, the foreplay, the falling at your feet. Is there anyone you can think of?'

'Actually ... There's this guy who comes into my work, and I don't know, I just like him. I've often wondered if we could have a relationship that really bends gender norms.'

'That sounds perfect! But is he fairly masculine still, like tall, good body?'

'He rides bikes.'

'That's fine then!'

'And he wears his shirt buttoned a bit at the top, which I find quite manly. And he is way taller than me.'

'Excellent! Finn, I am really happy with this!'

'But I don't know how to instigate anything. I've been trying to get this guy's attention for months. Sometimes I think it would just be easier to chase women.'

Celeste gave herself a quick fan. 'It's easy. Just look him in the eye. Let your gaze linger longer than is acceptable. It's a very clear signal. Now your X-ray eyes will bore into his soul. You will draw him into a state of vulnerability. He'll want to hunt you down and conquer you. He will want to rip your clothes off, make you just as vulnerable as you made him. He will be ready for the chase now, it's just up to you to invite him. Look, let me show you.'

Celeste took Finn's shoulder and looked into her eyes. It was like she hit a mute button. Sounds of chatter fell away. Thumping house-music became the thump of Finn's heart. The gaze was far too long. Finn became weak, sore, tingly, bubbling, diluted, ready to be washed away. Maybe she was jealous of Celeste. Jealousy can be a powerful teacher; it can show us those parts of ourselves we are lacking. Finn placed hands in her lap, hoping Celeste didn't notice the invisible erection.

'Finn, what's happened? You've completely stiffened up. Just relax. Breathe.'

A knowing smile played on her lips. The skin on Finn's shoulder was a patch of warmth, like when someone pissed in the ocean. The warmth was spreading all over her body. She wanted to pull away, was ready to turn, stand and run away, when Celeste released her grip.

THE BOAT

Richard pulled the laptop onto his belly, staring at her profile picture. He was lying in bed, listening to an album of healing throat-singing Eve had loaned him, an empty packet of orange creams crumpled nearby. He and Celeste had been chatting off and on, since that night. It had all been fairly superficial though. They had dodged the topic of her failed seduction attempt. But Celeste had been very curious about the members of IEWA, and particularly Finn. Like him, she seemed to think Finn was special.

As he typed, he felt the chance of something happening, something changing. The change might be great. The change might be terrible. The change might slip through his fingers. Maybe he couldn't fight it. But what would the change be? Was it time for him to leave IEWA, to start a relationship with this bliss ball-making guru? Would someone else take over the circle, maybe someone who was better at boat repairs? Or perhaps it was time for IEWA to close. But he would need somewhere to go. What would it be like, two healers living together in unholy matrimony? But was he entertaining a thought without the appropriate feeling, Richard wondered? Maybe she wasn't even interested anyway.

Richard pulled off his glasses and rubbed his eyes, before beginning to type.

@RICH_NOT_YET_IN_HEAVEN

I owe you an apology for the other night. Sexual intimacy is an uncomfortable area for me. I'm very sorry, but it doesn't mean I would not be up for trying again. x

@CELESTIAA_DAVINAA

I can help you work through this if you like. Not in any serious relationship sort of way. It's just, there is a soul connection here, isn't there? And soulmates make terrible life partners. I just wonder if we can somehow speed up this lesson-learning process and get on with our lives. Dating can be quite distracting.

@RICH_NOT_YET_IN_HEAVEN

Oh so you're not interested in a relationship? I'm sorry. I didn't mean to distract you. You seem so focused.

@CELESTIAA_DAVINAA

Thank you! Relationships aren't really my thing. They are just opportunities for growth. After all, we're only here to learn the lessons of life. We could think about learning some lessons together if that's what Spirit wants.

@RICH_NOT_YET_IN_HEAVEN

I don't know if I can learn lessons so quickly! Some things you can't force, I suppose.

@CELESTIAA_DAVINAA

We could just follow my lead? I could come around there now if you like? Touch can be very healing. It could help you sleep better too.

@RICH_NOT_YET_IN_HEAVEN

I didn't realise I'd mentioned my sleeping problems. Did I? Or did you just sense it?

@CELESTIAA_DAVINAA

I suppose I did. You do look very tired sometimes. It doesn't take a medical intuitive to diagnose that one! But if anything is bothering you, it's okay, you can tell me, healer to healer. It can be really hard for us to be vulnerable about our own suffering. Never forget though, healers are just humans with superpowers! We're not any greater than that. Yes, sometimes we manage to connect up our direct line to Spirit. But we are here too. We are here with everyone else.

@RICH_NOT_YET_IN_HEAVEN

I know! Thank you for reminding me Celeste ☺

@CELESTIAA_DAVINAA

It's okay, I present a lot of the 'up there' side to spirituality, and really you know Richard, that's what sells. People want to know how to escape their current crises and feel amazing.

@RICH_NOT_YET_IN_HEAVEN

That's what sells???

@CELESTIAA_DAVINAA

I don't mean that in a crass sense. I need to make a living just like everyone else, and if it's in healing, I need to really work out what kinds of spirituality are giving the best return, for me as well as the client.

@RICH_NOT_YET_IN_HEAVEN

I'm sorry, I have been very lucky – living on an inherited property and not having to worry too much about money. Maybe it's given me the opportunity to become set in my views. I suppose I've always felt we're in this for God rather than money. But it's possible my attitudes come hand in hand with privilege. So I'm sorry to question you on that.

@CELESTIAA_DAVINAA

Don't say sorry, just take me on a date! Perhaps a walk in nature.

@RICH_NOT_YET_IN_HEAVEN

I find nature stressful. It's all too busy, too much demanding my attention.

@CELESTIAA_DAVINAA

Okay, maybe dinner then?

@RICH_NOT_YET_IN_HEAVEN

Dinner sounds much better.

@CELESTIAA_DAVINAA

Phew! I'm glad we've sorted through this. Well, good night Richard. My medicine drum is calling me.

@RICH_NOT_YET_IN_HEAVEN

Okay, a pleasure as always Celeste x

He wasn't being entirely truthful. He wasn't sure that talking to Celeste was a pleasure. But Richard wasn't sure what his feelings were at all at the moment. With the laptop still open, he switched the camera on again. He found himself needing to explain what the hell was going on.

'Well, I've gotta say, Ross, this whole video-blog thing isn't really coming together as planned. But it's nice to be preaching again, if only to myself.

'But who the hell are we? Who are we in ourselves, when we are alone? Who are we in togetherness, when we come alongside each other? When do we begin to lose ourselves? When is it right to go within ourselves, and when is it wrong? And where does togetherness begin and end?

'She left a note, but it was far from an explanation.'

Richard stared out the porthole. It was dusk, and the streetlights flicked their warm glow onto the sky. Things were changing, but it didn't feel like they were getting better. He didn't bother pressing pause. This wasn't going to be a video for anyone but him. He sighed, and began again.

'I booked the taxis, hostel rooms. I looked around in wonder; the noisy streets of Delhi. Kids with no legs, smiling up at me. Maybe it was all too much for her, seeing people in poverty, when all I was seeing was riches: happy, smiling faces. She'd often grow faint. Once she keeled over on the street. And more than once, she'd say, "I'm having a stomach migraine. I need to lie down."

'I'd let her rest, and go back out on my own. I moved amongst the bright lights, meeting strangers, falling in love with uncertainty. Did that upset her? Once I was out all day. The sun was so intense, the world around dripping with significance. I came back to find her, curled up in a ball on the bed. Window closed, curtain closed.

'Look out here, on the streets! Come out, into the world! This will cure you!

'I didn't tell her that. Maybe I should have. I opened the curtains, just enough. She moaned.

'"Hello my little spirit woman," I kissed her cheek. "Can I do anything?"

'Her eyes were closed, face pressed into the pillow. Her lush brown hair was a greasy mess, but she was still beautiful.

'"I'll get up soon. Maybe when the sun sets we can go out for dinner."

'It wasn't always like that. She wasn't a sickly person. She was bold, intrepid. That's what attracted me to her. It was a pool hall. Her dangly earrings knocking about. Big confident smiles. Red lipstick. Leaning against the cue between shots, like it was a pitchfork.

'She winked at me and it was all over. We understood each other. We were odds and ends, shaken out from the handbag that was the church.'

Richard smiled, and began to laugh. He needed to see her. Trudging out to the main cabin, he collected the photo from the shelf, bringing Serena back to his room. She smiled as he resumed the story.

'I knew her. I knew her so well, but there were the things I was not aware of. How could I see? How could I know if she didn't tell me?

'I heard the sighs. The small comments. After I'd finished the day, I left my clothes on the floor.

'"It's not my job to pick up after you," she said sternly, one time, looking down.

'"Those clothes are in my past now, and I only concern myself with the present," I joked. She didn't laugh.

'Every day she would make the bed. I guessed she was unhappy about that too, the way she held her head down, tucking, fluffing pillows.

'"You don't need to do that sweetie. This is a hotel – *making beds* are its middle names!"

'Again, no laughter. Not even a glance in my direction. "I have to make the bed. It's self-respect: getting up in the morning, taking care of our things, taking care of ourselves."'

Suddenly Serena's face didn't seem to be smiling, but looked hateful, unhappy. Richard placed her facedown on the bed.

'Then there was the washing!' He found himself roaring. 'She was happy to organise it, she'd said in the beginning. Once a week, we needed to get our clothes laundered.

'"I just wish you noticed," she said. "I wish you noticed your clothes were dirty, that you might need to wash them. I wish you took responsibility. Or said thank you. Or can I help you with that? You just don't show any interest."

'"Oh forgive me for not being interested in the washing!" I probably yelled.

'God I was childish! Why did I say that?' Richard grabbed at his hair, pulling it. 'I was a fool! I waited until there was some word I could pounce on. *Interested*. I wanted it to be funny, but I knew I was walking a fine line. If she laughed, cool. If she got upset I could say, "Oh no … Sorry! I didn't mean it like that!"

'You just can't take back what's been unleashed into the air. After my shit words had flown about, she would be quietly forming ideas, opinions about my true intentions. *When he says this, he means that.*

'"You're so manipulative!" she screamed at me more times than I could count, towards the end. I pretended to never understand these outbursts, but I think, deep down, I did.'

Richard looked out the window again, 'And I always needed her to remind me of where I begin and end. Tell me what is good and bad. "You're doing the wrong thing right now." "Please don't say that. It upsets me. Say this instead."

'But she didn't want to be doing that.

'"Why can't you just understand that what you're saying or doing is inappropriate, without me having to tell you? I can't be your conscience."

'"But how can I possibly know what is appropriate and what is not?"

'"It's common sense."

'"But I'm uncommon!"

'I know now. I do this thing where I push things too far. I push until someone has to say, "Hey, this is more than enough. Really, this is just too much."

'I was an only child, a child with a wife, is that why I was so unwilling to change? Am I still a child now? I speak words that weave a net around me, protecting me and my will. No-one else can come in, I won't let them. I will talk to Ross until he tells me to shut up. I will let Finn clean my home until she says she's had enough.

'"I just, I get sick of feeling like I need to spell these things out for you." That was the closing line of Serena's final argument with me.'

He picked up her picture again, and found himself speaking softly.

'Things became darker,' he whispered. 'You spent more days alone in our room. The part of you that was mysterious – attractive in the beginning – became frightening, unknowable. When I kissed you, my tongue felt like a turkey baster, planting itself into a non-responsive throat. Trying to plant a garden in barren soil.

'For so many years, I was only able to have meaningless sex with spiritual women, like I could thrash the memory of you away. Then eventually, I couldn't even have meaningless sex. I couldn't bring the heart and flesh together. I still can't bring the heart and flesh together. I just don't know how.'

Richard pressed stop and watched his face shrink away.

THE SHOP AND THE HOUSE

Ethann came in to Pure Source at a bad time. It was the day after Finn's appointment with the gynaecologist. Her name was Lucy, and within five minutes of entering her office, she had put something between Finn's legs and confirmed: there was a problem. An operation was required. She should come to the hospital next week.

Finn had nodded, signed the form, listened to the instructions. She went through the motions, but secretly, she couldn't imagine going through with it. Booking the week off work was easy, she had plenty of sick days owing. She didn't tell anyone what was happening though, just that she needed to support her mum after a medical appointment. Old bodies are the ones that need extra support, Finn said to herself. Hers was an 'old body', wasn't it? She was a young woman in an old body, but now she was old inside too, because her body had made her feel that way.

No, she quite possibly wouldn't go through with the operation. She might instead take a week to herself, putting whatever food she wanted to in her body. Allowing it to grow as wide and soft as she liked. Being bigger and softer seemed like very nice things actually, she was thinking, right when a customer had opened the jar of valerian. The awful smell, like crushed vitamin B tablets, wafted through the shop. Loud nineties pop was blaring.

Customers began to cough, covering their noses. Spotting Finn, a crowd of them huddled around her. Half of them still wore bike helmets.

The customers cried in almost-unison, 'What is that smell?'

'Valerian,' Finn called back over M People's 'Movin' On Up'. 'To help you sleep. Someone must be buying in bulk.'

She smiled up at the grimacing, healthy faces, wishing she could grimace too. Finn turned back to the lady who had just enquired about a product called Gut Shot.

The customer had been describing her long history with autoimmune illnesses, all the side effects of the medication, and her friend's advice to get into fermented foods.

'I can get the store naturopath for you,' Finn had said, eager to get back to stocking shelves.

'No!' She grabbed Finn's shoulder. 'I don't want her to see me like this! I don't have my face on!'

Finn chuckled. Annette, the store naturopath, was always a glowing, radiant goddess of natural health. Finn could relate to wanting to be 'presentable' in front of her.

'I don't think you need to wear makeup in front of her,' Finn smiled. 'She is all about natural beauty.'

'No, I prefer talking to you. You make me feel comfortable, because you're just real.'

Finn felt a pang, wanting to ask, *What do you mean by that? Do I make you feel beautiful by comparison?*

Finn felt herself slipping, as she often did. It's as though she was moving away from the centre, swinging just to the left of things, just to the right of things.

'It's like a pickling brine,' Finn muttered.

'Sorry?'

'The Gut Shot.'

'Really? It's eleven dollars and it's pickling brine?'

'It is probiotic, and organic,' Finn countered in a tone which she herself would never be convinced by. She noted the lady had matched her pink earrings with pink blouse and shoes. Finn felt a small sadness for how much time and effort her outfit-curating must take.

'Ah ...' the lady gave a satisfied nod, dangling earrings scratching her neck.

In the past, Finn might have said, 'I agree, that's expensive. You could make your own.' But she'd been called up on that in the past.

'I get it, honesty sells,' her supervisor had said, overhearing Finn's exchange with a customer about choc-buckini cereal. Finn was explaining that despite the fancy packaging, there wasn't much to the cereal.

'I was just letting them know, you know, it's just buckwheat and cacao.'

'I get it, I do. But just be careful,' her supervisor had said. He was a young man surely the biological age of thirteen, who permanently radiated positivity; Juicy Jesus, the girls called him when he wasn't around.

'We don't want them to go away and dehydrate their own buckwheat and make their own delicious cereal!'

Juicy Jesus had laughed, while he held Finn's shoulder, looking into her eyes. It was like the touch and eye contact was supposed to provide a soft place for Finn to sit while she was reprimanded. Her shoulders had tightened as she endured the touch but she smiled, nodded, and didn't give her suffering away.

But the point was, the majority of customers would not find out how overpriced the buckwheat cereal was, then go away to make their own. Because the cereal box was matt-pink on recycled cardboard, the font pleasing capital letters that looked like they belonged on an indie-movie poster. And the box felt so good to hold, not slippery and shiny, but slightly rough textured, like it should be stowed away in a pantry at a farmhouse, alongside jars of house-preserved fruits. It felt good to start the day, picking up the pleasantly textured matt-pink cereal box, and listen as buckwheat kernels clopped into the cereal bowl.

Finally, the woman with the pink shirt and scratch earrings put the Gut Shot back in the fridge, chose instead the sauerkraut with juniper berries, and nodded at Finn – a nod of deep understanding – before walking up to the cash register.

The whole experience with this customer left Finn uncomfortable, and it was difficult to understand why.

Before and after this exchange, it was an incredibly busy morning at Pure Source. The camel and bath milk deliveries had arrived simultaneously. Betty, a regular customer who never removed her bike helmet, overfilled the noticeboards with advertisements for cacao ceremonies. Vegan pet food was over-ordered and Finn had to stash excess stock beneath the nut-butter stand. It was only eleven o'clock, but she'd already been asked about whether arthritis existed in the pre-agricultural record (I'm not sure), if green banana resistant starch was adequate in powdered form (I'm not qualified to say), if raw vanilla protein powder with lucuma tasted as nice as the chocolate flavour (I have only tried the chocolate flavour, but that really is quite good), why the caveman granola was named so (because it's 'Paleo'), if horny goat weed really worked as an aphrodisiac for humans (I can't say, but I'm not sure if it's genuinely used by goats for that purpose), whether breastfeeding tea was safe to drink if you were not breastfeeding (I can only assume so), which bush flower essence spray was best to use when cleansing a space (I would go with 'emergency'), if bamboo underwear felt clunky (many customers report it's the most comfortable underwear they've ever worn), when next year's moon planting calendars would arrive (you can pre-order one, just leave your details at the counter), and if apricots kernels were the best cure for cancer (we are not allowed to make any comments on cancer cures). One woman had scoffed at the twelve-dollar charcoal toothpaste.

'That's what they used in the time of Jane Eyre.'

I think you mean the time of Jane Austen. Jane Eyre is a fictional character.

The smell of valerian had finally dissipated when he sidled up. Finn's imaginary rebuttal about the toothpaste was still hanging in the air when an arm draped over her shoulder. The music was so loud. Was he shouting?

'So I've finally finished my dreaming workshop!'

Ethann seemed more interested in Finn than usual. Perhaps there had been someone else in his life. Perhaps she was no longer.

'Oh cool. I don't know if you got my message, Divine and Dateless?'

'Oh yeah, I saw it. That's a weird site, I do flick through it occasionally. But yeah, I thought I'd come in, you know, reply the old-fashioned way.'

Spice Girls' 'Wannabe' was blaring. Gillian walked past, doing the rap. She eyed Finn suspiciously, Ethann's arm still awkward around her shoulder. The arm was just there, purposeless, lingering, pleasing.

'Well, the circle is on Wednesdays, so you've just missed this week.'

'That's okay, we've got time. How about we hang out before then?'

'Sounds great.'

Please get out of here as soon as possible, the shelves have ears, the tongues are wagging.

Ethann grabbed her number. They arranged to meet at Kombu Bar at seven.

After he left, she overheard Gillian, who was restocking the millet puffs. She caught sight of Gill's lush armpit hair, creeping out from her tiny mauve slip dress.

'He just wouldn't get the message,' Gill was saying. 'I had to tell him to fuck off.'

There are some things a girl can't compete with. That is, if this is a game, if the game is on. Wit and charm can be worked, learned and built on. But without confidence in the moment, wit and charm are nowhere to be found.

Anyway, wit and charm can't compete with nice little tight triangular shapes down there. Those bouncing bottoms, every ounce in your hands just wanting to go up to them, pat them, bounce them like little basketballs, all pumped up, tight and muscular, but still soft in just the right way.

Soft and sweet, nourishing and biteable. Wanting to touch it, hating that, hating herself, hating the skin that tried to contain and tame her, skin that could never really do the job.

'Finn, are you okay?' Gillian was standing so close to her all of a sudden. Up close, Finn could see she was concerned. But she could also see something else. There was a line on Gill's neck, just beneath her chin, where the colour of her skin changed. Finn stared into the line, and then she realised.

'Gill, are you wearing makeup?'

Gill threw her head back in laughter. 'Of course I am! I have to! I wish I had perfect skin like yours.'

Finn didn't know what to say, but tried to smile.

Gill smiled back at Finn, then shook her head. 'You have no idea how beautiful you are, do you, Finn. We're all so jealous of you.'

'Shut up,' Finn laughed, straightened a box of cereal, looking away from Gill.

'It's true. Believe what you want. You're the true natural beauty.'

'Don't we all know it!' cried a voice from behind a shelf.

Finn began to laugh nervously, feeling that tingling between her legs.

'Please, Finn, don't put up with anyone who makes you feel otherwise.'

She gave Finn a light punch on the shoulder, and strode off in time to the music.

❁

Finn crashed onto her bed, lying across her potential outfit – a loose flowery dress, some faded jeans and a large brown cardigan. She grabbed her phone and looked for another Kinsey quiz.

Who do you feel comfortable socialising with?
I DON'T GET OUT MUCH.

How do you identify yourself to others?
I DON'T LIKE LABELS.

What do you think of yourself as?
I TRY NOT TO THINK ABOUT IT MUCH...

Finn wasn't sure what she'd done differently, but instead of receiving her usual notification of being 'more than incidentally attracted to women', the Kinsey site declared that she was 'not really heterosexual or homosexual. You don't necessarily fall on the spectrum of sexuality, which is okay.'

She let her phone fall to the floor.

Remember, Doctor Laura said first one finger, then two fingers, one more and that's roughly the same size as ... She lay on her bed, on the outfit she was never going to wear, watching the clock, a huge shuddering in her chest. The minutes ticked over, from the moment before to the moment after they had agreed to meet. There was no other way. Now she knew there was something wrong with her body, what confidence she'd felt had slipped away. She would go through with the operation. Then, maybe, she could meet Ethann.

She texted and got one back – *it's okay, meet up again soon then x*

Finn was angry and wild and hurt. As a silver tear swept down her cheek, the shapes rose straight out from her chest, sparking up into the air.

THE HOUSE AND THE HOSPITAL

The day before, the shapes followed like a kite on a string. Sometimes the string uncoiled to its furthest reach, other times it drew close, shapes waving and flapping by Finn's face. The night before the day before, her belly ached. It was bloated, rising like a golf mound. Lying in bed, Finn pushed a special point on her lower back – just above the tailbone. This point was raised also, forming a discus shape under her skin. When she pressed, there was a creaking sound, like a door ajar in the wind.

The sound of gas releasing went on for a long time; it was a small orifice for such a large procession to pass through. As the sound continued, Finn thought of dromedaries and needle eyes, chunks of regurgitated carrots stuck in basin drains.

The chain of shapes seemed endless as magicians' handkerchiefs. They finally assembled – bobbing and dancing – encircling the light. With the creaking over, Finn's stomach-mound had become flat, and she was able to sleep through the night, which all felt like a good omen.

Everything is going to be fine.

But the following morning, when she asked the shapes to come back, it was like yanking a dog on its leash; a dog insistent on halting, smelling recently marked territory.

She called and called.

I don't want to come, they said.

When Finn got out of bed, they followed. She felt like a clown with a bunch of balloons, bumping and squealing behind her.

And there they were – inappropriately cheerful – bouncing around her face as Danielle broke the news.

'There's a yurt in a friend's backyard! It's meant to be! I'm moving out next month. It has proper wooden flooring, a small sink, washing area and even an outdoor kitchen!'

Finn was bleary-eyed, not yet caffeinated, a fact which Danielle was oblivious to. Caffeine was probably never on her radar. She woke up before sunrise, already bouncing off the walls. Danielle spoke with such an intense, incantatory drive that Finn wondered if she was casting some 'good vibration' spell, making everything about the dream-yurt-palace sound so right, that to speak negatively, or just realistically, about little things like leases would be a dream-crushing move.

It would place Finn in the realm of 'bad energy' that 'I don't need in my reality' and shows 'why I need to move on'. It was like the whole thing was some great circle-of-life, self-fulfilling prophecy that she would recount to her friends, as 'everything falls into place'.

Danielle was still talking. Woven gypsy rugs and Indian pillows. Plenty of space to hold heart activation ceremonies. Drinking tulsi tea on the yurt veranda and looking out at the zucchini flowers.

The prospect of not living with Danielle was a good one, but posed some serious difficulties too. Finn deliberated on the alarming task of finding a new housemate, while she smiled and nodded.

The incantation seemed to work, because all Finn could say was, 'That sounds perfect for you,' while her troublesome shapes knocked and thudded by Danielle's face.

What about my two a.m. nocturnal-pain-relieving showers? Will they annoy my new housemate?

Danielle's judgements were far from pleasant, but Finn was used to the sighs and the glances. It took energy to get used to people, and she was tired, wondering if she would ever have the energy to be close to anyone, ever again.

But then, some quiet excitement rose in her chest. Maybe this was all she wanted. Maybe this was all she had ever wanted. She pictured herself, in underpants and a T-shirt, lying on the couch, the television blaring, devouring a greasy chicken burger, licking her salty fingers, burping after sculling her Diet Coke. This felt like an image of heaven.

'You'll find the right person,' said Danielle, walking into Finn's thoughts. 'I just know. They'll come through that door, and you'll know.'

You can't argue when someone 'just knows'. The shapes were bright and dancing, cheeky and defiant. They hovered near Danielle's face, while she talked. They reminded Finn of a child pulling faces, making it hard to focus.

Finn knew she could play tough, like a teacher yelling at funny-face kids. The shapes would eventually form a line, single-file, marching onward into her body. But then she would risk ending up in pain later. It was all costs and balances and risk assessment, she'd learned over time.

'You know it's tomorrow, don't you?'

'What's tomorrow? Oh no, is it Earth Hour? I forgot to mark the date,' said Danielle.

'No, my operation.'

'Oh, that.' Danielle resumed squeezing almond milk from the nut-milk bag.

On leaving the house, the shapes wafted up into the sky. They were wispy, streamer-like lines dancing across the blue. Sometimes so far away, Finn needed to turn around and squint.

A few times, they looked like confetti, tiny fireworks, coming close to her ears, teasing her, before scattering off into the sky.

❁

She lay back, already kitted out in the waiting area. A nurse looked her up and down, then handed over two magazines, *Country Life* and *Gardening For Beginners*. Finn took this to mean she looked scruffy, like someone with unruly hair who spends too much time in the sun. She ran fingers through her locks – which felt greasy – and examined her fingernails, which were lined with dirt, as always, though she could never understand why.

For a moment Finn longed to have given the impression of being a reader of *Cleo*, or perhaps just *Women's Health*. That would mean shiny skin, straight white teeth, large lips, coordination (being able to stand in heels), and non-chunky legs. She shifted in bed, adjusting the plastic underwear, which felt like an oversized shower cap.

It turned out the magazines were comforting. Flowers, lawns and birdbaths, bowls of rustic vegetables, soup recipes and companion planting. But flipping through glossy pages of hairy vegetables, a dread crept in.

The specialist had confirmed Doctor Laura's suspicions. 'You have an imperforate hymen. It's quite unusual to be diagnosed as late as this. You have a good GP.'

Finn was booked in for surgery three days later. There was no time to think, no time to wonder what it meant – that her body was about to change.

She had finally talked it over with Gloria on the phone. 'Should I go through with it?'

'Are you serious? Would you actually consider not getting it?'

'Celeste reckons I should think it over.'

'What does she know about you? I'd be wary of someone trying to talk me out of an operation that could help me lead a normal life.'

Finn laughed. 'I've never managed to feel normal. Maybe this is my in.'

Gloria giggled. 'God I didn't mean it like that!'

'I know!'

'But if you don't go through with it, won't you be left forever wondering?'

'This all happened so fast, I haven't had a chance to think.'

'What's there to think about?'

'I don't even know. I guess you're right. It's all booked anyway. If I really start to get a strong feeling against it, I could pull out.'

Gloria snorted, 'What, pull out at the last minute? Like that ever works.'

Finn was silent, lost in her own haze.

'You know what,' said Gloria, 'ignore me. Ignore everyone. Just do what's right for you.'

'Thanks Glore. But sorry to just go on about my stuff. How are you?'

'I'm okay. I have a crush on a boy though.'

'A boy?'

'I know!'

'I just assumed, because you satisfied one side of yourself with John, you'd only crush on girls!'

'Who is he?'

'He's a guy at work. Just a regular guy. I have no idea why he has this effect on me. There's just all this flirting and giggling and I forget about it, and then I rest my head on John's chest at night, and all I can do is think about *him*. I'm a horrible person.'

'Oh ... We'll get there, won't we? We'll understand it all one day?'

'I hope so. What about you, how's that guy, Harry is it?'

'Ethann. He asked me on a date but I got scared off. Performance anxiety.'

'You do need this you know.'

'I know,' she sighed. For a moment Finn reminded herself of Richard, sighing like this. She found this an unpleasant thought. 'But I haven't really been thinking about Ethann lately. Not much. I just seem to be liking this girl lately. Well, I kind of like her, and hate her, but she's attractive.'

'Oh yeah, what's she like?'

'Older,' Finn said, hoping she was concealing the fact she

was talking about Celeste. 'Although, I'm not sure that she's a good person. It's quite troubling.'

Gloria laughed again, 'Yeah, feeling attracted to bullshit people sucks. It's so weird, but so real.'

Finn found she had been staring at an article on natural approaches to pest management. She flipped the magazine closed, rolled onto her side, and suddenly felt so tired.

❀

Sweet and sour. Pink and salty fish. She is punishing me, in her whites. I'm a naked animal, bell around my neck. She is pushing my face there, so I lick her. Some other grandma is coming from behind, I am trapped between the two.

She gives me a slap because I'm soft and young and being fucked, and it's been a long time since she felt someone as soft as me. She's all turned on and wild and so am I, because I'm just an animal.

My face is pressed there. She pushes deeper and deeper, making me drink, like this is an eternal well. She knows the truth. She knows her divinity is down there. The most special abode. The powerful site. Womanhood.

Every now and then she lets me up, for a suckle on her nipples. That thing keeps going in and out.

And I come now, I come and I know that's what it is. She has come on my face, and I am just so, very, hot.

When she is finished, her blond hair parts, and there are her eyes. Oh God, she is celestial, she is divine.

Someone was gently shaking her shoulder.

'Hello there, Finn, time to wake up.'

Faces were moons, suns and planets appearing around her. 'Hello, Finn. I'm Dave and I'm an orderly. I'll be wheeling you down the hall into theatre today.'

The orbit began. So much white and blue. Beeping and some energetic beats.

'Hi Finn. I'm Jean, and I'll be assisting in your procedure today.'

'Hello there ... Finn! My name is Alex and I'll be your anaesthetist today.'

The planetary arrangement beamed down on her. They smiled because they were all – each and every one of them – more in charge of Finn's body than she was. Planet Lucy was the biggest, nearest, and she spoke a few words, seeming excitable.

They began to cover faces. Counting back from ten. The snap of latex gloves. A mask came over her nose and mouth.

I don't know if I want this anymore. Did I ever say I wanted this?

A gauge, a dial, numbers, a red line jumping about. A rising anxiety, leaping, cool air coming from someplace.

Finn tried to climb from the bed but instead she woke up. The room sounded different. The colour was different. There was a different beeping and no energetic beats.

'Is there something wrong?' Finn asked the nurse.

She didn't remember being introduced to this planet-nurse. Burly and stern, she glanced over, lips pursed, then continued ticking things on her clipboard.

Finn called out again. 'What happened? Why am I here? Is there something wrong? Are they not going to cut me open after all?'

The nurse didn't even look over at Finn.

Suddenly Lucy's big, shower-capped face appeared. 'Finn! Welcome back. It's all done now. Your opening was actually one third the size it should be!'

Finn tried to talk and finally heard herself. It was only croaking.

'It's okay, you just need some rest.'

Is it over now?

'It's all open now. There are stitches. They might get itchy. But don't worry, you don't need to get them taken out. They're just plastic and will break down in the next three to five days. They'll just wash down the drain when you're having a shower.'

Are you sure? How can you have taken something from me if I don't even feel the empty space?

'I'll give you some Panadol to take home. We're just going to monitor your blood pressure, so keep lying back for a while. We'll get you some sandwiches, and you've got your post-op in two weeks. So this is it, Finn. I will see you soon!'

Lucy's face disappeared, the blue curtain drawn. There was no applause, no call for an encore.

As her foggy mind began to clear, she realised. Finn was just taking a bite of a curried egg sandwich when she knew. The shapes were gone.

THE BOAT

'Close your eyes. Observe the breath. Don't try to control it. Let it not be rushed. Let it not be slow. Let your breath fall into its natural flow. Okay. I have located the sites of pain, and the energy centres presently affected. Acupuncture pins have been placed at the appropriate site, which for you Joan, is not the location of pain, but is the Shining Jewel chakra. As I've explained many times now, we are treating your arthritis, which I cannot guarantee will be cured. Though I can say we will cast off this deposit, which is threatening your ability to honour yourself. Now, all there is left to do is release. This is the moment I ask you to reflect. What does this deposit mean to you? How is it speaking to your life in the present?'

It had been a long time since Richard conducted the extraction component of a healing session. Extractions could be quite long, drawn-out processes. He'd always found it difficult to stay focused. A good few years back, when Finn expressed interest in helping out at IEWA, extractions were quickly handed over. This gave Richard a chance to rest after the tiring process of identifying deposits, their places of lodgement in bodies, and their accompanying meanings. But Finn hadn't been available so much lately. She'd had her operation about a month back, and took a week off afterwards. After that though, she'd missed a few IEWA meetings, which was unlike her. She'd been busy once or twice when he'd asked her to help.

August had been quite available, and spending plenty of time at the boat. But Richard couldn't help feel there was something slightly different about her too lately. She seemed quieter, her eyes wider than usual. And her artworks had changed: not such big and bold sculptures and paintings. Instead, she'd been sitting in the main cabin often during her visits, hunched over a sketchpad with an ink pen, drawing tiny detailed patterns, shapes interlocking, tiny beings with eyes and no mouths. Whenever he asked how she was, she smiled and said she was fine, just waiting.

'I'm just so glad it's not too hot,' she said one afternoon. It was mid-November, and after a few weeks of heat in October, there was a welcome cool change, before what would be the blistering heat of summer.

Today, with Finn and August both unavailable, Richard reverted back to the role of Mr Extraction. It was a simple procedure, though. What could go wrong?

The file needed an update. August and Finn had each made notes, a list of cues littered everywhere. Finn's handwriting was neat capital letters, while August's was a wandering script in coloured textas: *sea urchins, cephalopods, oranges, needles, pine cones, feathers, gum leaves, nuts, kernels, boxes, bricks, flies, the colour red or pink, the absence of all colour.*

'Joan, there is a list of cues here,' Richard sighed, leaning heavily against the wall. 'Do the girls usually read them to you?'

'Yes of course.'

Richard rubbed his temples and yawned. 'Okay, okay. Now, there are many, many forms that a deposit might take. What does it feel like to you? The flutter of butterfly wings? The scuttle of crab feet? The brush of a chinchilla cat's tail?'

'Are you reading from the file?'

A blanket covered Joan's body. Most clients like a blanket covering their lower legs. Joan felt the cold though, and requested the blanket be tucked in, up to her chin. She looked straitjacketed. She always seemed to struggle with letting go, more so than other clients.

Maybe she enjoys the feeling of restraint; maybe it makes the eventual release more powerful, Richard thought.

'Sorry, Joan, right there I was improvising. Is that okay, or would you prefer I read from the file?'

Joan sighed. 'Just go on please. But you don't need to ask such direct questions. Just run off a string of free associations.'

Richard closed the file and took a deep breath, the kind of breath that sounds like a request for patience. 'Okay.' He spoke rapidly. 'Cat whiskers. Dog paws. Dripping hair, falling leaves, stabbing knives, glowing embers ... quacking ducks, gorillas pounding fists on chests ...'

'Okay okay! That's enough! I'm getting somewhere. You can sit down now.'

Yes your Highness.

Richard slumped back into the chair.

Ah, the waiting game.

He drummed fingers on his right leg, gazing at his purple pants. Many healers prefer to wear all white. It helped to 'get into character'. For Richard, this *was* his character. What you see is what you get. The one, the same – the man, the healer. Did that make him more or less genuine, he mused. But there was something missing here. Transformation. Richard missed transformation.

He remembered those first feelings, getting up as a young preacher. When he stepped up to the pulpit, he became New Richard, and was born again and again, every time he stood there. Reaching the pulpit was like stepping up to the dais to receive yet another gold medal.

There were nerves. Those feelings, small particles flying about, searching for order. But once he spoke, those particles settled. Like audience members milling about, nervous energies found their seats as soon as he spoke.

Richard never understood why some people didn't like public speaking. It's your chance to show the world who you really are. To hold everyone in your palm, tiny little people.

It would be so easy to blow them all over. But that's never what he meant to do. Some sermons he wrote were like works of art. The seed of an idea, growing into a metaphor, parable, or a cautionary tale, taking root in the contemporary world. First, there was bliss in conception, and another bliss in the performance. And it was so easy for members of the congregation to be swept up, believing that every word really was the Word of God.

But when Richard met fellow preachers, when they talked and compared notes, there was a shared understanding about the Word of God. The Word wasn't consistent. The Word worked in different places at different times.

A certain portion of the Word might have a contemporary relevance that suited the minister's own interests. An old railway carriage on the church ground was getting in the way. The congregation were attached to it for 'heritage value'; it's where the old Sunday school was run. But the minister was well aware it was a losing battle; the council wanted the carriage moved. And so, the minister would speak about Moses, the staff left lying on the ground too long. The staff left lying on the ground so long that when Moses picked it up, it had turned into a snake. The congregation would now think of the carriage as Moses' staff: as they held onto it, it would become a snake, it would become something that could harm them. Soon, the congregation would want to get rid of the carriage too.

It always ended up sounding like God's opinion, but really God wasn't the one making the argument. God wasn't the one who assigned a story from the Bible to the contemporary world. It was someone else – whether an older minister, the church itself, or the preacher – that had the job not only of interpretation but of transplantation – taking a seed, moving it to another place.

But that was the beauty of it. Richard got to make his own point. He got to take the seed and plant it where it was needed. He got to create his own reality. It was unique every time. It was free-form, flowing. He was spreading his own message, feeling those zings, those special sensations you get when you create, when you make a difference.

Richard knew he was still making his mark, but it was completely different now. No-one would ever plant a regular church in a little boat like this. Churches are supposed to grow. That is their vision. Cast the nets wide, ye fishers of men.

But you don't keep all the fish in the boat. You take your catch back to shore. You keep feeding, feeding and feeding until the five thousand have fish in their bellies. Then they go back and tell others. Fishes keep multiplying, flipping from mouth to mouth. It's like a fish-chain-letter. The whole thing just keeps growing and going.

Really, could there ever be buildings that adequately housed the kinds of exponential church growth the Bible demanded? Ideally, buildings need to shrink and grow, magically, guided by demand. Huge half-empty churches are terrible advertisements. Tiny ones bursting at the seams work much better – but who really can stand the smell of each other's armpits?

Richard had been, over the years, limited by these walls, but felt that setting boundaries was a really good thing. The circle wouldn't ever grow much bigger. How he would be criticised by the Church! But what if the boat, and what if the Circle of IEWA, were just the right size? What if this is the cream of the crop, genuine people, making a genuine difference? But how could this possibly be true, when Richard himself had not been touched for so long? Richard had never told anyone how long ago it was, the last time he had a deposit. It was over two years ago, shaped like a jellyfish, floating out the window – blandly, indifferently – without any indication that this would be the last time.

But what good was it, a healing centre that was unable to attract new visitors? Sure, it's good to be surrounded by genuine Receivers, but what was the point of his work if he was just preaching to the converted? And how was he going to sustain the centre? How was he going to get it up to whatever kind of impossible standard that the council probably wanted him to live up to, without that income generated by new Receivers?

Celeste had presented him with ideas for what she called a 'more sustainable business model'. She had come over on the weekend, and Richard was ready to attempt physical intimacy again. Well, he was open to the idea at least. But Celeste seemed to have other things on her mind.

She had sat at his table, produced a diary and glasses from somewhere, and then stepped into a very serious persona.

'What if you're wasting Star Seeds?' she asked, tapping her pen on the table. 'What if you're flushing divine matter down the toilet?'

Celeste pointed out that Richard was treating the deposit like a waste product. The message, ideally, would be retained by a Receiver, yet the deposit was cast off – like a husk thrown away.

'What if we could keep it? What if we could repurpose the deposit?' she asked, then laughed, playing with her hair in that flirty way. 'Richard, I think you need to get better at upcycling!'

Celeste really was a shrewd businesswoman, Richard realised. He didn't mean to poo-poo her whole idea. The word de-poo-sit did roll like film subtitles in his mind's eye some days.

'What if we have two, three therapy rooms. We could treat several clients at once. Let them relax. Just leave them on their own for the waiting game. Start working on a new client. This could be really big, Richard! Of course, we would have to seek out new premises.'

Richard felt his body tense up at the suggestion. He knew she could see it; he was holding onto something. The boat, this scrapyard, as a site for spiritual renewal. Is that really what he must let go of? Could he move away from this boat, move in with Celeste, and build a new centre with her?

'Fine then,' she snapped, closing her diary. She must have read the overwhelm in his face. 'I understand. You're not ready for this change. But you should think about it. There really is so much potential here. Maybe change is ready for you, whether you like it or not.'

'What do you mean?' Richard countered. He needed to move, and did so, scraping slowly out of his chair. 'Why do you think we should keep the deposits? I mean, I'm not saying I don't agree with you. I wish people coming in here were more interested in what it means to receive. To listen to the teachings of pain, the lessons that this deposit might bring into their life. But that would mean holding the deposit in the body as long as is needed for the learning, and still letting go. Letting go is important, at the right time, isn't it?'

'I haven't figured out everything Richard. I'm just acknowledging the potential here. You extract deposits. You say it yourself: these things are divine, and one-time Receivers just don't get it. They get caught up in the prospect of release. But what if we were doing the opposite? What if we were calling the deposits in?'

'How the hell do we do that? Anyway, do you seriously think there will be a demand for that? You've come to the circle. There are six of us. Well, seven, counting Joan. And that is the sum total of people I've come across who have wanted to seriously invite an experience.'

'No, no. Listen. I've been thinking. Seeds. Star Seeds. Seeds contain so much information. But they need to be activated. They need to have the right conditions to come to life. If the deposits are the seeds of stars, and as seeds, are able to disperse more seeds, seeds and seeds to infinite, then isn't this whole thing about *growth* rather than *release*? Perhaps when you expel the deposit, the shapes which emerge are seeds we might capture? I'm imagining a vibrational therapy here.'

Richard laughed, though wasn't quite sure why.

'Please, Richard, hear me out. What if, for instance, Finn –

we have her in the room. She calls out her deposits. Now we know they won't go far. What if we are able to hold the deposits in the room, with large bowls full of water. The bowls would need to be very wide and shallow, so that we maximise the surface area exposed to the deposit's vibration. The presence of the deposits will perhaps change the state of the water. We call the water an 'essence' and treat people with it. Treatments, much the same set-up as you do already, just inverted really.'

'But we don't know that would work! The treatments I do now, they're tried and true. They were born from my own experience, and reflect that truthfully. I mean, your idea is interesting, but it's not based in reality.'

'But think of Finn! You are fascinated with her, with her ability to draw her shapes in and out! Although, I forgot. What did she end up deciding about the operation? I've sent her a couple of messages seeing if she wants to catch up.'

'Oh, she's already had that. Done and star-dusted. She's been a bit quiet actually. I haven't seen her much, I think she's having a little break from the world.'

Celeste's face broke into a frown. 'What about her shapes?'

'What about them?'

'Are they okay?'

Richard's face screwed up. 'We don't go into every intimate detail.'

'Well, this whole idea I've come up with really hinges on her involvement. I'm sure we'll find a way.'

'Well, maybe there is potential for a whole new healing modality. Maybe Finn will create it, the way I created this one. If it were her having this idea, I would say, "Great! Let's nut this out." She owns this experience, not me. And Finn is someone who just won't do something unless she really wants to. It has to be her choice. Whatever she does in her life, it will be all in her own good time.'

'Well, there's our time and there's Spirit time. Some things are out of our control.'

'That I will not argue with.'

Finn and Celeste had something in common: they both seemed capable of managing Richard. Finn – youngish, boyish woman. Sarcastic, deep-thinking, honest and spiritual. An embodiment of spiritual cynicism. A woman who doesn't have an orderly appearance, but her thinking is crystal clear. Then Celeste: Earth mother with an edge. A hippie with a head for business. What if the three of them – Richard, Celeste and Finn – were able to form a healing collective?

Maybe it could enable Richard to use his other skills. Get out of the therapy room. Back to preaching, helping people through words. Maybe he could write again. There were still so many sermons in his head. Waves of words, desperate to move from chaos to order.

He knew the power of editing; it doesn't all come from the divine. Yet some things truly feel divine. Once he thought of a good line, even if it was in the middle of the night, if he allowed it to actualise, it would become imprinted on his mind. It would reach its truest, fullest form, and would never be lost.

He needed to do these sermons. What would he call them now? Talks? Lectures? Maybe it was time.

'Something special is happening here,' Richard called out to Joan. He leaped from his chair, beginning to pace.

But what about the space issue? How can a healing space be just the right size for the people who are visiting it at any one time? Goldilocks said it all – people only like things when they are just right. It's true, it wouldn't be possible to cram large crowds desirous of becoming Receivers in here. But what if a new space felt cold, clinical, or empty? He pulled out a notebook and scratched down some thoughts.

'Richard?' Joan sounded stern.

'Mmmmm ... Yes, Joan ... How are you doing there?'

She was looking over at Richard. Arms hidden away, her eyes glaring.

'Richard what are you doing? Are you writing?'

'Yes, Joan, I am writing, is there something wrong with that?'

Her lips pursed. 'Look Richard ...' Suddenly she rose up from the table, like a mummy resurrecting. 'This just isn't happening for me right now.' Her arms wriggled free from the grey.

'I am sorry Joan, did I not tuck you in properly?'

'You just don't get it Richard! Do you know anything about IEWA?'

Richard's mouth fell open. 'Well Joan, I think I might, since it is my very own healing centre! Is there some kind of problem here?'

'Yes there certainly is!' she snapped. 'I haven't had a deposit in years, and I see that as a problem!'

Richard laughed and ran fingers through his hair. 'Oh Joan, Joan, why are you getting worked up like this? I've seen you, I've been with you in here, crippled in pain, walking out of here, spine upright and happy after your extractions.'

'Yes, I know,' Joan brushed grey strands off her face and began slipping off the therapy table. 'I am not denying any of that Richard. I'm not denying the significance of all this,' she motioned her hand about the room.

'Well what's this about then, Joan, what the hell is going on?' Richard rose to his feet, surprised at the thumping he felt in his chest. Why was he so angry?

'A deposit. I haven't had one in years! That's what this is all about?'

Richard's fists began to coil, like snakes in the grass. 'Why didn't you mention this before?'

Joan stared at him, sitting on the side of the table. Her legs dangled, the legs of a young woman, carefree. Legs that did not seem like they belonged to her. 'I'm sorry,' she said quietly.

'God!' Richard dropped his notepad and began to squeeze

his nose. 'You're just, you're blowing my world apart here, Joan!'

'I like it! Usually! I used to like it here! You were a great healer, Richard. I always found the treatments soothing, and your helpers, they do a damned good job! Really, they pamper me!' Joan snarled.

'But why did you come here today if you don't have a deposit?'

'I haven't had one in three years!' Joan was shouting now.

'What?'

'Yes, I have been faking it, that's right faking it!'

'But, you ... I hear you call out, I've heard the table shaking, Joan, I've heard it from the couch!'

'I do regularly experience something quite special, and Finn and August are wonderful assistants in creative visualisation. And so yes, maybe it is all just a bit abstract for me!'

'This is absurd!'

Richard's hands were on his hips, as Joan pulled on her coat.

'I'm quite aware of that,' she spoke quietly, adjusting her collar. 'Today,' her eyes bored into his, 'I did not get what I wanted.'

Joan began to rustle about in her handbag, Richard following her out to the kitchen. 'I won't be needing any milk or yoghurt today: warm, hot, cold, raw, unpasteurised. Nothing you could offer me would make me want to stay.' She slapped a fifty-dollar note on the bench.

'I don't want your money!' Richard lied. 'All that yoghurt and warmed milk! Warmed orange juice even! And you're not even a real Receiver!'

Joan rolled her eyes, 'Oh big deal, Mister Big Pants. Why don't you go buy some new happy pants? Those ones have become very see-through! That's right, I see through you!'

'I am sorry Joan,' he said sarcastically, eyeing the money, trying not to look down at his pants. 'I am so sorry that I don't have as impeccable a dress sense as you.' He waved his arms towards her long, flowing floral skirt and tiny tee with the words LIVE LIFE ON THE VEG.

'Thank you for your time,' Joan was just turning out onto the ladder. 'Thank you for introducing me to Celeste. I am booked in to see her next week.'

Richard watched her stern face as it sunk from sight.

THE HOUSE OF CELESTIAA DAVINAA

'Wow, I love these colours!' August exclaimed.

'Thank you.' Celeste flashed her perfect white teeth. She flicked a strand of blond-grey hair behind her ear, and looked around the bright room. 'They carry holographic energy.'

August was pulling off her helmet, admiring the neon-pink counter and hyper-green walls. Celeste looked somewhat out of place in the colourful abode; she was wearing a long white flowing shirt, loose white pants, and white slippers.

'These colours are the result of the pull of the photon belt. We're coming closer to the fifth dimension all the time. It's completely out of our control.'

'Yes, I read your article! Well, I had a look all around your website.'

'Fantastic!' Celeste looked down at her own outfit and chuckled. 'I like to remain open and white when I'm conducting a healing session though. Who knows what colours are going to come up with a client? I need to dress plain, so Spirit can flow freely through me.'

Celeste seemed more friendly today. August felt as though they'd got off on the wrong foot, although she couldn't figure out what she'd said or done wrong. August just had the feeling she was tiresome company, perhaps not quite the calibre of people Celeste usually hung out with. It was probably a sign that Celeste was on a higher spiritual plane, and didn't want to be bothered by people stuck on lower vibrations. But August was feeling calmer today. Maybe that was it. She knew, it was likely that she put people off when she got 'a bit intense' as her mum called it; when her eyes widened, when her speech became loud, her movements too fast, her heart thudding in her ears.

But then August felt that, since moving to the city, she was always the one who was 'a bit intense'. And she was always in the position of looking up to, in awe of, others. That's what she loved about Richard. He was intense, and didn't apologise. And he didn't mind August's wildness; he even encouraged it.

August had waited a few weeks to call, as Celeste had instructed her to. After that, it was another two weeks until the appointment. All up, there was a month between her meeting of Celeste, and her session. Some days August didn't know if she was going to make it. Some days she didn't know if she was going to be okay this time around. But when she asked, Tom always reassured her: this was the right thing to do. She was stronger than she knew. She was surrounded by love. Everything was going to be okay.

She trailed her fingers along the pink wall. 'Richard never talks about photonic energy.'

'No,' Celeste laughed as she opened her refrigerator, pulling out a jar of bliss balls. 'Richard and I, we believe the same things essentially, but we certainly have different ways of talking about it. Would you like a bliss ball? I've just been working on a new recipe: spirulina, cacao, maca and acai, with dates and almonds of course. I'm thinking of calling it "Supramundane".'

August took a bite, small brown clumps dropping on Celeste's counter. She felt an energetic frown, hovering in the air. 'Mmmm ... Sorry.'

August tried to cover her mouth when she realised that Celeste wasn't eating one. She was just watching. August began to panic, realising one of her worst fears: she was eating, alone, in front of someone.

'This is delicious,' she panic-mumbled. 'Do you sell the balls at cafés?'

Celeste raised a hand, signalling 'stop', and shook her head.

'Oh, you just make them for yourself?' August was speaking more clearly now.

'Sorry,' Celeste began, 'I didn't mean to say no to your question. I was trying to get you to stop all that talking and eating. It was painful to watch.' Celeste smiled. 'But yes, I do sell them, to a couple of conscious-eating establishments.'

She pressed a napkin into August's hand, then dabbed the corner of her own mouth, indicating that August had some food on her face. She smiled, seeming to enjoy August's struggle to locate the bliss-crumb. 'Great. Come through to the therapy room.'

Bansuri flute was playing, the air full of sage and fresh paint. A chart of the meridians took up half a purple wall. The therapy table was studded with lights at the base.

'Lie back, when you're ready.' Celeste tapped the table, indicating that actually August should be ready, right now.

August clambered up, suddenly afraid of falling. The carpet – white and shaggy – looked fairly soft at least.

'Okay.' Celeste sighed, running fingers through her shining hair. 'Look, I honestly never know what's going to happen when a client comes in. I always play it by ear. But I like to start with some free spoken word. Kind of a call-out to the universe. Does that sound okay?'

August nodded. Celeste pulled out what looked like a large roast carving fork. She tapped it with a metal rod, and it began to shudder in her hand, making long, high-pitched, resonant tones. Next, she waved it up and down, allowing tones to wash over August's body. She dragged the fork from her head to her toes and back again. Finally, she nodded, comprehending something.

'I see. Let's start.' Celeste closed her eyes and spoke in a hushed tone. 'God loves empty space. God loves me. God is love. I am love. God is in me. I am God. You'll probably think I'm crazy if I tell you, God told me to paint this wall lavender. One feature wall. A women's meditation wall.'

'I don't think ...'

'Sshh. Please. It's okay. Purple is the royal colour. Have you ever had a women's dream, where you squeeze your nipple like it is a pimple, and purple paint shoots out, splashing everywhere?'

'No, I ...'

'That is a special women's dream. The more paint the better. Any shade of purple. In my dream I looked in the mirror as I squeezed. Paint splattered over the mirror and began filling the basin below, a constant stream. Well, there are all kinds of womanhood dreams, but that one is fairly common. You will have it, or a similar one, eventually. The reason I mention the wall is, God told me in prayer-time a few weeks ago to create a women's wall. It is very important, the differences between men and women, the masculine and the feminine. And what people don't realise is that when they say "I love you" in one lifetime, it doesn't just mean they will be unified in that lifetime. It means they will be together, lifetime after lifetime, until the death of the soul, which is less like death and more like completion.

'This is not a completion lifecycle for you. It is a completion one for me, which is why it's such a difficult lifetime for me to have relationships, children, family, anything that will tie me to this earthly existence. But now, this session is for you ... Phew! Let's take a deep breath together! August, why have you come to see me today?'

'I have problems. Anxiety. I think too much. But I also get excited too much. But I like being excited. I like it because it gets me thinking about big important things. But then I get so anxious and so excited that I get tired out before I get anything done.'

'Monkey mind,' Celeste nodded. 'I have a good kitchari recipe for that. But what about something deeper?'

August felt heat growing in her body. She didn't know, she wasn't sure. What if she opened herself up to be cleansed, and was cleansed of the wrong things?

'I can't think of anything right now,' she mumbled.

'That's okay.' Celeste smiled. She began to run her arms through the air, about fifteen centimetres above August's body. She closed her eyes, as though listening, taking in information, from head to toe. 'But you did come here for a reason. I am just collecting body data through my hands. Let's begin.

'August, why are you attacking yourself? Everything happens for a reason. You know that. Some people are too proud to admit it, but I know, they know, deep down, the spiritual cause of their health problem. I can see you have a problem in your mind. It's not something I can diagnose, but that doesn't matter. All problems of the mind are the same.'

August began to squeak in nervous laughter. Celeste frowned, then squeezed August's shoulders. 'What's funny?'

'Nothing! It's just, no-one has ever spoken so directly to me before.'

'That's usually what we need. We need to hear the truth. You have brought this all on yourself. The problem with your mind has stopped you living your life. You're saying, "I'm not good enough. I don't deserve the good in life. I am guilty. What I have done can't be forgiven." But self-attack with the kind of focus and clarity I see in your system? This self-attack is having dreams, knowing your life purpose and not letting yourself near them.'

August felt her body becoming rigid, and Celeste seemed to notice. She walked around the table, to August's feet, and commanded, 'Open your eyes.'

August looked up to see the small figure, doused in white. Her eyes were very large and her hair seemed to be shining, as though heaven had opened up and chosen her.

'August, your other name is Resistance. You are halting the development of your true selves. You keep inviting spiritual lessons but you are unable to learn those lessons.

'Receiving is inviting challenge. Pain means something. Pain is speaking to you. But don't forget, the pain is not real. It is the lesson that hurts. Even the threat of that learning can inflict suffering if you're not wise to the ways of pain.'

Celeste leant over and turned up the stereo, the flute now piercing. She took a grip of August's big toes. August winced; her hands were so cold. Celeste smiled.

'Really, the pain is pure distraction, a safety mechanism. It is our body, comfortable in its own ways, trying to protect itself from the challenge of a lesson. The pain is not real. It is just something you have to endure. You are, and have been, fixated on pain. Let us get past this sickness. This is your chance to grow and become a more spiritually productive being. Is that a cold sore coming up on your lip?'

August was startled by this change in direction. She had been ignoring the tingling sensation that let her know: a blistered lip is imminent.

'Yeah, I get coldsores when I'm stressed,' she said, reaching up to touch it. But Celeste grabbed August's wrist, and pushed her arm back onto the therapy table, smiling.

'Let's do a deep hum together for a second. Focus all your clean energy into that cold sore. Think good thoughts into that little lip-demon! Let's deactivate it together.'

After Celeste counted down from three, an eerie discordant sound was struck. She inhaled deeply at the end.

'How does that feel? Still tingling?'

'A little.'

'Okay, let's do it once more. This will be my proof to you, that physical and mental problems are manifestations of spiritual dis-ease. I want you to really, really focus on that point on your lip now. Focus on that tingle, like waves of electricity, like shards of lightning, slowly beginning to dissipate, until that tingling is no more. Just focus, I'll do the sounds this time.'

Celeste used the fork again, then resumed humming. Some bells sounded, somewhere in the room. The soundscape lasted a few minutes. August tried to imagine what dissolving might feel like.

'How is it now?' Celeste asked.

August touched her upper lip, and registered no tingling. 'Oh, it's actually much better, I think!'

'Fantastic! Okay, sorry, let's get back to business. Now, don't just put cream on a cold sore. Don't take Panadol or use heat packs. These all give illness attention; really, these things are just like fertilising a plant. You need to stop treating spiritual problems with physical things.'

Celeste pointed towards the ceiling, where some glow-in-the-dark stars were stickered.

'Focus on a higher vibration. This is all happening on quite a low vibration. Oh!'

'What?' August panicked, a flute crescendo rising.

'I see. August, I've seen the knowledge behind your eyes. If it were all unlocked in this one lifecycle, it would just be too much, too much! But, just looking at you ... Such contradictions in you, such strength and such suffering. I really need to cut some cords here, but God, these cords are tight and tough! You have always been so strong and lonely, wanting communion with others but not wanting to give yourself up to that. You are blocked in your Muladhara chakra, and that causes this lower back pain and a lack of belonging. I don't see this lifetime for you is about a life-companion, a family. It is about a soul journey, about ascension. But that ascension isn't working at the moment because your Crown chakra isn't working properly at all. I want to talk to you about ascension, but ... Oh. Oh, I see now.'

'What? What is it? Celeste I ...'

'August, you are holding onto something. You shouldn't be. But you know that already, don't you? You are inhabited. Now, I am not going to name this being, but I can see it. This entity is here inside you. Wow, this is actually quite complicated! August, there is a great battle going on in your body. On the one hand, you are experiencing ascension symptoms, and on the other hand, this being is halting your ascension.'

Celeste looked down at August, smiling and shaking her head. 'What terrible trouble you've been in.'

'I just can't see a way,' August found herself choking back tears. 'I can't see a future without this. It's not what I meant to get rid of, coming here.'

August suddenly felt an urge to be standing, to not be stuck, a helpless Receiver. She tried to pull her body up, but Celeste seemed to have glided over to August's shoulders and was now pressing them down. Celeste laughed, 'You are really trying hard to resist!'

August closed her eyes. 'I'm sorry.'

'What does the IEWA creed say? "Seeing isn't all there is to believing?" Faith is trusting, when we can't see and know. Isn't that right? Now I can flush this entity, but you need to know, you will still be your whole self, however wounded, without it. In fact, you will be more whole. Do you trust me?'

'I think so. I am just not sure I trust myself.'

'You don't need to trust yourself. You only need to trust me. I will be your guide. I will perform the flush. But first, August, let's talk about this problem of ascension.'

'How is ascension a problem?'

'Well, ascension symptoms are like growing pains. Growing pains happen when our muscles are growing too fast and are not supported by our bones. We are changing and growing at different rates, in different parts of ourselves. But because we are changing, we are not always one in ourselves, in our own bodies, and of course, it is so hard to be one when we have three subtle bodies. But we are not all, always, in process. Some of us are finished, though this is rare, and a true state of enlightenment. But remember, to be touched like this at all, by higher beings, calling to us from a higher vibration, that is a sign of being advanced.

'I know you've been doubting yourself, lacking trust. But now, all you need to do is trust me. You are ascending slowly, but you are also holding yourself back. This entity problem is keeping you stuck in a small part of your subtle body. I know that being halfway can feel like safety, but let me assure you, it's not truly safe. People sit on fences because it feels easier. But sitting on a fence for a long time? Eventually, your cheeks will fall asleep. Don't be scared of awakening. I can read it in you, you're an open book. An awakening process began, and it's still well and truly alive, but halted. It's a bit like the awakening was frozen; all we need to do is thaw you out.

'Do you know the reason for the halt, August? Don't worry, there is nothing strange here. You are not alone. Many people are afraid of light-exposure. Pure and clear light is healing, but it also shows up our imperfections. Healing can be terrifying. Besides, we all like the smell of our own waste. We keep returning to the past, to dead and gone relationships. When it was alive, the relationship held us back. Now the relationship is gone, and we hold ourselves back by returning to that relationship, in thought, in heart. It's time to work, work, work on ourselves, so we might learn how to behave in this world. August, I can see now. You are so close to moving from a Pain Body to a Light Body.'

'Where are you?'

'I'm right here, in the present.' Celeste seemed to glare with something like pride.

'I mean, where are you, on the Light Body to Pain Body spectrum? Is it a spectrum?'

'Oh, I move between the two. I tend to stay in my Light Body for long periods. Eating sentient foods helps to keep me up there, but sometimes I get tired. It's a bit like flying. You know, it is very tiring for birds to fly. We look at them like they are free, but birds actually have very hard lives. I feel if I wanted to, I could stay up there, but my interest in helping people keeps me down here.'

Celeste took another deep breath, closed her eyes and gripped August's shoulders tight. 'So back to here. You know, this entity. If you want to ascend, it has to go.'

'I know that, I understand that,' the fear was rising in August's throat. 'I've just never been able to let go.'

'Well, it's not your choice anymore. Do you realise this is embedded deep inside you, enmeshed with your own cells? Even if you wanted to let go, you couldn't! You need someone to drive this from you. You definitely came to the right healer!'

August wished she could just ask Tom. She wished he was standing here, in the corner of the room. All she needed was for him to shake, or to nod his head. Celeste's fingernails were digging into her skin.

'I get it,' Celeste continued. 'You don't feel ready, but none of us are ever ready. And the longer we wait, the less ready we become. But this other part of you, that two-thirds of your subtle body you haven't been in contact with, it is just so ready.'

'Two-thirds? Really? That is so much! It is hard to believe. This is all I think about. This is all I know.'

'I know! But if you leave it, August, your conscious subtle body will keep shrinking and shrinking. Without an adequate, nourishing life source, it will become one quarter, one eighth, and eventually, you won't be here at all. Any chance to lead a spiritually productive life, to function well and easily in this world, will be lost. This is how we become shadows and shells. But that third of you, that fragment of you, August, it has been ready for such a long time. And so, the question is, do you trust me?'

'I think so?'

'Do you trust me?'

August closed her eyes and saw Tom. He was standing in the corner of the room. He didn't nod, and he didn't shake his head, but just his presence was enough.

'Yes,' August said, a lightness moving all through her body.

'Okay. I am going to make the room dark now. There may be a sound, a bit like a scuffle. Then the uncorking of a bottle, and sometimes liquid fizzing over. And then I'll turn the lights back on.'

Celeste began to hum. And then the rain came.

The roads were streaked with water as she rode away. It was that special post-rain light. Pink clouds were reflected in puddles. Golden light sparked off the awning of houses as August tore past. The landscape reeled around, like film unspooling from a camera. Sparks and stars were twinkling everywhere. August felt so fast, so light, and so empty. Everything looked new after the rain, but this world might in fact be an old photograph, overexposed. A photograph blotched with white, like a ghost crept over the lens. It could be that this wasn't a new world, but an old world that has burned up, that would soon lose all its light, that would soon be gone.

August stopped on the side of the road, letting her bike clash onto the ground. She took out the phone and held it to the sky. She wanted to hum, she wanted to sway, but she didn't feel calm enough even for that. She knew there were sharp edges charging through her being. You can't calm yourself if you are full of razors. All she could do was hold the phone in the sky, close her eyes, and wait for a message. This was her openness, this was her receiving. But was it all gone? Why would Tom do that to her? If it was wrong, why didn't he shake his head?

August jumped back on her bike, and kept riding, up, up. She didn't know where she was going: home, to the boat, or somewhere else. She hit the top of the hill, and stopped again, catching her breath, taking in the view. Far away, she saw something shiny, that might be the roof of Richard's boat. But was that boat enough to save her? And how long did Noah really sail around the globe? Did the animals keep mating, or did they abstain? Did Noah throw unwanted babies, cubs, piglets overboard? Were the original animals he took on the boat the same animals that stepped off once floodwaters dropped? Horses and camels grow old. He'd check their teeth. Were they fit? Still good examples? Look at this young stallion, what a testament to the breed! Throw this old one over! There must have been the threat of illness. But young ones die too! People and animals always get sick on boats. Maybe he needed to keep an extra of each animal as spares. What a nightmare. And rabbits breed so easily. Maybe they were dinner. And hares. Hares too.

God knows each hair on my head, August thought. If you did a hair analysis on me, would you read in the results that God made me? That we are all one? Or will you read what really happened? Is what happened, is that already written in my coding? Has it changed my DNA? Or was it written in the stars, before any of this?

God sent the flood, then a rainbow, to say, 'I'll never do that again.' August never understood why he said that. Everyone knows that floods still happen.

The phone remained silent, held against the sky. It had been too long. There was too much emptiness. Messages used to come quickly, whenever she needed them.

Looking down the hill, she saw a patch of light, like a spotlight. What was that? Could it be that the light was waiting for her?

August got back on her bike, and let herself float down the hill. The wheels spun like crazy, and she began to laugh. She let go of the handlebars, and closed her eyes. She felt it, everywhere in her body. Tiny little suns, all connected. Laced and chained together, a circuit, firing through every surface, inch, internal, external. Firing through every part, every fold, and every depth.

Then there was pain, some pain, but mostly noise. It was the sound of crashing metal, spikes and spokes, twisting and jagged, chain and oil, as the bike hit the ground.

THE BAR

Being alone felt more okay during the day, Finn thought. She was waiting for Ethann, drum and bass with didgeridoo rumbling through Kombu Bar.

The operation was a month ago, and the shapes still hadn't returned. She'd taken a week off work; a week spent feeling groggy, watching TV and eating hash browns. Danielle had gone. Finn could afford paying double-rent, for now, and wondered how long it would be till she started to worry about money. It was amazing, actually, to have a break from everyone, everything, she realised. To just do nothing. To not be expected by anyone, to do anything.

The follow-up appointment had come and gone, where Doctor Lucy showed her photos of all the pink and white. It looked like newborn marsupials.

'What's that?'

'That's what's inside you!'

'Oh God.'

'So, are you going to have sex?'

Finn must have looked shocked at the question.

Doctor Lucy's smile faded. 'Well it will be good to have sex. To make sure it's all working properly.'

'But what if it's not working?'

Lucy smiled. 'I'm quite confident that everything will work well.'

Finn was bursting to tell Lucy about the shapes. How they hadn't returned. And she also wanted to talk about the strange new sounds. Rolling around on the yoga mat weeks after, a noise came from between her legs. It was like gas, but not gas. Rows of tiny hands clapping together. Was it air caught in her newly widened road? *This body has changed.*

Finn knew what she had to do. She messaged Ethann, and he quickly responded. He suggested Kombu Bar, and it was a date.

'Hey!' Ethann appeared from nowhere, sliding into his seat. 'Sorry, I got held up at tai chi.'

He wore a leather jacket, and a shirt that opened to a V, showing off a large pendant.

'What a beautiful crystal!'

'Oh, thank you.' Ethann assumed a serious tone. 'It's azurite, for awakening and accessing intuition. I use it for manifestation and dream states.'

'Wow! I have a lovely moldavite piece but I'm getting it cleansed at the moment.'

'Moldavite? I haven't heard of that. What are its properties?'

'I have no idea.'

Ethann frowned. A waitress in a miniskirt and combat boots brought over menus. Her earrings were feathery dreamcatchers. Ethann ogled. Finn would have liked to tell him about how her shapes were sometimes like dreamcatchers. The shapes. It was probably too soon for the shapes to emerge in conversation. If only they'd emerge in real life. For a moment she closed her eyes, trying to imagine the shapes in formation, bobbing at her ceiling. But all she could see was a giant hairy armpit.

Finn opened her eyes, and buried herself in the menu.

'I think I'll get the Primal Plate,' she announced.

'You're not vegetarian?'

'Oh usually, but anything pre ... agrarian is fine.'

Ethann frowned.

'I just need some protein sometimes, you know!' Finn gushed. 'But it's okay, if you're not comfortable with it.'

'I was just looking at the Vegan Plate. Kraut, pulled jackfruit, dehydrated buckwheat lavosh, basil dip, rocket. Sounds great.'

'Yeah, fresh. Make it two.'

The next time Combat-Girl came round, Ethann ordered two Vegan Plates and two Cosmos Kicks.

'You know the couple who brew this booch bless every bottle as they lid it.'

'Really?'

'It's so important to keep it pure. But not much kombucha is live you know.'

'Oh I know. We get crates at work that don't need refrigeration sometimes and it's like, what's the point?'

Ethann raised his eyebrows. 'Hmmm ... I wouldn't have thought an establishment like Pure Source sold non-active kombucha.'

'Well, mostly not. Just every now and then we try a new brand. Customers are savvy though. If it's not active, it won't sell.'

Ethann nodded, satisfied. 'So you enjoy your work there?'

'I think it's a good job. I mean, I studied writing and the only prospect was to teach. It's nice to work in a growth area.'

'Ah, writing. So do you write much?'

'I keep a journal, more like what I'm feeling, stories, stuff like that. It's hard to keep a day-to-day diary.'

'I suppose you read books then?'

'Not as much as I'd like.'

'But you can read books?'

'Yes, I am literate.'

'You could make a lot of money. Being able to read books.'

'What do you mean? Did you never learn how to read?' Finn giggled too loudly, then gulped some water.

'No I learned ...' Ethann shrugged. 'I just can't read books. It doesn't feel right for me.'

'How do you think I can make money reading?'

'Well, there are lots of ways to make money. The money is just out there. There's plenty of it, you know. You just need to learn how to get at it. It's all in books. You just read the books that teach you how to make money.'

'Oh you mean like *Rich Dad Poor Dad* and investment property stuff?'

'Exactly,' Ethann nodded knowingly.

'Well I can't read those books, just the way you can't read books at all.'

'Surely not, if you can read, can't you read anything?'

'Maybe ask yourself that!'

Finn smiled and laughed, knowing her smile was too big, too satisfied, the laugh was too loud, unhinged. Ethann looked confused.

'I'm sorry ... But what do you do if you don't read?' asked Finn. 'You're clearly curious about the world.'

Ethann smiled at that. 'I certainly am! I listen to lectures and podcasts. I do research online. I take courses. I've studied electromagnetic therapy, neuro-linguistic programming. I'm actually doing a weekend course soon to get my NLP practitioner certification.'

'Cool!'

How can you study if you refuse to read?

Combat-Girl commanded his attention again, swaying up to the table. Finn downed some Cosmos Kick.

'So, with NLP, aren't you ever scared about changing yourself too much? I would be scared about losing parts of myself. I like to read over old journals to be able to make sense of things. It takes me a while to digest things I guess.'

'You look through your journals to find how to live? NLP will get you there, just faster.'

'Get you where?'

'To the point! Finn, what do you believe in now? Do you believe the same things you always believed? Can you cast off the things you want to move away from, like heavy winter garments you don't need anymore?'

'Do we have to want that? I always wonder if snakes forget

a part of themselves when they shed skins. Do they feel sad about the loss? Aren't we all just hoarders of life-things because we're scared without those things, we won't mean anything anymore?'

Ethann stared. The stare was blank space, and Finn's words poured forth, eager to fill it in.

'Isn't that what happens when we meet someone, get married, have children, get careers and jobs, pay for the things we need and want; really we are paying to be sure of what is going to happen? "This is what will happen next in my life, I will do the work, I will do everything right, I will build foundations, walls, a fortress to protect myself, to protect myself from the unknown."'

A furrowed brow. 'I'm not sure what you're getting at.'

Finn sank more Cosmos. 'You mentioned making lots of money. I just don't know that all the money in the world could pay for the sureness of what happens next.'

'You're right! Every minute could be our last, so we should always live as if there is no tomorrow.'

'I find that idea stressful.'

'Why? Isn't being present to now the ultimate freedom?'

'But if we always thought we were just about to die, wouldn't we spend every moment rushing around, trying to see every significant thing, trying to get every important thing done? There would be no breaks, it would be like, "It's okay, I can see the Eiffel Tower tomorrow. Actually, I could be dead tomorrow. I'd better hurry off and see it now." It would be nonstop sightseeing, risk-taking and adventure. I just like sleep too much for all of that to be possible.'

'You've misunderstood the saying.'

'Probably. I usually don't get sayings.'

The didgeridoo and bass seemed intensely loud. Finn wondered if they were getting along, if this was a successful date, if she was panicking, if it was common to say 'fresh' when you like something, if Ethann could tell that she also found

Combat-Girl attractive, if she was in with a chance with him at all.

'Whereabouts in Scotland did you grow up?' Finn coughed.

'Oh!' Ethann chuckled, stretching out, bumping into a bearded man behind him. 'That's a bit awkward, actually. I grew up in Victoria, but my parents sent me away to school. This teacher I really looked up to was from Scotland. And now I have his accent. Don't worry, I get it all the time.'

'What?' *Is that even possible?* 'I'm sorry, I need to unexplode my brain ...'

Ethann laughed. 'What about you, Finn? Tell me something I don't know.'

'Well, I think one of the most remarkable things about me is how many times I've come out as gay then had to take it back. Just to close friends, not to the whole world or anything. People always used to think my first boyfriend was a girl, so we went into cafés and they'd say "Hi girls!", like making sure we knew they were liberal and open-minded. So I got a bit of an idea of what being a lesbian might be like I guess. Maybe it just put the idea in my head. But then, alas, after I'd freshly come out, I'd crush on a guy. Again and again.'

'That's so personal! How can you say things that are so personal?'

'Maybe the embarrassment just catches up later.'

'And you're talking so fast, just, slow down! Do you have high blood pressure?'

'I actually have low blood pressure, but it has the opposite effect to what you'd expect. It means I just bounce around between lethargy and overdrive because, you know, I have to push myself to keep moving. If I slip down to cruise mode I'll just crash. At least I can sleep like no-one else. If there were awards for sleeping I'd definitely be hot competition. That's my blessing, I sleep deep every night. And I can fall asleep very suddenly. Sometimes I need to know there is a bed nearby because I might crash at any minute. Except, a lot of the time,

I actually sleep very badly. That's usually when I'm in pain, which is a lot of the time.'

What the hell am I talking about? Finn giggled, then downed the rest of her drink. When she looked up, Ethann was smiling.

'You're a wildflower!'

Together they barked in laughter.

'But Finn, what do you want? What is standing between you and what you want? There is self-sabotage, and then there is the motivation behind that sabotage.'

'Sometimes I feel like I'm suffering from abundance, the sense that everything is well; good things perpetually coming to fruition, like it is eternally spring. But isn't that why we need the seasons? The restfulness of winter? All this abundance does confuse me. I feel overdone, overstimulated.'

'Are you shy? You seem nervous. Are you low in self-esteem?'

'Isn't that a bit personal?' Finn said cheekily.

Ethann laughed. It seemed he was smiling more. The Vegan Plates arrived: colourful bites of food, nothing touching anything else.

'This looks great!' Ethann noisily tucked in.

'No, I think I have a certain amount of ... well-distributed self-confidence. Not too much, not too little. I am really quite self-sufficient, but there are some things I don't have.'

'What don't you have?' Ethann asked through mouthfuls.

'Nothing, it's silly. Let's eat.' Finn resigned herself to the fact: this conversation was going nowhere. They weren't connecting at all.

Ethann fork-stabbed some sauerkraut, like it was alive, and threw it down his throat. 'I think I forgot to eat today. It was supposed to be a fasting day yesterday so maybe that's okay.'

Finn tried to mop up some basil dip up with the dry lavosh. It cracked and crumbled all over her skirt, her floral corduroy skirt, the skirt she thought might impress him. But he hadn't even seen her stand. He hadn't seen the skirt at all. She had arrived early after all, seated here, on her own, unfashionably early, always out of step. She could get up to go to the toilet, then he would see her skirt. But who cared, really. She sighed, dropped the lavosh. She could try the eyes. It seemed extreme, but according to Celeste, it always worked.

'Were you going to ask me something before?' Finn stared into his eyes. She caught him flinch.

'I was, I was going to ask you a question, the question, the question ...' Ethann munched as he spoke, while Finn continued with the eyes.

Ethann began to smile, catching a spark. His shoulders relaxed. 'My question Finn, is *the* question, and *the* question is, what is it you, Finn, what is it that you want in life?'

A small smile played on her lips. The music dropped away in that strange way, following their mood somehow.

'I would ...' She looked away for a moment. 'I can't believe I'm going to say this ... I'm going to say this.'

'What Finn! What are you going to say?'

'I would like to become a sexual being.'

Ethann laughed. Finn wanted to look away, look away, but no. *Don't give up.* They resumed the intense eye-moment.

'Is that still in a state of becoming?'

'It is. Long story. A complicated story, but yes. I would like this moment of transition to pass.'

Ethann laughed again. All of a sudden he seemed very relaxed. Much more attractive. He glanced around the room, arms folded, drumming fingers on biceps.

'Okay ... well, let me pay. My treat. Then I can certainly help you with that.'

❀

'You're so wet!'

Finn lay, heaving and panting, on his makeshift bed – wooden pallets with a mattress on top. He was on top of her, shirt off, clean and white. Finn was clean and white too.

Together, they were a mass of white, slippery limbs.

It felt like pool balls, gently kissing at first, then sinking into the pocket. Netted pockets on old pool tables, balls sacs, balls knocking together, knocking up against her, inside, sinking.

He was thumping frantically. Finn pictured him at a pool table, lining up the shot, pushing the cue in and out, in and out, the cue rubbing along that curved line between thumb and forefinger – whoops Tommy, whoops Tommy – never taking the shot.

She squeezed at the mounds of his chest. He stripped her hands off, slapped them onto his cheeks. So muscular. Hard. She held his hips instead, reaching that smooth plateau, the small of his back. Something happened inside her, something began to twist, melt, fall apart, when she held his hips. It could be the other way, she realised. He could be the woman, riding her power ...

'Fuck the light ... Fuck the light,' he whispered, again and again, and Finn wondered if that meant something. He was staring into her eyes, then there was the feeling of something caving and blooming.

The shapes! But when did they come back in? It was not the shapes. The floorboards creaked. They were flowers, all these tiny flowers are blooming, littering, that place, what Celeste calls 'the special abode'. Finn screeched, her body beginning to melt too, her body becoming small, tiny little pieces.

Ethann kept going with the cue, in and out, in and out, forever lining up his shot. 'Yah!'

Soon he pressed deep, deep, deep and whispered, 'Oh God ... I'm coming ... I'm coming.'

He collapsed. Finn shifted and realised. It was wet, everywhere.

'Fuck!' She sat up. Ethann pulled her back down. He tucked her head, neatly under his shoulder. Armpit sweet.

He lined her hips up against his. 'That's weird,' he whispered, breathless, stroking her damp forehead. 'We're just the right shape for each other. Our heads to our hips, the same length exactly.'

'You must have really short legs.'

He smiled. They fell asleep.

When Finn woke he was watching over her, sitting beside the bed in 'Parvatasana – seated mountain pose', he let her know, arms stretching up above his head. His chest was puffed up, but his eyes were concerned. Something in Finn sank.

'Look, in here, in this bedroom, we are just the right shape for each other. But out in the world, we just aren't,' he said.

He climbed on top again, grinning in a way which felt wild, out of place.

'How was it? How was the experience? Your first experience. I am so glad I was a part of it. You won't be able to wipe that smile off your face all day.'

❀

'Finn! Oh Finn, how do I get myself into these situations! I have said the wrong thing again! I know it's my life purpose to stir things up for people, but sometimes it's just unbearable!'

She had fallen back to sleep. The phone vibrated loud against the floorboards. She grabbed it, a polite reflex. *Stop the noise!*

She answered, and wished she hadn't. 'Celeste? What's going on?'

'Haven't you heard? She's in hospital and Richard says it's my fault, my fault!'

'What are you talking about?'

'I don't know exactly what the problem is ... All I know is he is very unhappy with me. It's just so hard for me. It's my job here you know, to complicate people's lives just enough to really let Spirit in. You know yourself, Finn, it's pain that happens before cleansing! That's what happens with any process of detoxification; all the toxins will rise to the surface.

We need to get sick before we get better ...'

Celeste sighed. There was a fuzz, distorted loudness in the phone. Finn sat up in bed. Out in the garden she saw Ethann. Hair already slicked back into a ponytail. Still no shirt. Eyes closed, the posture of a gymnast who had just completed a routine. Pleased with himself. Welcoming the sun's rays. Finn took in his gleaming body and realised. She didn't like him very much at all.

A kettle was boiling. A neighbour's dog barked, Geraldton wax brushed against the window. The smell of tempeh and seaweed floated in, someone's breakfast. Or was it lunch?

'I don't understand, Celeste ...?'

'Well, he's saying he feels a duty of care with August, like he's her parent. But Finn, she is an adult! She knew what she was doing, just like she knew what I was doing in the treatment! I always ask "Do you trust me?" and she said yes! Really that's all I need. This is probably her true moment. Her life will change now. This is her near-death experience, and now her colours will be so bright. One day she will thank me.'

'Where is she? Where is Richard? What hospital is she in?'

'I mean, she survived! Nothing has been lost! I don't know why Richard doesn't see that. He will soon. Oh Finn, maybe it's all gone! Look, this might not be the right time to tell you, but I was actually really disappointed when you went and had that operation, even when I warned you it may permanently damage your Star Seeds!'

Finn's mind was whirring. 'Celeste ...'

'I wasn't happy with two things: first that you went ahead and had the operation, and second that you didn't even tell me about it! If you'd told me you were seriously considering it, we could have talked it out! Have you even considered how much general anaesthetic interrupts our personal dream-times?'

'But Celeste ... It was my choice, wasn't it? The doctors I saw really made me feel it was the best option.'

'Oh they would! They won't see through what they believe, even when evidence contradicts it. What do they know about all that is beyond our physical bodies? They are trapped in their way of seeing the world. Medicine is always chasing its own tail!'

'But I remember you saying it's important to see a doctor to rule out serious illness?'

'Yes that's right, rule it out! Was this a serious illness for you, Finn? Was it?'

Finn looked out to Ethann again, his body doused in sun.

'I'm not sure.'

'You're not sure! Well, it was quite possibly a gift from God! Look, I can't handle this right now ...'

'Celeste ... Celeste ...'

Finn heard some more thumping down the line. She wondered if Celeste was turning up some healing music. 'Do you know which hospital she is in?'

'Oh God, I can feel these cords coming around my neck ... Look, Finn, maybe I'll see you in some other reality!'

She hung up, stood up. Her phone was full of messages.

Come to Fremantle Hospital.

THE HOSPITAL

August heard cracks and bangs, crashes and rumbling. Lightning flashed through the black. Back then, that really was Genesis – the beginning of new life. Back then, it was almost three years ago now, she woke up in that hospital bed. Everything was white and new and she was tired. It was like she'd been born again, again and again. Maybe it's possible to go through conversion many times, because energy converts and converts and never actually dies.

Back then, the blanket felt rough on her skin. The plastic band rubbed against her wrist. That's what it felt like then. That's what it felt like now. How many chances do we get, to live our lives right, August wondered. Celeste says it is nine times. If people kill themselves in nine different lifetimes, then they will cease to exist. But August only wanted to make things right in this lifetime. Why was that so hard?

Back then, when she woke up in hospital, it wasn't because she had tried to hurt herself. It was because her mind had fallen apart and all the golden brain-stuff had floated out. She had lost the sense of where she began and ended. But because her brain and body had become so open, she had also begun to see and feel things that came from outside. That's when she began to receive. That's when she met the Pleiadians, who were always smiling, wisps of hair flowing across the walls. The Pleiadians wanted her to know, it will all be okay, in the end. Will it feel even a little bit okay, soon? August asked them. But when she tried to speak, the Pleiadians faded away.

August began to draw everything she saw emerging from

the walls. They were beings from an eternal place. These beings were reborn, given new life as perfect creatures, emerging from the ink of her pen, like humans rising fully formed from the mud. Every stroke was confident. She held the pen so tight, but her hand never tired. Because this art wasn't of her. It wasn't of this world. All August was doing was providing her body as a vessel; she was opening herself up to receive.

August drew constellations, dots that linked together to form the shapes of boats, suspended in black space. The boats were there so she could float above it all. But the boats cast nets, nets to catch beings when they drifted; nets to ensnare. Mostly the beings were clear, wispy and fluid. Some were just tiny faces growing from pea-pods – thousands of tiny peas, thousands of tiny pods. Spiralled patterns of faces, waves of pure light.

August's mind was noisy with the memory of this vivid life. The rolling sighs, all in time, all out of time. This was the heaven-place. This was ecstasy, but different from the one she experienced in church. This was a slow ecstasy. It wasn't crashing into the sun. It was a slow drip of golden feeling, moving through her veins, for one day, three days, one month, three months. She was in hospital, back then, for three months and one day. Her hand kept pace with her mind, her mind that was visited by all this holiness. Her hand held the pen, and the pen let holiness flow forth. There was nothing more and nothing less. She was conceiving the universe, shrinking and expanding, rocking back and forth, inside time, outside time.

Did the slow ecstasy really last three months? August didn't know anymore. And she didn't know that this wasn't recovery. Nothing would be recovered. He was gone. Nothing would be okay.

August knew, and the beings knew – their space on the paper, their place in the universe. A shape carved out perfectly, just the shape of their own shape. August wanted to believe that we all have our place here, that there is a divine order. *We all have our place, we just don't know it yet.*

She was lying back, on a bed, but also moving. She was shooting somewhere, hurtling through space.

What about Tom? It would never be fair that he was gone.

The sounds of beeping became louder. There was chatter rising all around.

'For I have not left you, I have just moved to another room.' That is what the man at the funeral said. But it wasn't true.

❁

'You're not wanted here! Apparently I didn't make that clear on the phone!'

Richard was standing in the hospital corridor, shouting, thrusting his arms through the air. The walls were lined with photos of freight ships, patchworks of shipping containers.

'I just want to help!' Celeste stamped her foot on the floor, her fists clenched at her sides.

Richard belched out a laugh. 'Oh, I think you've done enough already!'

'But what? What is this all about, really? Are YOU okay, Richard?'

'Celeste, it was you, you pushed her too hard!' Richard believed that. He believed the words that were coming out of his mouth. It seemed likely that Celeste did push August too hard. But another part of him, a second, invisible Richard moving through him, had no idea why he was shouting at all.

'What I'm hearing from you,' Celeste said, now more calmly, head cocked empathetically, arms folded across her chest, 'is that this has really upset you deeply! Is your feeling of upset, disappointment, is that really about me? Or is that about yourself? Why aren't you owning this?'

'What are you talking about? What have I done?' Something

in what Celeste said – or was it her body language, or the way she had said it? – made Richard uncomfortable. Perhaps it was that her demeanour was more relaxed, as though she knew something he didn't, saw his weakness – which would be her way of wresting the upper hand.

'It's like you said, Richard, it's your duty of care, darling.' She stepped closer to him now, speaking gently. 'And she obviously looks up to you. Have you ever considered she might have feelings for you? When I came along, it meant the thought of losing you. Maybe that was all too much.'

Celeste reached out for his arm, and Richard flinched. 'I'm old enough to be her grandfather!'

'Plenty of young, vulnerable women are attracted to older men. And plenty of people would find your close relationship questionable!'

'What are you talking about? She has a boyfriend!'

Celeste's face screwed up. 'Does she? Are you sure?'

'Of course I'm sure! His name is Tom!'

'But she makes your bed!'

'Sometimes! I never asked her to!'

'It's boundaries, Richard, you are terrible with boundaries!'

'I can't believe you are making this about me!' Richard again felt that perhaps these words didn't make sense, because perhaps this *was* all about him. But he shook away the thoughts. 'Just please, she needs space. I need space! She has been pushed too hard.'

'Okay. What if I don't agree? What if this is exactly what she needed to really wake up to herself?' Celeste had stepped away again, but she still seemed so calm, a kind of quiet conviction in her clear blue eyes.

'I respect your words, thank you for sharing. Please fuck off now.' A heat was rising through Richard. He needed to take the power back. He needed to protect his own. August was part of *his* healing circle, not Celeste's.

'I should fuck off, why should I fuck off?' Celeste shrieked, then laughed wildly. 'Why don't you fuck off! Why are you suddenly the one in the right, and I'm just like ... dog-sick on the floor?'

Celeste squatted all of a sudden, pointed at the floor, then stood up again, clicking her heels together three times. She closed her eyes and opened them again. Richard felt a pang of fear, that she had just downloaded a message from the universe. Why was the universe sending her special messages and not him? Did that mean she was in the right? She opened her eyes and spoke calmly.

'How could I have done all this damage? I've only been around for two minutes.'

'That's a good question, Celeste!' Richard giggled, looking around at the nurses' station. Three women stood there, peering over glasses and paperwork, with slightly bored expressions. Perhaps healers argued in hospital corridors all the time, Richard mused for a moment, before remembering his outrage.

'Celeste, how *did* you manage to do *so much damage* in such a short time? You are so efficient with your bullshit!'

'Oh,' Celeste shook her head in disbelief, then pulled her palms. 'I'm not hearing this.'

'Yeah well, August has been part of *my* healing circle for two years, and she's going to continue being part of it for long after your two minutes of fanning the flames have passed!'

Celeste's jaw clenched. Richard took note of the loose blue jeans she wore, a long cardigan and runners that seemed far too big. In a split-second, an urge to curve his body around her, protect her, rose and fell.

She seemed to sense the chink in his armour and crept closer, arms folded, speaking softly. 'Look, don't you think it's more likely that you've hurt yourself and others, over a long period of time? Isn't this problem chronic rather than acute?'

He drew a deep breath. 'Celeste, she came away from you and she crashed her bike. Now you need to think about that.

About pushing people too hard. What does your website say? "There is intention in all things?"'

Celeste was quiet, staring off at the nurses. 'Look at them, looking at us. I'm getting out of here. This is no place for healing.'

She strode away down the hall.

'Finally! Thank you!' Richard called out after her, wondering why he had to do that. He wished she'd pull a finger or yell back so he could look like the righteous one.

As it was, the petite woman pulled her cardigan close, shoulders hunched and forehead drawn down, an old man yelling after her.

❖

'Finn! I've never seen you move so quickly!' Richard was pacing the corridor as she dashed in, red-faced. 'Thank God you're here!'

He pulled her into an unwanted hug. Finn's arms remained stiff by her side.

'Okay, Richard, you can let go now. What's happened?'

Richard flung her away. Finn felt her ankle buckle, nearly falling. A feeling of rage swept over her. Just for a moment, she wanted to scream at his carelessness, his seeming inability to think of others. But maybe it wasn't the right time.

Richard shifted from one foot to another, looking down. He had the appearance of a basketball coach, frustrated with the way a game was unfolding. 'She was just here, we yelled at each other.'

'More importantly, is August okay?'

'Celeste said this is my fault,' he choked.

'Oh, she called me too. I couldn't make sense of anything. But Richard, is August okay?'

He squeezed his nose in a bizarre way, nodding. 'Yeah, she's okay. She's okay. She's not okay. She's resting. The doctor says she'll wake up soon. I haven't been allowed in there. Her mum and dad, and someone called Kaye, are floating around, somewhere.'

'Richard! Richard, this isn't your fault,' Finn said hesitantly, like maybe these words weren't true.

He continued pacing, squeezing his nose. 'Yeah, well, I do sort of believe you. But I feel guilty too. I feel partly responsible. If anything happened to her ...'

Richard's voice was squeaky. He pulled Finn into a hug, kissing the top of her head.

'You know, you and August are like daughters to me.'

'You've never kissed my head before,' Finn said weakly, not enjoying the touch. She felt he wasn't kissing her head so much as attempting to suck some energy from her.

A nurse power-walked past, calling over her shoulder, 'You can go in now. Be gentle!'

Richard's face squashed up. He ran fingers hurriedly through his hair, took a deep breath, then returned hands to pockets, a homecoming gesture. 'Yes, be gentle, be gentle. Come on, Finn.'

Richard stepped towards the room, as Finn turned her head, back to the nurses' station. She caught the eyes of a young woman, wearing large black glasses, looking over the edge of a folder. Her eyes were smiling, but she seemed to be trying to repress a smile. Finn smiled at her, not quite understanding the feeling that rose up in her chest.

'I shouldn't laugh,' she called out to Finn. 'But you just missed quite a scene.'

Finn chuckled nervously, embarrassed, that she was here with Richard, that Richard was her person she moved with in the world. 'You see what I have to put up with?'

The nurse laughed. 'But *do* you have to put up with it?'

Finn felt something in her body, move and change. Did she have to put up with it?

Finn shrugged, feeling suddenly awkward. 'It's very Freo,' she said, unthinkingly.

The nurse laughed, shaking her head. 'That is just one kind of Fremantle. I see plenty of other versions here.'

She tapped her paperwork bundle on the bench, like it was a deck of cards, all the edges coming into line. Finn felt lost in the presence of this nurse's knowledge and competence, as though it was a shadow she was disappearing into. She felt herself going red, smiled back at the nurse, then ducked into the room.

August was upright in bed. Her eyes were nets cast wide. Her left arm was plastered, and there were scrapes and cuts on her right.

'August! My dear August!'

Finn shot Richard a look, like *tone it down*. But August seemed oblivious.

'What happened?' Finn asked.

August closed her eyes, and began to speak in hushed, rambling monotone. 'I wake up here again. At least, it feels like again.'

She looked up at Finn and Richard, pointing to the chairs beside the bed. Then she stared down at her blanket, as though lowering her head in prayer. 'It feels like here, but I can't be sure anymore. My head throbs and I feel foggy and no, no it's not before.'

'What's that?' called Richard, who was swiftly kicked by Finn.

'The white-walled mazes that go on, in endless possibility that isn't dizzying, but is eternal and profound. This moment is not eternal, it is not profound. It's more of a light, dull thud on the earth.'

August looked up to the ceiling for a moment, and began to smile. 'This happened, this happened,' she said. 'There are forces, there are laws and I have been warned before. Gravity can't be argued with, no matter how much you feel like picking a fight. We never stopped being close, we never stopped talking. And maybe that was a problem.'

'But he became my second voice and I needed my second voice, and the voice that always slowed everything down. Without the second voice, I keep being the girl who goes for walks and registers so many beautiful things, a flower here, a pebble there, the dancing shadow on the pavement. I kept being the girl who needs to stop each time beauty is registered, giving a short hum, a nod back, saying thank you to the universe, to the point where I am humming all the time, I am nodding all the time, caught in a perpetual and crazy gratitude, that is really saying, "There is so much beauty, I cannot find my place."'

'August, August, honey ...' said Richard, reaching over to hold her hand. 'August. What do you mean?'

'Mum, Dad, Kaye. This is Richard and Finn. Richard and Finn, this is Burt and Shirley, and mum's cousin Kaye.'

The couple had shuffled in with such gentleness, no-one noticed till August addressed them. They were followed by a woman who jangled as she walked; her dress was covered in tiny bells, her wrists lined with bangles.

Richard and Finn turned, following August's shaking, reaching arm. The couple was grey-haired, dressed in beige, black, grey and white, and smiling in a soft way that betrayed a deep hurt. Burt's arm was around Shirley's shoulder, while Shirley clasped her handbag, a gesture of quiet pride. Kaye couldn't be more different from the two; she smiled broadly, and announced 'G'day!' at a volume that competed with Richard.

'Mum, Dad. Please come closer. Meet my friends. This is Richard and Finn.'

The meeting of parents seemed to switch Richard into meet-and-greet evangelical mode. Finn's blood boiled as he shook their hands, ushering them into their daughter's hospital room.

Once they were seated close to the bed, Burt and Shirley reached for their daughter, Shirley's curling fingers round her daughter's, Burt brushing hair from her face. It all seemed as though they knew their place here, understood this pain and how to help.

Richard sat back down next to Finn, and tried to drag her into a hug. Finn's body didn't melt into the embrace; rather it hardened, defending itself against affection.

'Where is Tom?' Richard queried, eyes bounding from August to her parents.

Shirley's eyes were shiny behind her large glasses. She had a large mole under her right eye, and shot a confused look at Burt.

'What do you mean?' Her voice was as soft and scratchy as a woollen cardigan. Richard turned to August. She had pulled her hands away from her parents, engrossed in the blanket's weave. Shirley's eyes were razors, and a glare at Burt seemed to conduct electricity – a charge for him to speak, take control.

Burt looked over to his daughter. 'You haven't told them, love?'

August shook her head. 'He still speaks to me. He still sends me messages.' She looked up at Finn suddenly, as though defending a point. 'That's why I need it. His phone.'

Burt and Shirley looked at each other.

'That's why there were two phones.' Shirley whispered. 'She still has his.'

August closed her eyes and lay back, heavy into the pillow. 'Of course I still have it, I asked to keep it. I hold his phone up to the sky, and that's how I receive. The message just comes, and my fingers know how to bring it to life. Then the message is sent to my own phone, a message from Tom. He's up there now,' August looked up to the ceiling.

Burt reached over, his hand gentle on hers. 'August, dear. Is it okay for us to talk about this?'

August closed her eyes, for a long time, before she nodded.

'Would you like to tell us more about Tom?' Burt asked.

She shook her head.

'Well, is it okay if I tell your friends about what happened to Tom?'

August was still a moment. Her chin became dimpled. She began to nod, tears running down her cheeks.

Burt looked over to Finn first, then Richard. Shirley looked down to her handbag, as though in prayer. 'Tom is gone. He died, a few years ago. It was a tragic accident. These things happen on farms, in the country, to young people especially. Sadly, it's a part of life in the wheatbelt. The whole thing has been terrible for August. But she has been doing the best to make a new life for herself. It's just, we're coming up to the third anniversary now, and the last two have been tough. After he died, she needed to go into a special clinic to recover, and then she stayed with us for quite a while. The first anniversary she broke down again. By the second, she'd managed to stay with Kaye in the caravan for that year, but come the anniversary things fell apart, but not so badly. She didn't need to go into hospital. This year, she'd been doing so well. But she will always be sensitive, she will always be fragile. What did she tell you? Did she tell you Tom was still alive?'

Finn and Richard shared a look of wonder.

'What did she say to you, Richard?'

'I don't know, I can't think if she ever said either way, dead or alive ... She just, she seemed to imply that he was living.'

Shirley was shaking her head. 'It's not right to lie,' she spoke, barely audible.

'I am very sorry,' Burt said. 'What happened, well, we are not sure really what to make of it all. We are not sure if, why don't you come back home, love? Just for a while, until you get back on your feet?'

'Well it was really late, and it was hot.' August had burst into life, vocally at least. Her body lay still. 'He was at the farm, over the summer, helping his dad with chaff-cutting. He was working so he could save enough money so we could rent our own house together, and really make a home. But sometimes, he'd go quiet, and I wasn't sure that's what he wanted.

'I stayed living in the city and we saw each other on the

weekends. And things were hard, things were hard for me. My brain hadn't been working, and I really needed him. He was always my soft place to land. I was so tired and unable to really self-console without him. I don't know if I was just tiring him out, was I tiring him out? I wanted to call every night, and it just wasn't easy to talk on the phone. He was so tired after a day of being all manly and one of the blokes, and even though he was tall and a beautiful man, he wasn't like that, he was weird like me.'

August sighed, looked up the ceiling and smiled, then closed her eyes again. 'And there were cracks and crack-ups for him too, I'm sure there were, and I just wasn't seeing it. It's not like he was ever brushing me off. He was always there for me, but maybe he was exhausted. Sometimes when we talked, he said things – in a laughing way – like, "I don't really know how to be a man, you know." He laughed about it, but maybe it was serious. Maybe he felt he needed to escape from his own body. But I don't know for sure that's how he felt.

'He found it really hard adjusting to the city. But when he was back there that summer, he knew that home wasn't home anymore. He felt caught in this exhausting limbo. So he went for his walks at night, under the moon, when things all felt clearer. He would call me at two a.m., sounding excited, awake to life. It upset me because I knew he needed to wake up early. It made me freak out. I was anxious for him. He probably wasn't sleeping because of anxiety, and then I just threw the anxiety back at him.

'So I knew he was having trouble sleeping. It didn't feel like trouble for him though. It felt like he was getting to know himself. Everything was beginning to make sense. The last time he called me, he was walking down the gravel under the moon. I could hear the crunching under his feet.

'He said, "I know now. Finally! I know what we should do. Let's go travelling. I want to see the world!"

'I was excited and like, "Where? Where shall we go?"

'"Anywhere! Let's go to Paris! Let's go to Canada! Let's go somewhere really cold where we can dig tunnels in the snow! I am saving good money now. I'll come back to the city, we can both work and save a few months, it will be amazing!"

'We were capable of this crazy, laughing high together. It's like everything was a private joke. There was no reason for me to believe that we, with all certainty, would go travelling. Plans change. But it was the happiest he'd sounded in a long time.'

August trailed off. Finn looked over to Burt, who had wrapped his arm around Shirley. She rested her head on his shoulder, and together they seemed like one.

'He said some things that made me wonder, later. He said, "I love you very much, little August. Never forget that." Never forget. It was odd, looking back. But it didn't seem so at the time. Maybe it didn't mean anything particular at all. I went back to bed so excited, closing my eyes with this big smile on my face. I don't know that I was genuinely excited about travel. I was just so happy that my Tom was happy. It was really hard to get to sleep, I was buzzing to my toes.

'I got the call from his mum in the morning. They found him lying on the ground. Next to a tree. Next to a motorbike. Near the pipeline. Odd. Why would he be lying there? What was he doing? Did he wake up for an early ride? Then, no, he's actually there, but not there. This isn't Tom. This is Tom's body. Tom is dead.'

August bowed her head low. Finn cast Richard an accusatory look. *How could you not know about this?*

'We all came to know he was riding the bike really, really fast. In the dark, dark, dark. That itself wasn't too weird. Tom was unusual and sensitive, but he grew up on a farm and loved motorbikes. So I thought, maybe it was just after we talked. Maybe he wanted to tire himself out. An adrenaline rush, then off to sleep. He hit a tree. Why did he hit a tree? He was smashed out of existence.

'Then people began to talk. He must've done it on purpose.

Why else would he ride so fast when it is so dark? It was the top paddock. There is no human-made light around. There are quite a few trees around the fence lines. If he wanted to go for a joy ride, why did he choose that paddock? And why that bike? It could go very fast but wasn't in the best shape. That's what everyone said.

'I had to tell his mum about the phone call. She asked so many questions. She needed to know, exactly what he said. "I love you. Never forget that." She latched on to those words. She screamed at me. It was my fault. It was my fault he was feeling like this. Well, she didn't say that exactly, but I felt that. But I only felt that for a moment, not for long at all. Maybe it was just self-protection, to not believe in things being my fault. I never believed, and I still don't understand that he killed himself.'

August looked down again. She needed to stop, close her eyes. She needed to open them again, resume the story. 'What I believe now is, he was doing a gamble, a Russian roulette.'

She turned to Finn. 'Why did he make those plans with me, if he'd wanted to die? I know what he was doing – riding that bike in the dark – was very risky, I know that. But what were his final thoughts? What were his intentions? Maybe he said to God, "Let me live through this, and I'll take it as a sign."

'I don't remember much straight after that. When I woke up I was in a hospital. I knew I'd been to some heavenly place. I didn't try to hurt myself. I just … cracked. And it was beautiful. Once I cracked, once I'd been to that place, it's like I brought him back. I went to heaven and brought him back.'

At that Shirley sighed, and reached for her daughter's hand.

'I didn't know when I went to see Celeste that she would see straight through me.'

'Who is Celeste?' asked Burt.

'Good question! Who the hell is this Celeste!' Richard raged, rising from his chair. Finn reached over and pushed him back down.

'Celeste saw through it all. She knew I had an entity inside me, straight away. But I didn't think she would be flushing him. I thought it would be flushing other lingering molecules of darkness. But she emptied me. I called out to him, and he was gone.' August's face was streaked with tears. 'She took Tom. Away. Again!'

Richard tore off the chair noisily and began to pace, squeezing his nose. 'Why do you have to let go? Must we really let go?'

'It's okay, I know, she was right. It's all about flushing entities. I was holding myself back. This thing, I wasn't letting Tom pass.'

'But what if Tom doesn't want to pass?' asked Richard. 'What if he wants to stay with you? And what if it's not him anyway? What if it's just something in you, something important that you hold on to, that helps you live your life? And what is wrong with that?'

Burt and Shirley had risen to their feet too. Burt drew his wife in close on his left, reaching down to his daughter's hand on the right. Richard tried to sling his arm around Finn, who ducked.

'Well,' Richard said, embarrassed. 'Finn and I might go get a coffee. Is it okay though if we stay a while? If we come back?'

August nodded.

'We will do whatever our daughter wants,' Burt said.

Finn was almost at breaking point when she and Richard reached the vending machine. Richard began a fierce search for coins in his pocket. Finn pushed him out of the way and used her bankcard, ordering two flat whites.

When she turned back round, Richard looked stunned. 'Finn, are you okay?'

The machine whizzed, sending a stream of hot milk into a paper cup. And Finn broke.

'You are just so shit sometimes! But thanks for finally asking, Richard; actually, I'm not okay! Did I mention to you that my shapes never came back after the operation? That you've been acting like a weirdo since Celeste has been around? That Celeste confuses the hell out of me, and I don't know whether I can't stand her or if I'm in love with her? Or did I mention that I've been beginning to think this whole thing is bullshit, and that maybe my shapes were just some kind of weird pain-management technique?

'Or maybe I forgot to mention how I don't feel cut out for any of this stuff, this hanging around vulnerable people and acting like we have all the answers when we can barely tie our own shoelaces ... I really don't know how or why or what I'm doing here anymore. I'm only here because of August now. But everything is just shit, shit, shit.'

Finn reached over to pull the paper cup from the machine. But it was too full and hot, and her movements were too jerky. The beige liquid pooled over the white floor and she began to sob. Why was she sobbing? In part she was sad, in part she felt guilty for lashing out. Everything had just been too much lately, and here was Richard, who was always there, even though she wasn't sure that she wanted him to be, wasn't sure that she wanted to be close to him, ever again.

Richard reached over to her, and she beat her arms on his chest. He stepped back, tried again. She beat his chest once more.

Richard stepped back, drew a breath, then tried to hold her again. And Finn held him back.

❀

Finn and Richard returned to August's room about an hour later, when Burt and Shirley went for a quick sandwich. No-one seemed overly worried. August was a little brighter. It was as though there was medicine in being surrounded by loved ones. Kaye was sitting next to the bed, sipping tea from a thermos.

'Oh Richard,' Kaye said when they came back. 'Can I talk to you outside?'

Richard nodded at Kaye and followed her out. August and Finn sat in silence for a moment. Finn felt too warm, uncomfortable with August's gaze on her.

'Well,' Finn coughed. 'What actually happened?'

'I fell off my bike. Well I took my hands off my bike, going down a hill. I put myself in God's hands.' August was still smiling.

Finn shook her head, not knowing what to say. At that moment, Richard walked back into the room, hands in his pockets, his gaze vacant.

August patted the bed and said to Finn, 'Come on. Be my personal space invader.'

Finn laughed. It was actually funny. It was a good joke. She turned to Richard, expecting him to burst into laughter on hearing her repeat the wordplay. But he was staring out the window, a million miles away.

'Are you okay?' August called over. Finn seemed to be the only one to register the problem here. The sick trying to look after the well.

He looked over, then away again, sighing. August patted Finn's leg. Waves of guilt felt like nausea. Finn thought of her chronic desire to push August away.

'I see you, not seeing me.' August spoke quietly, looking down. 'I don't know how to show you who I really am. Maybe I try too hard, but I just want you to see me, because I see you.'

Finn reached out to August, taking her hand. She usually endured rather than enjoyed the touch of others. It was the needs of others, not her needs, that dictated touching. She would only touch others in attempts to console, because it's what she had learned. It's what she'd been shown. *This can help.*

She looked into August's eyes because that was the right thing also. The guilt went through metamorphosis, becoming butterflies.

She actually wanted this, Finn realised. She wanted to hold her friend's hand. She squeezed tight, and August squeezed back, a puddle of warmth that each stepped into, feeling rainbows and the nearness of treasures.

'I am so sorry, August,' Finn said.

'It's okay, it's not your fault.'

They looked over at Richard. He was squeezing his nose again. Finn felt her jaw clench. Was he trying to hold his breath? His face was turning red.

'What's wrong?' August called out.

'I'm sorry. It's just, this all brings back Serena for me.'

'God, Richard, are you really going to make this about you?' snapped Finn.

August patted Finn's leg. 'It's okay.'

'I know, I know, I am making this about me,' Richard laughed wildly. 'You know, that's something Serena would have said!' He slumped onto a chair, sighing. 'I know this is a problem. I see that this isn't all about me. I know it's terrible, but I can't help it. I need you to tell me off. And I know I'm not over her. I never will be. And then I went and chased down Celeste, and then I chased her away. I think it might be over between us.'

'There are more important things to care about right now, Richard!'

'Sorry. Sorry.'

He jammed himself onto the other side of the bed.

'How did you two meet?' asked August sweetly.

'Who, me and Celeste?'

'Divine and Dateless!' shot Finn.

Richard shrugged. 'It was Ross. He set it up for me. Must have thought I needed some help.'

Finn was smiling into her lap, shaking her head.

'I've seen *you* on there, Finn. "Freo Dreamer"?'

August and Richard began to laugh. Finn's face was hot.

'God!' She pulled at her hair and let go, falling into the laughter. 'I am ashamed of myself!'

'Me too!' chimed Richard. 'Ashamed of you, I mean, not me!' Bells of laughter rang again.

Then August wiped a tear from her eye, calling out, 'I guess it made me feel like shit! I didn't want to go around telling everyone, "Hey, he's dead! Maybe he even did it to himself!"'

'Yeah well, Finn's been walking around acting all superior,' Richard threw about his arms, underlining his sarcasm, 'but then she calls herself "Freo Dreamer". Do you really enjoy skinny-dipping by moonlight, Finn?'

August started to giggle again.

'I just wanted to be special, I just wanted to be like everyone else!'

August laughed the loudest and Richard swept Finn into a hug. Finn knew if she didn't laugh now, she wouldn't be the person she wanted to be.

'Are you two angry with me, that I lied?' August asked through laughter. 'That I led you to believe Tom was alive?'

'August, you never actually lied,' Richard corrected her. 'You just never set us straight when we assumed you were talking about a live boyfriend.'

August wiped a giggle-tear. 'But this is what I miss. I miss laughing. How can I be laughing now? I felt so guilty when I was happy the first few times, without him. And now I'm sick, but I've probably been sick a long time, since before he died. But I miss having a place, for myself. He's been all small and shrunken, something I carry around in my pocket, hoping if I just add water, this tiny little powdered Tom will shoot up. But it's not quite everything. My parents don't know the half of it.'

'It's okay, August,' Richard assured her, placing a hand on her shoulder. 'You are still allowed to keep some secrets.'

'I know, but I want you to know, it's just I had a feeling ... When I met Tom, my first thought was, *Okay, he is a gay man.*

But then, we were both getting deeper and deeper into church, and the idea of homosexuality, it just stopped existing in my mind. Being gay was not possible within that church. It's the way it was talked about, and not talked about. We were all washed anew. If those thoughts had existed, they were our old selves. If those thoughts were creeping back, it's because we hadn't been properly cleansed.

'I don't know, I don't know what it felt like to be him ... But sometimes we talked about it, the possibility. He would shut down, and really, we were more like friends, the best of friends. It just took so long for us to get together, and I wonder now if all that time he was struggling, with being a Christian, with feeling different, maybe with liking men, with also being in love with me, all the while told by the church elders that we were meant to be together, doing it the right way ... The pressure was from all directions ... And I will never really know the answers to all this. At least, I won't share this story with the people who knew Tom. It's just, it's just a feeling I have. I don't want to go blurting it out. Sorry. Sorry.' August was frowning, her eyes closed.

'Don't say sorry. Why are you sorry?'

'I am sorry I got you all worried.'

'Tom sounds really cool,' said Finn. 'I would love to have met him.'

Richard nodded, 'Me too! You have been through a lot, my August. One little spring chicken with the weight of the world on her shoulders.' He stood, stretching into a yawn.

'I thought I was hearing voices,' August spoke quietly. 'I realised it was you and her. I know what you both said. I'm not in love with you, Richard.'

'Thank God for that,' muttered Finn. 'Not that I thought you did love Richard.'

'It's okay,' nodded August. 'I can understand how Celeste might have misunderstood the situation. But Richard, she didn't even know I had a boyfriend, dead or alive. She didn't realise what she was doing. If she knew my story, maybe she would have been more gentle.'

'I think as a healer, she should have made a point to know your story.'

August was fiddling with the blanket again. 'But *you* didn't know it, Richard.'

'That is true.' Richard sighed, nodding.

'It's just, I miss him. I miss being close to someone who knows me so well. I feel at sea so much of the time. People don't understand what I'm trying to say, because I can't make the person I am inside really show on the outside.'

Richard sat down again, placing his hand on hers. 'August, you can't go back to that caravan. There is too much mould, it's not healthy. Kaye had a word with me outside. She will talk to you later, but she said she'd made up a bed for you in the lounge, that is, if you don't want to go back to your parents' house.'

August stared off into the ceiling. Finn glared. *Nice timing, Richard.* And then she remembered. Could that work? Could she and August get along well enough to live together? She herself had been firm with August many times. If you've been firm with someone once, it's much easier to do it again. That could be a good thing. That meant she'd be able to draw lines. They could both draw lines.

She took a deep breath, resolved. 'August, my housemate moved out recently, and I kinda need a new one. There would be room for you to have an art space and a bedroom. I have a bedroom and a lounge room. It was meant to be for writing, but ... whatever.'

August beamed at Finn, eyes shining in disbelief. The butterflies devolved into squirms of guilt. If kindness was this surprising, it was also alarming.

'That's a great idea, Finn!' Richard slapped her on the back.

August laughed and gasped – the sound of being winded, excited or both.

'That would, that would be,' she looked at Finn imploringly. 'Would that really be okay?'

'I don't know. I don't know if it will be okay. We'll just have to try. But just please, try not to look at me like that.'

August gave a huge grin, which turned quickly into a look of fatigue. Finn wondered why she had to be so blunt with people, Richard stared out the window, and August fell asleep.

❀

'I need to tell you something,' Richard said. He and Finn had stepped into the corridor. 'August should know too, but I didn't want to mention it to her. Not now. It could be distressing.'

'Oh,' Finn folded arms across her chest. 'Shock, horror! Are you showing some tact here? Some consideration? Hang on, Richard, this might be too much to take.' Finn looked around. 'I need to find a chair.'

'Finn ...' Richard sighed. He looked truly exhausted.

'Sorry, I'm sorry, Richard. It's been a long day already.'

'Let's just find a seat,' said Richard, sounding much more firm than Finn was used to. 'I have some bad news.'

'What's wrong?'

But Richard had walked off ahead, down the corridor, towards the waiting lounge. There they found an uninhabited couch and sat. Finn felt an awful fear. Something like another rejection was coming.

'I'm getting worried, Richard,' she laughed, sounding more nervous than she wanted to. 'You sound like you want to break up with me.'

Two rejections in one day would just be too much. But how could Richard possibly reject Finn? He could say to her, 'Stay away from IEWA.'

What if she heard those words? What then? She closed her eyes and felt something like a deep relief, heaviness and rest, moving through her legs, feet and fingertips, as she sank into the couch. Maybe this was what she wanted after all.

She sought out Richard's eyes, but they were fixed on his feet, which were large, bulging, slightly red. Shiny and swollen in a way that was worrying, in well-worn leather sandals. They were the feet of an older person, too old to be Richard's. And his feet touched her heart.

'What is it, Richard?' Finn spoke with the kind of gentleness she always wished she could find in herself, but rarely seemed to be there.

Richard took a deep breath, touching his fingertips up against each other, considering. His eyes looked sad and tired, behind his glasses.

'Well ...' he began. 'Something has come up. I have been getting these letters.'

'Okay.'

He closed his eyes. 'From the council,' he whispered.

Finn staved off laughter. 'What do these letters say?'

Richard shook his head, as though he was attempting to shake the letters into another existence.

'I haven't opened them. But I know what they're all about. The council aren't happy with how I am living. They want me to clean up my act, fix up the boat, or move on. You've seen how the world is changing. There's no room for an old healer like me anymore.'

He spoke with an injured pride that Finn found sickening. She had to swallow something rising in her throat. His red, swollen feet caught her eye again. A moment ago they touched her, and now, they were just his feet. He was just a person. Did he need to matter so much to her?

Richard turned to Finn suddenly, grabbing her arm. She found herself pulling away.

'I need your help, Finn,' he pleaded.

'How?' Finn spoke loudly, still pulling away. 'What am I supposed to do?'

'I need help keeping IEWA alive, Finn! Celeste, you see, had all these ideas, to expand, to move to a new premises ... I mean, I was never really sold on what she wanted to do, but for a brief moment there, I got quite drawn in to her, and I could see her helping me to really move forward ...'

'Oh great! That's fantastic Richard, you are actually admitting that you want to use me!'

'What? No, it's not that! It's just, there are things that you are good at! I think, if you can just help me to write lists, things to do, things to fix, then hold some committee meetings, organise some busy bees ... If you could just start by sitting with me and opening the letters, so we can see exactly what steps I need to take ...'

'But why do you care about this *now*?' There it was. That rage. That rage that leapt up, inside her. 'How long have you been getting these letters?'

'It's been a few months now, but ...'

'A few months?' Finn laughed, becoming breathless, running fingers through her hair. 'What the hell? And all of a sudden, right now, today, when August is in hospital, and you seem to have had some kind of break-up, you think it's a good moment to start pressuring me into cleaning up your fucking boat!'

'It's more than a fucking boat,' Richard said gently. 'It's a healing centre. I am asking you to help me keep IEWA alive ... Think of everything we have been through ...'

Finn was perched on the edge of the couch now. She felt like she might cry and kept looking straight ahead, at the water cooler. She didn't want to wipe away tears. He would notice. And she didn't want to turn to him, because he would see the power of his words over her.

'I can't,' she said quietly.

'You can't what?'

'I can't do it. I can't help you with this. This is your problem. I'm not so sure this is my path anymore.'

'Is this because of your shapes? Just because they are gone you know, doesn't mean they're not coming back. And even if they never come back, it doesn't mean you can't be a healer. Anyone can be a healer, actually.'

'Well, if anyone can be a healer, what's the problem with me not being one? There must be a long line of hopefuls, just waiting to do that work.'

'No no,' Richard said. '*You* are special Finn. *You* are the one I want.'

She turned to him. She looked him in the eye. She reached for Richard's hand. It felt so different when it was on her terms, she realised. When she was the one reaching out.

'Richard, I just don't know what I want … It's been such a long time that I've filled my life with work, with IEWA, and with looking out for you.' She felt that rage again. 'You know, my life used to be more empty. I had time to myself. But just because I had free time, it didn't mean I wanted it to be filled. And just because I haven't set goals for my life, it doesn't mean I will take your advice and become a healer.'

It was all making sense now. She felt the words pouring forth. 'I've realised, my whole involvement with you, with IEWA, is something that has happened in the absence of other plans. But what if the only thing I really want, is to just be alone?'

'But Finn, Finn,' Richard began, sounding at sea. His eyes were glassy. 'You have, you have something so special, and I just really need you …'

'I can't,' Finn choked. She was resolute, and almost shocked with herself. Just a moment ago, she was scared of being rejected by Richard, and now she was the one doing the rejecting. 'I just can't.'

There was that thing in Richard's eyes that she loved. It was that look that was tired, smart, sullen, knowing, and full of a quiet kind of love, that felt close to resignation. It was like he had really heard, and really understood.

He sighed, not heavily, but just to himself. He sighed a sigh that didn't impose on everyone and everything in existence.

Richard took her hand, and said, 'Okay. That's that then.'

Finn closed her eyes, and he closed his. They still held hands, and became still: a limestone figure, the river of nurses, doctors and patients, buzzing, beeping, clanking, words, smiles, laughs, faces, chatter flowing round them.

THE BOAT

'I have roots. I am connected. I am part of a thick forest of trees. I am a light, bouncing, weaving around the branches. I am light. I have light. I am love. I have love. I have beauty. I am beautiful. I have eternity all around me, from here to eternity. I have light, love, beauty, inside me, and all around. All I need to do is breathe, and I am part of everything.'

'Wow, August, that was beautiful!' Jessica said.

'Thank you, I wrote it myself! Now it's time to close down the eyes. Let's try to visualise this deposit. Is it scratching inside you, eager to come out? Is it like a wet, slimy baby chicken, pecking at the warm inside of her egg-home? Or is it spiky, like a sea urchin? At once heavy, solid and soft, like cream cheese? If you were looking in an aquarium, is there a particular fish it would resemble? Is it like an orange, an apple, tiny forks prodding, feathers tickling, ants building cities ...'

August took a deep breath. The ants built their colonies, all around the graves. August had gone back home, with Finn and Richard, for the anniversary of Tom's death. Burt and Shirl drove them out to the cemetery. Terry met them there too. He was the only one from church who still came, on this day, each year. Terry hugged August, shook hands with Richard, kissed Finn on the cheek, and there was a tear in his eye. The earth was dry and cracked. Gravestones were like crooked white teeth, emerging from the ground. Plastic windmills whirred, framed photographs and ceramic flowers were dotted about. On Tom's grave were peonies and hydrangeas, from his mother and grandmother.

August laid flowers too. It was a large bunch, handpicked around Fremantle: geraniums, jasmine, lavender, kangaroo paw. Birds passed overhead, their shadows black dots, flitting over the graves. Knowing Finn and Richard were there helped somehow. She was able to sit, in silence, and remember: Tom died, but she lived. His leaving wasn't a single act, but a slow process that stretched like a veil, over the clouds, stars, moon. His leaving was a spiderweb that gradually floated down to earth, keeping August, and all around, quietly and gently captive. August looked over and waved at Richard, as a willy-willy picked up earth, spinning a whirl of dust around.

'August?' Jessica said.

'Sorry!' August closed her eyes and let a tear roll down her cheek. Tom was still here, but he was like a wind, spinning up an emptiness inside. She looked up, across the room, realising the door was ajar. She saw a sliver of her painting *The Pleiadian Goddess*, the blond hair of the deity flying in all directions. She suddenly couldn't breathe. The picture made her remember, how when Tom lay in his coffin, his long hair fell down around his shoulders. Finally, his hair was laid out, long and free, but she wished it wasn't.

'Are you okay?' Jessica asked from the bed.

'I'm okay. Not perfect.' August smiled faintly.

'I'm glad you're not perfect!' Jessica laughed and closed her eyes again, August continuing to scan her body. She waved her hands up and down, from head to toe. August enjoyed this movement, seeing it as a kind of dance, swaying her hips, rolling her head from side to side.

'I was beginning to see something,' Jessica said. 'It's strange really, maybe I was just distracted.'

'What was it?' August stopped.

'A giant watermelon?'

August squealed, clapping hands together. 'That's fantastic! Well, have you been eating the seeds? My mum always told me if I ate them, a watermelon would grow in my tummy.'

Jessica gushed, 'My mum told me that too! I think I'm still afraid, so I usually buy the seedless ones. Anyway, when I buy watermelon it's because I really want to chow down on it, and I'm not going to want to get slowed down by the seeds.'

'Well, maybe this watermelon is trying to tell you not to be afraid!'

Jessica and August erupted into laughter, though neither were exactly sure why.

'Okay, let's do this,' August spoke, still giggling. 'Let us hum together.'

She reached down to grasp Jessica's hand. 'I want you to pick a tone, any tone. I'll pick mine and count to three. I like to call it hum-onising.'

Jessica shrieked in laughter. August had learnt this humming technique from Celeste – that day she didn't like to think about, but felt important to acknowledge. But one day a pleasant memory from the session had popped into her brain. August remembered how much she enjoyed the humming-harmony, before everything fell apart. She decided to bring this activity into her extraction work. It was her way of saying, 'This happened. This is a part of me. I can make something new from this experience.'

'We'll start to hum at the same time, so our hums may be dissonant. But I don't want you to correct your hum, bring it in line with mine. I want the two hums working together, to get this thing moving. I find that works best. Okay, are we ready?'

As Jessica nodded, August felt a knock in her chest. It was the way Jennifer looked up. She looked the way August felt – permanently caught, looking up to others. August hadn't felt someone looking up at her like that, not since moving from the country.

'Are you okay?' Jessica asked. 'Your eyes ...'

August wiped a tear, smiling. 'I'm okay if you're okay! Let's do this, okay. One, two, three ...'

The humming duet was such a unique sound, every time. Jessica's tone was a long, low note, speaking of safety, constancy, a soft place to land. August was high, thin, bright, like sparks, stars crashing and burning.

Jessica's hum began to swell, then broke into a cry. August imagined the shattering of watermelon. Pink flesh, black seeds. Green, white and yellow, shiny fragments. Bursting mess, flying up at the ceiling.

Jessica's eyes were wide, looking up. 'Oh God, it's beautiful. And the pressure, the feeling. It's gone.'

She jumped off the therapy table, but was unsteady on her feet. August reached out for her shoulder.

'Careful now, Jessica. Don't panic.'

Tiny, shimmering flecks. After their Big Bang, they gathered, and began to float, slowly migrating towards the porthole.

'Nooooo!' Jessica cried out.

'It's okay, it's okay,' August said, a slight panic rising in her. Would Jessica be sad too, would she mourn her loss?

Jessica leapt up and dashed to the porthole, looking. Hills, pine trees, houses, the crisscross of roads. People walking dogs past the new housing development, a red car driving past rollerbladers, women digging in their gardens, children sucking icy poles, all under a pink sky. The green, black and pink matter floated into the scenery.

August placed her hand on Jessica's shoulder. She remembered how it felt, when Tom placed his hand on hers. How it made her feel small, contained.

'But, they were inside, they were *inside* me? I didn't realise it would be like this!'

'It's okay,' August felt the quietness in her own voice. It was her own voice, she could feel that, she knew that. But it wasn't rushing, pushing, zinging the way it used to. It was a part of her, body, mind and soul. These parts were all travelling the same speed, in the same direction. She was able to say the words she meant.

'It might not feel okay right now,' she said slowly. 'But it is going to be okay.'

❀

Richard sipped his coffee and stared at the photograph. August had convinced him to create a special space for Serena. Next to her was Tom, a wide cheeky grin over a birthday cake. The two frames sat on the rooftop – each on their own chair – surrounded by wisteria, nasturtiums and morning glory.

August still didn't know about the letters, and Richard didn't want to tell her. He preferred the idea of just waiting, seeing what happened, if the council were bold enough to actually approach him on his property.

After finishing the pre-extraction on Jessica Morton – a young woman suffering abdominal pains, with a tendency towards seeing lights at night – Richard did some cleaning. It took all his energy just to begin, but once he started, he realised it wasn't too bad. He managed the dishes – rinsing plates, soaking plates, wiping plates down. Then he spread out his doona on the roof, an airing-out overdue by about nine years. The vines needed pruning too, he noticed, and were beginning to encroach upon Serena's face. But that could wait. Now it was time to enjoy his coffee.

'Just a little bit every day,' is what Finn used to say.

'I try to set timers when I'm cleaning,' said August.

It doesn't have to be perfect, he realised.

In the past, this made cleaning seem pointless: why vacuum the floor when you know it will just get dirty again? But there was something about raising the mean standard of cleanliness. It just felt better. It was easier to sleep at night. And it made the breaks from cleaning time seem well deserved.

The ocean wasn't visible from here, but Richard closed

his eyes and tried to imagine it. Sun, water, sand and grass. Travellers parking their vans, hand-painted cockatoos and balga bushes on the sides. Propping open their boots with mops, switching on gas cookers, boiling water in saucepans for cups of green tea. Shirtless men in Thai fishermen pants squeezing accordions, juggling, or twirling fire-sticks in circles of clapping. Full-moon drummers gathering early on the grass, wielding bongos and djembe drums. Dreadlocked gypsy women ready to jiggle, screeching out in laughter. Later they would raise their singlets, welcoming the moon's rays onto their bellies and breasts.

Large-eyed dune cats would be waiting for handouts of canned tuna. Some beachgoers would have tins stashed in their calico bags, leaving small platters for mums and their kittens. Flocks of scuba divers from the military base would be trudging in flippers – over the hill, into the water, disappearing like submarines into the waves. Dogs would look on at these strange land-animals – goggle-eyed, flesh tucked into black rubber – moving into the water.

Fiery masses of a meteor-like substance would be crashing into the road. Upset mothers would be forming huddles, blaming the military base and their covert operations.

Detectorists would be rolling up jeans, swinging their rods, searching the water for coins, aluminium, things that harm the ocean, or things that could make one rich quick. Helium balloons would be hovering alongside owls and heavy metals, even though there were the signs that said 'BALLOONS DON'T SEND MESSAGES TO HEAVEN'.

Kestrels would be thrust about in odd-shaped thermals. Men with shaved heads and tattoos would be running through the dunes with knives, looking for anyone living in tents who might have stolen laptops from utes.

It was all the way over there – up hills, down hills, across roads, beyond powerlines, mansions, beach shacks and kerbside rubbish – at South Beach that he first met Ross, which led to the purchase of *Richard's Ark*, and the beginning of IEWA. And it was there at South Beach that he laughed and flirted with a blond-grey healer named Celestiaa Davinaa. It was all the way over there that he came close to reopening his heart.

THE BEACH

Thank you, for everything. I will be forever grateful. I will certainly never forget you.

The lines ran through Finn's head – days, weeks, now months after. She let them run like a stream, hoping that stream would soon run dry.

Finn liked Ethann best when she heard the news about August. A friend was in hospital, she needed a lift. He knew just how to be. Strapped the seatbelt across his bare, gleaming chest. Tore noisily down South Terrace. Finn noted that his van needed a muffler.

When he dropped Finn, he gripped her hand and looked into her eyes. 'We'll stay friends, yeah?'

It was like hearing an assurance they didn't have to.

That was just before his face changed. Ethann became gawky and awkward, as he asked, 'You don't happen to have that Gillian's number, do you?'

And she slammed the door in his face.

Maybe that wild feeling was anger. Not anger with any big thing, small thing, a misplaced piece of skin, a person. It was anger with her own meekness. A meekness that gets in the way. A meekness that just happens.

Get to know people, speak your mind in the right place, hold your tongue when it matters. Meekness means you don't know which way to be, who you are, the right and the wrong time. Meekness didn't suit her, it didn't make sense, and she knew that. Still, it hung around just the same.

The meekness was there, right up until that last moment. The door slammed. His face would have been shocked, surprised, she was sure. But she didn't get a chance to see it. The meekness turned straight into a wild, free feeling that just wanted to fly away from everything.

She began to picture Doctor Lucy's face, excited, in her post-op appointment. It was like she had performed a makeover and was handing over a mirror. 'Just look at yourself! Look at all the possibilities in your life, now that you have all this new space inside!'

'And how did the sex go?' the imaginary Doctor Lucy asked. 'Was the penis able to just slip in?'

But how would Finn answer a question like that, when she had nothing to compare the sex to? There was no 'slipping in' in the past. Chances slipped away, like this space had the stubbornness of Cinderella's shoe, and it didn't need the right shaped foot to inhabit it, but needed a surgeon to make that space just the right shape for anyone to enter. It needed a surgeon to make it just the right shape so that it wasn't special at all.

But according to Doctor Lucy, the space was wasted before. It was like a poorly designed apartment, where you walk through the front door, straight into a wall. There might be a nice open area just beyond, but you just can't get there. Doctor Lucy was responsible for activating that space, and she would probably like to hear: 'The sex worked well. I am in full working order.' Doctor Lucy would probably like to say, 'My work is done here,' before floating off into the stars.

Yes Doctor Lucy. You can say that. You can say yes, the sex worked. The sex worked beautifully. It was easy. Too easy. You wouldn't believe how beautiful and terrible it was.

So Lucy wouldn't need to worry about writing a referral for genital physiotherapy, not for Finn at least. But Finn wondered if she might request a referral for something else. And she wondered, too, if one day Lucy would find out about floating building-blocks, or the glowing plankton that watches over a sleeping face. Maybe Eve would walk past her in the street, and see a fire burning in some part of her body.

Finn meant no harm, thinking these thoughts. She just wanted her shapes. But why did she want them back? And what were they all about anyway? 'My periods are different,' she would report, if she saw Doctor Lucy again. 'They are less painful, even though you said my physical problem isn't related to my pain problem. And there is no brown and dried blood like there used to be. It's all more fresh, bright red blood now.'

But the operation didn't change the other pain. The pain that travelled all across her body, like the body was a map of the world. Like toes, knees, the forehead, ankles, were sites to colonise. That pain still came and went, throbbed and quietened, without rhyme or reason. Stabs, spasms, stiffness, shooting. Stress could make it worse. Eating too much bad food – you could call that another kind of stress. But then stress could be so all-consuming, that all physical pain, all physical sensation even, could fade out of existence.

Pain, pain, pain. You get so sick of that word.

'Pain isn't real anyway,' is what Celeste would say. The kind of answer designed to trump everything, or allow sufferers the luxury of self-blame.

The sun was setting. This was the place for letting go. Finn pulled her beanie down over her ears. It felt itchy on her skin, but the wind could do worse. Don't let the wind in, or the toothache, the earache, the tight jaw. Let them away, let them all away. Because everything is connected. If one falls down, we're all going down.

Finn had arranged to meet Celeste at six. The ocean was pink and yellow, glowing waves everywhere. Lights blinking in the distance. Black-blue water and mauve sky. Sand stung her legs, the taste of salt on her lips.

Celeste was standing alone, facing the sun, a fiery orange ball. Finn stood beside her. Blond-grey hair blew about her face. The wind and waves made their own layer of silence. Hands in the pockets of her rain jacket, she turned to look at Finn, smiled briefly, then looked away.

'Thank you for agreeing to meet, Finn.'

'That's okay.'

'This isn't easy for me,' Celeste said quietly.

'Really, everything is okay.'

Celeste sighed. 'It's a women's sun, you know. This is a special sun. A special sun for healing.' She looked to Finn. She looked more fragile than Finn remembered.

'How is she? I do care, you know. I know, maybe it seemed like I didn't at the time. I was reacting. I felt attacked, so I defended myself. I don't think I was completely wrong though.'

'She's doing well. She's moved into my house actually. I think she really needed a friend.'

'Maybe you needed a friend too.'

Finn smiled, wondering if the tingling would return. 'That's probably true.'

Celeste smiled, a hint of smugness, and turned to face the sun. 'So, she's okay.'

'Actually, I think she's doing much better,' said Finn.

Celeste shook her head, rolling her eyes in a way that betrayed her pride. 'That's exactly what I expected would happen. But would he listen to me? No.'

'She's been helping out more with healing sessions.'

'What!' Celeste's jaw dropped, though Finn somehow didn't find her surprise genuine. 'Richard is letting someone who recently attempted suicide be part of a healing practice?'

'I guess you could look at it like that.' Finn shifted her feet, looking down at the sand. 'But I haven't been so involved lately.'

Celeste nodded, now looking genuinely sympathetic. She took Finn's shoulder, and looked into her eyes. 'And I understand. I understand why.'

Finn was surprised she didn't say *I told you so. You've lost your shapes, you've lost your divine connection with the universe.*

But that wasn't Finn's reason for pulling back from the healing. She wasn't sure what it was, exactly, this barrier that came up inside her, and stopped her from wanting to be at IEWA. She felt guilty about leaving, and wondered if that guilt would be around forever. She knew Richard was probably telling Jsun, Rhodda and Eve that she just needed a change. But what was that change? Finn had no idea, and that was painful in itself. All she knew, was that she was still at her happiest when she was alone at home, in front of the television, wearing as little clothing as possible, and stuffing her face with as much junk food as she could.

Celeste began to wiggle her legs, power-walking on the spot. Her footwear seemed incongruous, large black Wellingtons.

'I can't stand sand, actually,' Celeste said softly, seeing Finn's glance. 'I walk barefoot on the beach sometimes because I know the negative ions revitalise me ... But all the sand between your toes, in your car, in the house, in the shower! If I wear my gumboots, I take them off when I get to the car and put them in a plastic box I have in the boot. A nice, sandy plastic box where all the sand stays.'

'That's good thinking,' said Finn.

'Desperate times call for desperate measures.'

Finn laughed and Celeste joined in, laughter passing to a small smile. 'And how is Richard?'

Finn felt her face warm. There were so many feelings about Richard. She still hadn't decided how she wanted their relationship to be. It's not as though they were blood-relatives, but Finn sometimes felt stuck with, or to him, in a way she imagined one might with their own parent. You can't choose your family, but maybe you can't choose your friends either, Finn had been musing lately.

There was no need to go into all this detail with Celeste. But she was looking closely at Finn's face. Finn thought she saw a glint of pleasure in Celeste's eye, as though she had found something in Finn to pounce on. But Finn didn't want to let her in. She looked into the horizon, and Celeste looked away too.

'I don't see Richard too much at the moment. I drop in at IEWA once in a while – mostly just to pick up or drop off August. She's become a bit scared of bikes. I told him I was meeting you, actually. He said he was glad. I asked him to come but he said he's not ready. I'm sorry for what happened between you two.'

'Why are you sorry?' Celeste's eyes were piercing blue.

'Well,' Finn considered, not wanting to say anything that could offend. She really didn't like the idea of an argument with Celeste. 'It seemed you both wanted to try to be together, but it ended up hurting.'

Celeste flicked her hand dismissively. 'No, no. It's okay. We had a soul connection, and soulmates are never supposed to stay together.'

'Well, I am sorry about that argument then, in the hospital. I caught the tail end of it, and it was unpleasant.'

Celeste breathed deep into her collar. 'It's okay. I don't believe he was truly angry with me. He just wanted a way out. He was looking for a reason to explode, and what happened with August, that was it.' She shrugged. 'He's a drama queen.'

Finn didn't completely understand Richard's anger with Celeste either. It's not that his anger wasn't justified. She could see that Celeste had pushed August over the edge. But Richard's reaction seemed to come not just from concern. It seemed almost territorial. It was as though August was a piece of fruit hanging on *his* healing tree. Celeste had picked, and needed to be punished for that. But who knows, Finn thought. She had spent too much time – these last few years – being around people with confusing behaviour, always trying to understand it, when perhaps that behaviour didn't make sense to anyone. What a waste of time and energy, she thought.

The sun was just peeking over the horizon. Spools of pink flashed across the blue.

'Oh, I almost forgot.' Celeste drew something from her right pocket. 'Here you go. Just returning what's yours.' She thrust it towards Finn.

Panic, panic, but that tingling isn't there. The warm, electrical feeling. Have I reset myself now?

'It's your moldavite.'

'Oh!' Finn clasped the stone. 'Wow, it feels so light!'

Celeste laughed, her face lighting up like it did the day they met, here, on this beach. 'It doesn't just feel lighter, it *is* lighter! I've lifted a lot of energetic weight from that thing. There was seriously a lot going on there.'

Finn draped the chain around her neck. There was the tingling, against bare skin. 'Thank you.'

'You're welcome.'

Finn wondered if this moment would pass without a mention of that phone conversation, when Celeste rang Finn and moved so swiftly from the topic of August's hospitalisation to criticising Finn for having her operation. The setting sun called things into closure. But there was a hardness now between them, like something had already passed.

'Well, it's good to see you, Finn.' Celeste spoke smooth and soft, looking down, tucking wisps of hair behind her ears.

'It's really good to see you,' Finn found herself croaking.

There was a tall ship on the horizon. The water was glowing.

'I should go,' said Celeste. 'I've got a new bliss ball recipe at home. My kitchen is covered in date paste and soaking macadamias.'

Finn gripped onto her moldavite. 'This feels truly different.' She looked down at the pendant. 'Thank you.'

The sun had gone. The sky was pink and milky. Celeste

turned away suddenly. Finn watched as Celeste walked away, her boots leaving deep impressions in the sand.

The waves grew louder. It was getting cold and windy. Maybe the crashing of waves sounded louder with the loss of light. Out at sea, a faint pattern of light appeared. It could have been a coastguard boat, or a small vessel of some kind.

Finn squinted. It was a small constellation, seeming to dance and flit on the surface of the water. Excitement rose in her chest. Perhaps, she thought, these were the shapes. Finally, they were back, ready to return.

She stared out across the water, seeing the lights, noticing them dip, blink and fade. And then they were gone.

Finn felt deflated, but then that sensation quickly passed. Why would she need, or want, the shapes back? What did they mean anyway? Maybe if she could figure out what they meant, all her understanding and wisdom could lead to a career as a healer. Being a healer would mean she had purpose, a sense of direction in life. But really, Finn was never convinced that's what she wanted.

THE BOAT

By the time Finn pulled up at the boat, it was raining hard. She let the engine run, headlights pushing through the black, picking up faint outlines of scrap, sheds, tractor wheels, and the form of the boat.

She hadn't been inside since August's hospitalisation. There was something helpful, though, about sitting in the car with the engine running and looking at Richard's *Little Mother Earth Ship*, seeing it for the basic thing that it was.

Richard would usually dash out to the car when he heard her arrive, plunging his head in the window to say hello, which Finn tried hard not to recoil at. Still, after everything, she didn't want to hurt his feelings.

His eyes were always wide, his breath reliably garlicky as he asked, 'Are you coming back?'

'I'm not ready,' was always the answer. She didn't say 'yet', because 'yet' implied that at some point in the future, she would be ready, and Finn didn't know if that was true.

Right now, Finn couldn't see much. The sky was dark, and the rain was so heavy it was creating a thick layer of grey. There appeared to be no lights on in the boat, which was odd. Finn pulled on the handbrake and turned up the heater. She sat on her hands, and in the warmth of the car, began to fantasise about eating hash browns in front of the television. That's exactly what she would do when she got home: turn on the oven, cover the frozen hash browns in oil, put on her pyjamas and lie down.

She could be in her own space so easily, she'd found, living with August. It turned out that August was quite a different housemate from what she'd expected. They met in the kitchen, chatting over a cup of tea. But August was just as keen on retreating to her own space as Finn was. Sometimes Finn found herself even wanting more of a connection, to hear about Tom, and what it was like, growing up where she did, and moving to the city. Finn realised that August had been through a lot, and even though she was just twenty-three had already reinvented herself. Finn found that inspiring. Maybe Finn was the cause of all that awkwardness between her and August in the past. August just wanted to be seen, nothing more.

Finn glanced at her watch. She had agreed to meet August at seven thirty p.m. It was now seven forty, and Finn felt slightly worried. Why weren't there any lights on in the boat?

Then she saw them. There were two flashing lights, from mobile phones, waving up and down through the air. Finn switched off the engine and drew a deep breath, before running through the rain.

After trudging through puddles, and nearly slipping on a sheet of tarpaulin, Finn ducked under the makeshift gazebo. She found August and Richard, their faces each lit up by phones. The pair were laughing, and their eyes were wide, big drooping shadows across their cheeks. They each clasped a framed photograph: August held the picture of Tom, Richard held Serena. Finn felt that rage inside her again.

Once she was afraid that rage was some kind of jealousy, that she was secretly in love with Richard, and upset that he hadn't truly gotten over his first love. Now she saw the rage differently. She had devoted time and energy as an apprentice-healer to a man who seemed to love the smell of his own shit.

Finn dug her fingernails into her palms. She felt her jaw tighten, but tried to smile.

'What's going on? And what are you wearing?'

Richard and August began laughing maniacally. They were

each wearing large hooded jumpers – August's was bright purple, and Richard's was yellow.

'There's a bag of clothes here, I remembered when we left the boat,' August spoke rapidly. 'I don't know where it came from. Here, see if you can find something.'

She had no free hands, so August began to kick the large, open garbage bag somewhat in Finn's direction.

Finn raised her hands, 'No, no it's okay. I'm fine. I just don't understand what's going on.'

Richard belted out a laugh. 'It's *Richard's Ark*! It always *was* an ark after all.'

August joined in laughing, before catching Finn's serious eye. 'Sorry, Finn. Well, we were on the boat when it started to rain –'

'And then the lights went out –'

'And there were some really strange noises, creaking and groaning –'

'I have *never* heard a noise like that!' Richard declared, laughing again.

Finn looked up at the boat, thinking she heard a creak.

'August, the darling, managed to scuttle up on the roof and get the photographs,' Richard shrieked in laughter again. 'You saved them! The pair of photographs, saved them from the flood, so they may breed forth new life! This really is biblical, Ross won't believe it!'

'Well it's not really biblical,' Finn snapped. 'Because your boat is about to get destroyed in a storm, not save us all from one.'

Richard's face dropped, but he began to smile, and then thundered his laughter. He raised his hands to the air. 'It's the end of the world!'

August laughed along, as Finn shook her head.

'What are you going to do, Richard?'

'I invited Richard over for dinner,' August said. 'I hope that's okay? He probably just needs somewhere to stay for the night.'

'You know me, Finn. I have a tent, sheds.' He pointed to a rucksack on the floor. 'Look, I saved my computer and some food.'

Finn rolled her eyes. 'Wow, well done, Richard.'

He laughed again, now gripping the picture of Serena to his chest. Finn couldn't help it. She had to do something.

Still looking at the photograph – Serena's face smiling up in encouragement – Finn said, 'You can stay over, just for tonight. On one condition.'

'What is it?' August asked, sounding more than excited.

It happened so quickly. Finn reached out, wresting the photograph from Richard's hands. Then she flung it, as far and high as she could.

'Noooo!' Richard called, his laughter shrilling through the dark.

There was the sound of breaking glass as the picture hit the boat. Wind rose through the trees, and Richard's laughter went squealing through the rain. And then there was the other sound: something like wailing, scraping and moaning. The boat seemed to sway, and August's eyes were wide white moons. She grabbed Finn's hand, and Finn squeezed as *The Little Mother Earth Ship* listed to one side. And with a creak and a groan, the boat fell, sinking deep into the wet earth.

The rain was falling hard now. Everything smelt fresh and new.

ACKNOWLEDGEMENTS

I acknowledge that this novel was predominantly written in Walyalup, on Whadjuk Noongar Boodjar. I wish to pay my respect to Noongar elders past, present and emerging.

This book would not have been possible without the support of the Perth writing community, and in particular the Katharine Susannah Prichard (KSP) Writers' Centre. I attended a workshop with Chloe Higgins at KSP in 2016, in which I felt encouraged to work on an early draft of this novel. While visiting the centre, I learned of an upcoming Spring Story Retreat with Laurie Steed, and applied. I was awarded a position but was unable to attend the retreat. Despite this, Laurie gave me hugely helpful feedback, and pushed me to continue with my project. KSP then awarded me a writing fellowship in 2017, and it was at the centre that I completed my first draft. I further developed the work at KSP in 2018, on a First Edition (manuscript development) Retreat with Laurie.

Thanks are due to the Beta Reading Group of The Meeting Place in Fremantle, who anonymously read and gave feedback on the first two chapters of the novel in 2018.

Also, Rosina Wonglorz and staff at the Third Wheel made me feel very welcome to write every morning in their café across from South Beach.

Brooke Dunnell, manuscript-assessor-extraordinaire, gave me invaluable feedback on the novel in 2018; her critical eye helped me to find pathways to continue writing.

Thanks also go to my writing friends and teachers Nathan Hobby, Brenda Walker, Magda Wozniak, Jess Panegyres,

Meg McKinlay, Heather Bloor, Hayley Scrivenor, Emlyn Johnson, Kali Napier, Emma Young, Emily Sun, Rashida Murphy, Simone Lazaroo and David Moody.

Also, without Jane Underwood and Donna Hamilton's yoga classes, I would never have finished the book. (Shavasana is the time to write endings in your head, isn't it?)

I also must thank my editor Georgia Richter, Fremantle Press, the Four Centres Emerging Writers Program, which I was selected for in 2018, and the Fogarty Literary Award, which I was longlisted for in 2019.

I am also indebted to my family (all of you!) and friends, particularly Louis Inglis, Karen Cameron, Jae Criddle, Jason Snook, Merle Fyshwick, Kat Stewart, Laura Whittock, Nunzia Sorrentino, Amy Vinicombe, Dan Gladden, Ric Kostera, Kerry Leggett, Rhiannon Chalmers, Laura Bennett, Alex Vaughn-Taylor, the Philosophy Room, Leissa and Glenn Pegrum, Lewis Waters, Peter Carlino, Agatha Snowball, Myra Thomas, Tobia Beckley, Gabby Ho and Matthew Dwyer, who was excited about my book, but never had a chance to read it.

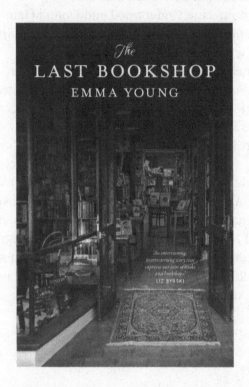

Cait is a bookshop owner whose social life revolves around her mobile bookselling service for elderly clients. Book Fiend is the last bookshop in the CBD, and the last independent retailer on a street given over to high-end labels. When James breezes in, Cait realises life might hold more than her shop and her cat, but while the new romance distracts her, luxury chain stores are circling Book Fiend's prime location, and a more personal tragedy is looming.

An entertaining, heartwarming story that captures
our love of books and bookshops. – Liz Byrski

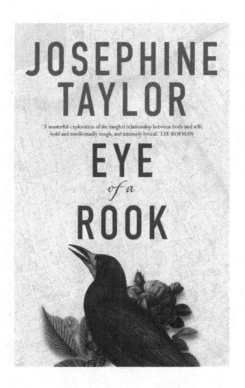

In 1860s London, Arthur sees his wife, Emily, suddenly struck down by a pain for which she can find no words, forced to endure harmful treatments and reliant on him for guidance. Meanwhile, in contemporary Perth, Alice, a writer, and her older husband, Duncan, find their marriage threatened as Alice investigates the history of hysteria, female sexuality and the treatment of the female body – her own and the bodies of those who came before.

A masterful exploration of the tangled relationship between body and self; bold and intellectually tough, and intensely lyrical. – Lee Kofman

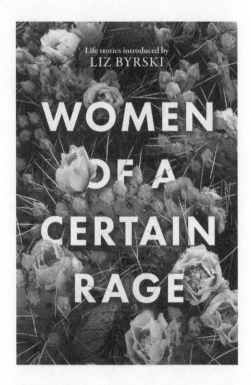

This book is the result of what happened when Liz Byrski asked 20 women from widely different backgrounds, races, beliefs and identities to take up the challenge of writing about rage. The honesty, passion, courage and humour of their very personal stories is engergising and inspiring. If you have ever felt the full force of anger and wondered at its power, then this book is for you.

A great read. Rage has never been this compassionate, absorbing and thought-provoking. When do I get to party with these smart, talented, wonderful women? – Judith Lucy

AND ALL GOOD BOOKSHOPS

Life sucks when you are a vacuum cleaner–salesman facing redundancy, and your wife of 40 years fills your days with incessant chatter. But when Gloria suddenly stops talking, the silence is more than Bernard can bear. In desperation, he turns to his ex–daughter-in-law for help. Meg has issues of her own, and her daughter Ella sometimes wonders if her mum's worrying stops them both from spreading their wings. Will Meg's suspicious nature thwart her chance encounter with the engimatic Hal? And is there still hope for Bernard and Gloria on the other side of silence?

An engrossing, moving and beautifully observed story of marriage, family and forgiveness. – Josephine Wilson

First published 2021 by
FREMANTLE PRESS

Fremantle Press Inc. trading as Fremantle Press
25 Quarry Street, Fremantle WA 6160
(PO Box 158, North Fremantle WA 6159)
www.fremantlepress.com.au

Cover images by: Maurice Pillard Verneuil, *Botanical Vintage,* rawpixel.com;
Gangway to a Romantic Houseboat in Copenhagen, alamy.com.
Printed by McPherson's Printing, Victoria, Australia.

 A catalogue record for this
book is available from the
National Library of Australia

ISBN 9781925816617 (paperback)
ISBN 9781925816624 (ebook)

Fremantle Press is supported by the State Government through the
Department of Local Government, Sport and Cultural Industries.

Publication of this title was assisted by the Commonwealth Government
through the Australia Council, its arts funding and advisory body.